Nomad's Trail

Nomad's Trail

The Saga of Simon Bolivar Grimes, Volume 1

E. Hoffmann Price

With an introduction by James Reasoner

BLACK DOG BOOKS

2011
Normal, IL

PUBLICATION HISTORY AND COPYRIGHT INFORMATION

"Tenderfoot" From SPICY WESTERN STORIES, November 1936.

"Treason's Kiss" From SPICY WESTERN STORIES, December 1936.

"Grimes, Outlaw!" From SPICY WESTERN STORIES, January 1937.

"Reward of Valor" From SPICY WESTERN STORIES, April 1937.

"Skeleton Creek Feud" From SPICY WESTERN STORIES, May 1937.

"Feud's End" From SPICY WESTERN STORIES, July 1937.

"Hoodoo Town" From SPICY WESTERN STORIES, August 1937.

"Salt Crazy" From SPICY WESTERN STORIES, October 1937.

"Too Many Cooks" From SPICY WESTERN STORIES, December 1937.

"Grimes Gets Religion" From SPICY WESTERN STORIES, February 1938.

"Hungry Valley" From SPICY WESTERN STORIES, June 1938.

"Nomad's Trail" From SPICY WESTERN STORIES, August 1938.

ISBN13 978-1-928619-62-8

Introduction copyright © 2011 by James Reasoner.
Cover art by Allen Anderson.

Book layout and design: Tom Roberts.
Proofreading: Gene Christie, Doug Ellis.

Black Dog Books, 1115 Pine Meadows Ct., Normal, IL 61761-5432.
www.blackdogbooks.net / info@blackdogbooks.net

Contents

Introduction

E. Hoffmann Price (1898–1988) had a long and successful career as a pulp writer, breaking into the market in 1924 with a sale to *Droll Stories*. Within a few months, he began selling to *Weird Tales* and became a regular contributor to the magazine. Perhaps more importantly in the long run, he became friends through correspondence with other *Weird Tales* writers such as Robert E. Howard, H.P. Lovecraft and Clark Ashton Smith. That correspondence led to Price actually meeting those fellow authors as he traveled around the country, and he was quite probably the only person who ever sat down and visited in person with all of them. His letters and memoirs have been very valuable for modern scholars who want to learn more about those authors, although some of Price's recollections have to be taken with a grain of salt.

Price was much more prolific than those three *Weird Tales* icons, spreading his work out to a number of different pulps and genres. His stories appeared with regularity in many of the detective pulps, as well as in general fiction pulps such as *Argosy, Adventure* and *Short Stories*. He became a master of globe-trotting adventure yarns, and one of his regular markets was the popular and notorious "Spicy" line. Having written for *Spicy-Adventure* and *Spicy Mystery*, it comes as no surprise that in 1936 Price also contributed to the newest of the *Spicy* titles, *Spicy Western Stories*. In fact, Price's story "Tenderfoot" (his first attempt at a Western, by the way), was the first story in the first issue of *Spicy Western*. It introduced one of Price's most popular characters: Simon Bolivar Grimes.

Grimes is little more than a boy when we first meet him, a gangling, callow youth from Georgia who has come to Texas to work on the ranch of his uncle Carter, who has a spread in Crockett County, near the town of Skeleton Creek. He has barely crossed from Louisiana into Texas, though, when he winds up in trouble and behind bars—the first of many times that Grimes's healthy appetite for beautiful young women and uncanny speed and accuracy with a six-gun will land him in jail.

Price's Simon Bolivar Grimes stories have long been known to have been influenced by the burlesque Westerns of his good friend, Robert E. Howard. The character of Grimes definitely owes a debt to Howard's characters Breckinridge

Elkins and Buckner Jeopardy Grimes. Note the last name, and know as well that Price lifted two-thirds of his character's name from the real-life Kentucky colonel Simon Bolivar Buckner, which is probably where Howard got the idea to use "Buckner" as part of *his* character's name. There's an unmistakable interweaving web of influence here, and not just in the names. Price's Grimes has a tendency of blundering into the same sort of complicated, broadly humorous plots that Howard's Grimes and Elkins did.

Don't make the mistake, though, of thinking that Simon Bolivar Grimes is simply a copy of Howard's characters. Price was too much of a professional for that, and he had a strong voice of his own that led him to take his stories in their own distinctive direction. This is immediately obvious in the first Simon Bolivar Grimes story, "Tenderfoot," which is told in the third person, rather than in first person, as Howard's stories were. This has the instant effect of toning down the comical, tall-tale qualities present in Howard's slapstick Westerns. By the end of "Tenderfoot," Price has wrenched his series even farther away from its influences by supplying some plot twists that give the story a darker, bleaker edge.

(Which is not to say that Howard's Westerns couldn't be dark and bleak— read his magnificent novella, "The Vultures of Wahpeton," if you don't believe me—but that element doesn't crop up nearly as much in his comedy Westerns.)

Price doesn't stop there in his efforts to make the Simon Bolivar Grimes stories unique. The stories in *Spicy Western Stories* featured few continuing characters. Grimes was not only a series character, but the stories that starred him often featured a strong sense of continuity as well. The first three stories, "Tenderfoot" (November 1936), "Treason's Kiss" (December 1936) and "Grimes, Outlaw!" (January 1937) appeared in three consecutive issues and form a larger storyline, each story flowing almost seamlessly into the next. Even though the other stories didn't appear at such regular intervals, they still feature continuing characters and plots that give the tales of Grimes's wanderings across Texas, New Mexico and Arizona something of an epic quality. Enough is resolved in each story that they can be read as stand-alone yarns, of course, but their effect is enhanced by reading them in order, which this collection, *Nomad's Trail,* enables us to do.

Although the Simon Bolivar Grimes stories are Price's first attempts at writing Westerns, they ring true from the beginning. Price had driven around Texas quite a bit in his travels, and Texas in the early Thirties wasn't that far removed from frontier days. Although his characters and plots are larger than life, his descriptions and settings are fairly accurate.

Grimes himself is a great character—gullible, hot-tempered, a little uneducated, maybe, but not exactly dumb. He may fall for a beautiful girl's lies when she's working with the villains, but it doesn't take him long to sort out the truth. He proves to be equally adept at gunfighting and kissing. These are *Spicy Western* yarns, after all, and Price was an old pro by the time he was writing them, able to come up with plausible reasons for his sultry female characters to lose their clothes again and again. Grimes can be distracted by such beauties, but not for long.

The Simon Bolivar Grimes stories continued to appear in *Spicy Western Stories* and its successor, *Speed Western Stories,* for about ten years, and Price's career as a pulp author lasted for several years after that, his final stories appearing in the early Fifties. He might have lived out his life in a well-deserved retirement, but in the Seventies, with the rise of pulp fandom, he became a sought-after contributor to various fanzines and books concerning pulp stories and the authors who wrote them. He began writing fiction again, starting with a Western novel, *Grubstake,* published in 1979 by Zebra Books, and half a dozen Oriental fantasies and science fiction adventure novels published by Del Rey during the Eighties, the last one appearing a year before his death in 1988, at the age of ninety.

For the most part, the Grimes stories have been out of print since their first appearances in *Spicy Western* more than seventy years ago. Now, Tom Roberts of Black Dog Books has gathered the first dozen of them in this volume, so you can enjoy their broad comedy, their colorful dialogue, their beautiful women, their bullet-blazing gunfights and their unexpected plot twists. These are some of the most purely entertaining pulp Western yarns you'll ever read, so settle back and enjoy the adventures of an innocent lad from Georgia who's fast on the draw and sometimes has too much of an eye for the ladies for his own good.

James Reasoner

Spur Award nominee James Reasoner is one of the most prolific and in-demand Western writers working today, with more than 250 novels to his credit in the Western and historical fiction fields, both under his own name and various pen-names, including books in the Longarm, Trailsman and Lone Star series, among others.

A long-time pulp fan, he has authored many detective/mystery short stories. Recent contributions to anthologies include tales of The Avenger, The Green Hornet and Kolchak, the Night Stalker. For several years, early in his career, he wrote the Mike Shayne novellas in *Mike Shayne Mystery Magazine,* under the famous pseudonym Brett Halliday.

He lives in his native Texas with his wife, award-winning mystery novelist Livia J. Washburn.

His website, with an extensive list of his work, can be found at: www.jamesreasoner.net, and he blogs at: http://jamesreasoner.blogspot.com.

James can be contacted at jamesreasoner@flash.net.

Tenderfoot

He had a coffin-shaped face, and like the thoroughbred he rode, his legs were long; but while the horse was graceful as a panther, the rider was gangling, slightly stooped, and his oversized hands did not know what to do with themselves when he dismounted at the hitching rack in front of Squint Eye Morgan's Sabine Palace, a dive so named because of its proximity to the river which separates Texas and Louisiana.

A .45 single action Colt was awkwardly strapped to his thigh, and its owner looked as though he must have picked a lucky day for his very recent first shave, otherwise he would have cut his own throat; yet somehow, he did not stumble over the hand-hewn planks as he strode to the bar.

Squint Eye Morgan winked broadly when the boy piped, "Whiskey, if yo' please, suh." Then, voice suddenly going bass, he boomed like a yearling bull, "I'm Simon Bolivar Grimes, suh, lookin' fo' my uncle's ranch in Crockett County in the next day or two."

"Not unless yuh kin fly," was Squint Eye's mock serious answer. "It's nigh onto eight hundred mile from here."

And that exchange gave everyone a chance to notice that the horse at the hitching rack was worth a thousand dollars of any man's money; that the buckskin poke from which Grimes took a gold piece to pay for his drink weighed at least four pounds, and none of it silver.

One of the half-dressed girls lounging on the bench at the edge of the tiny dance floor thought he was awfully cunning. The others had more practical thoughts, and debated initiating the yokel to what few mysteries their low bodices and short skirts contrived to conceal.

Grimes decided he might as well spend the night in Orange and rest up a spell befo' going on to the Box-A ranch; and then, after a crossfire of whispers, one of the players slid from his place at the poker table and raked in his winnings. Keno Charley, white-fingered and debonair house gambler, invited the boy to sit in.

"Thank yo' very kindly, suh," Grimes declined, "but my pap'd lambaste me if he ever heard of me playin' cards."

Which gave the girls a break, and Grimes a thrill. Thus far, he had never more than vaguely suspected white women of having legs; just skirts and feet.

A sweet-faced Creole with great black eyes and a passionate mouth was the first to reach the hillbilly. Her skin was pale olive, and her half-bared breasts were exquisitely rounded and firm. While Grimes reddened at the lovely stretch of silken legs, and a glimpse of thighs was momentarily revealed before her short skirt settled almost to her knees, he was eager—with the eagerness of youth.

It was entirely optional at the Sabine Palace whether the girls merely danced and hustled drinks, or took time out to show guests through their upstairs rooms, though such fine points never occurred to Grimes. He knew his elementary biology, but where he came from, it didn't apply to white women—not as far as boys and bachelors were concerned.

"Want to dance, honey?" she invited, betraying none of the hard calculation of her companions.

"I'd love to, m'am." She was lost in his long arms, a sweet parcel of tawdry spangles and warm flesh.

Lorette managed to dodge his heavy boots, and though she had to tip-toe to get her eyebrows to his shoulders, somehow that seductively writhing body, those swaying hips and shapely legs all clung to the best advantage. . . .

Grimes was breathing hard when the fiddle squeaking ceased, and tingling from tow head to cowhide boots. He was flushed and sheepish from knowing that she knew his eager glance was probing the scented shadows between her breasts. He gulped his whiskey and was shocked when Lorette drank hers. He didn't know she was taking tea at a dollar a drink.

Lorette's eyes had softened, and a little ghost of a smile sweetened her mouth. That gangling boy was reminding her that she was about his age, even though she did feel so much older. Her soft-voiced dance hall chatter died out, and she also began fumbling for words.

He did not know she was thinking, *Some night, I'll take too much real liquor, and forget to say no to Muddy Hawkins . . . .*

She shuddered, then laughed bitterly when Grimes rumbled, "Are yo'all chilly, m'am—"

He checked himself; he couldn't add, "with so much of you uncovered."

"Maybe you're right, honey." She caught his hand. "Come along, and I'll get a shawl."

But the trailing of her voice, and the clinging caress of her fingers hinted things that made Grimes' heart rise and choke him. The smokey, oil-lighted room seemed all awhirl. He did not hear the scrape of a chair, a man's angry mutter behind him, and another man taunting, "Keep yore shirt on, Muddy. That button won't know what to do with her, nohow. An' she never did want none of *you!*"

"Nor you neither!" was Muddy Hawkins' retort to Pinwheel Smith—the other one of a vicious pair whose friendship centered in Lorette's despising them both.

Grimes followed twinkling ankles and swaying hips up the narrow, one-way stairs. He was afraid of Lorette, so frail and dainty.

She did not light the bracket lamp on the wall. A pencil of moonlight made a blur of pillows, picked highlights from crude furniture. And then all that band of glamour centered on the shimmering ivory splendor that appeared as spangled silk rustled down about Lorette's ankles.

She was now quite close, and his awkward hands were conscious of the filmy stuff that still clung to her skin. Women were very wonderful and mysterious . . . he was glad he didn't have to speak . . . he'd not have known what to say.

Then her lips found his mouth, and her arms insistently drew him toward her. . . .

LATER, THOUGH HIS VOICE STILL CRACKED AT TIMES, IT WAS A FULL-GROWN MAN WHO told Lorette about Uncle Carter and the Box-A ranch.

"An' I'd sho' love to have you'all come along with me, m'am," he concluded.

"You foolish boy," she whispered, swallowing a catch in her voice. He meant it. "You don't know what you're saying. I'm . . . why—" There was no malice in her gentle mockery when she added, "Your pap would lambaste you, and me too."

"M'am," he protested, following her to the door, "I'd jest bust anyone's haid what said a cross-eyed word to you."

Lorette was composed when she reached the foot of the stairs leading to the barroom, but Grimes walked more erectly, head higher. His face was a revelation; and Muddy Hawkins knew that the girl had not even thought of rifling the buckskin poke. His fingers twitched as he snarled, "By God, he did—"

"Shet up!" Pinwheel Smith chuckled maliciously. "Jest shows he's a better man'n you be!"

His calculating glance shifted toward the thoroughbred horse at the hitching post, full in the glow of the front lights. When Pinwheel turned back, Muddy, now halfway across the floor, had Lorette by the arm.

"You dirty ______! You an' yore pertendin'!"

Lorette understood the cutthroat's wrath, and her face whitened as she saw Pinwheel in the background, grinning evilly, waiting. Muddy thrust her against the door jamb before she could retort. Grimes growled in wordless wrath, swung an awkward fist that no more than grazed the ruffian's cheek; but chairs scraped and men scrambled for cover. They knew that Muddy would blast the boy loose from his eye teeth, and get away with another plea of self defense—which he could, since Grimes was armed.

Pinwheel, however, had not moved. The kid wouldn't get a chance to draw, and he had to be handy for a deft grab at that poke of gold.

As Grimes recovered, there was a glint of blued steel and the muzzle of a short-barreled revolver blotted out all but those rattlesnake eyes. Time ceased in the Sabine Palace, and so did sound. Death faced Grimes—then the murky air burst into hell-roaring flame, and something jerked at his arm.

Before he knew that it was the blast of his own Colt, he wondered why Muddy suddenly spun, clutching his stomach, unfired gun clattering to the floor. He least of all realized that nature and years of boyhood hunting had given him the quick reflexes to make a delayed draw and win by an eyelash.

Lorette screamed, first terror, then quavering relief. Grimes half turned, but instinct warned him. He jerked back just as another blast shook the room. But

Pinwheel Smith's lead only raked the boy's shoulder; and his second shot was muffled by the thunder of Grimes' portable siege gun. A hammer blow knocked him sprawling, stomach tangled with his spine.

"They's mo' fo' any of you-all what wants some," announced Simon Bolivar Grimes, unshaken by the wild shot. "Raise yo' hands—you, there—"

The gangling boy's face was grim as his granite eyes. In feuds at home, he'd seen men killed aplenty, but never by his own hand. He still could not quite believe he had done it; but as Lorette drew closer, he remembered he was now a man.

"Git upstairs, woman, an' fetch yo' clothes," he commanded. "We're goin'. Quick!"

"But—" She gasped, blinked, still incredulous.

"Git!" he repeated, and she obeyed. Grimes remembered only his home traditions: there was now a feud between him and the friends of the dead, regardless of his just self defense.

"Listen, kid, take it easy," protested Squint Eye Morgan, to whom a shooting was just part of the night's work. But though his hands wavered harmlessly enough, Grimes had a single-track mind which was still reeling.

Wham! The back bar mirror spattered. Squint Eye, however, was untouched except for flying glass. He had ducked in time. The tension of waiting for Lorette was robbing the deadly youngster of his accuracy.

A stocky man with a horseshoe-shaped gray moustache came clumping in from the front: Mark Ferrell, the town marshall, who had been drawn by the thunder of the guns. Age and seasoning had made him confident. He arrived with holstered weapons, and when he saw a dozen uplifted hands, it was too late.

"Raise yo' hands!" piped the boy behind the long barreled Colt.

"Better do it, marshal!" croaked Keno Charley, and another added, "He's killin' us all—he's crazy—he done shot Squint Eye—"

Two men twitching in pools of blood made it convincing. Ferrell, despite his star, lifted his hands; but he warned:

"Yuh kain't do it, boy. If I don't git yuh, they's enough deppities to chase yah plumb to Pecos."

A stirring at the end of the bar warned Grimes, but not in time. He whirled as half a whiskey bottle, top shattered by his shot, drenched his face with bits of glass and stinging rotgut. The marshal's arrival had given Squint Eye his chance. Grimes' smoke pole roared, but harmlessly; blood and whiskey blinded him. A hurled cuspidor crashed against his head. That distraction gave the law its chance.

"Git on yore feet!" growled Ferrell, kicking the smoking gun into a corner and seizing Grimes by the collar.

Then he learned that conversation was out of order. Howling his wrath, the dizzied lad ploughed in, but boots and fists were too plentiful.

"He grabbed my poke!" yelled the vigilant Squint Eye, playing up the main chance; and once the hangers-on had their cue, they gave the marshal an improvised story of a daring hold-up. That'd settle the yokel!

With what Ferrell had seen on entering, that was plausible enough; so when pistol whipping had put an end to resisting arrest, he and a tardily arrived deputy dragged Grimes toward the door.

"I ain't held no one up!" he protested; then, recognizing futility, he added, "But yo'all feed my hoss, yo' hear?"

"What hoss?" grumbled the panting marshal.

"That hoss there—" Grimes blinked the blood and sweat from his eyes. The thoroughbred was gone, and not even hoofbeats lingered.

Once at the town jail, Ferrell demanded of the accusers, "Now, where's that *dinero* this kid grabbed?"

"Search him, marshal," answered Squint Eye. "Et's in a buckskin poke— don't know jest how much, but—"

But the bag was gone.

"Ain't no gold," frowned the marshal. "Mebbe he drapped it."

"Drapped, hell!" chorused a dozen voices. "We done looked fer it."

"Git that Lorette!" snarled Squint Eye. "Bet she grabbed it offen the floor whilst he was shootin' us up, jest before yuh got here."

"Yo' kaint call her a thief!" raged Grimes. Then he began to remember. He'd laid it on Lorette's dresser, and the thrill of the girl had made him forget it. "Yo'all go git her. She'll prove it ain't his'n. I done left it in her room, and that proves I didn't take it offen this here skunk. An' it's got my pap's name branded on it."

"Find the gal!" snapped Ferrell to a deputy. "But fust lock this jaybird in the hoosegow. Though mebbe 'tis his *dinero!*"

The door slammed on a battered but triumphant Grimes.

The accusers, muttering and plucking tobacco-stained moustaches, pulled long faces. Ferrell, though rough, was just in his own way; but Squint Eye Morgan, resenting a cut face and shattered mirror, was racking his crooked brain for a story to counteract the marked buckskin pouch, a kink that he had not expected, seeing that gold was gold.

"Yuh'll git yores yet," sneered Morgan, pausing for a final word before dashing back to the Sabine Palace. "Shootin' up two of my best customers."

And that left Grimes to brood over the loss of his horse. If his pap didn't lambaste him, his Uncle Carter would, when he got to Crockett County, where he was to learn how to run a ranch. His father's brother was along in years, and a younger Grimes had to go west to carry on.

Sweet mess he'd made of it, thus far; then he consoled himself, "But I'd not dast admit I'd ever let that skunk hit a woman, or he'd sho' disown me."

Presently, Ferrell returned, and his iron face was grim.

"Listen, jasper—that gal's done gone, and her hoofprints leads right up to the hitchin' rack where yore hoss was tied. Purty smart, havin' her sashay with the plunder, so's we kaint prove yuh took it."

He paused, spat a jet of tobacco juice at the bars of Grimes' cell, then added, "So we're holdin' yuh fer murder. Got plenty witnesses to swear you shot down two citizens an' tried to smoke out the owner of our leadin' barroom."

Grimes' indignant protests echoed in the emptiness of the corridor as the marshal made an impressive exit.

MURDER! THE GRIMESES HAD, IN THE PAST SIX OR SEVEN GENERATIONS, DONE A FAIR SHARE of killing, but they'd been honest feud shootings, not murder or robbery. And now, if they stood him on the back of a mustang, looped a rawhide *riata* about his neck, fastened the free end to a limb of a tree and smacked the temporary mount across the rump, he'd be left dangling, with never a *chance* to prove to pap that he'd killed two skunks for hitting a woman—even though she was a woman who'd stolen his poke and his horse.

That last was what really hurt. It took the edge from his newly found manhood; that, and the unjust accusation. Twice in a flaming moment he had beaten doom, which was a man's share of chances; and his breed was too stoical to fear the mere extinction of death. But the disgrace!

Morning came, and without any sign of Lorette. The greasy, pendulous-breasted Mexican wife of the town marshal bought Grimes his breakfast. Pity marked her fat face as she watched him stare frostily at the coffee beans, and sow-belly she slid through the bars.

"More better you eat," she wheedled. "They don' hang you till the trial. Maybe tomorrow, an' you should not die hongry."

A suggestion of vanished winsomeness brightened her smile. Grimes nodded, forced a half grin, and said, "Thank yo', m'am. Sho' looks good."

He wolfed it down, and the broad-hipped Mexican, picking up the plate, cheerfully added, "Sooch a nice boy. An' eef they hang you, I weel make you the *tortillas* weeth chili for the las' meal, no?"

Greasers were funny people, saying "no" when they meant yes. He didn't know that tortillas were corn cakes tough as leather, and that the chili would blister his throat like fire, but it was nice to get a friendly word. He fumbled in his pocket and found a five-dollar gold piece among his loose silver.

"Take it, ma'm," he said. "I won't have much use for it much longer."

She could hardly understand his words, but his meaning was plain. She left, shaking her head. Loretta's treachery could not help but arouse a touch of feminine indignation at another woman's work.

The jail was of brick; but even if Grimes had had a knife to work on the crumbling mortar, he would have had no chance to use it. The incredible killing of two cutthroats by an awkward hillbilly made him the sensation of the town.

The inhabitants came to gape; and while the better element muttered about there being contradictory angles, they were true to form and did nothing about it. That left Squint Eye Morgan and his clique to stick to their accusations, hoping that the criminal, trying to save himself, would give some hint as to Lorette's hiding place. They had the marshal in a bag.

They were sure he and the dance-hall girl had agreed to meet somewhere. The disappearance of the thoroughbred horse convinced them. And if Lorette returned,

Grimes' buckskin pouch of gold could be seized for damages to the Sabine Palace, or as a fine for disturbing the peace.

THAT FORENOON, TWELVE MEN, NEITHER GOOD NOR REMOTELY TRUE, MADE UP THE frontier jury. After a frantic scramble for a Bible, the witnesses solemnly swore that Grimes had held the place up and smoked out "pore Muddy an' Pinwheel."

The execution was set for sunrise. The delay was to give Lorette a chance to repent and return with the gold.

As Grimes was marched from the court, there was much applause and talk about the marshal's valor in subduing the outlaw; and that, with the close packing of the crowd, gave no one a chance to notice that the Law's Mexican wife slipped a Bowie knife beneath the prisoner's belt. Grimes himself, for a moment, wondered at the chill of steel against his skin; but he did not betray his surprise, and his manacles kept him from rashly using the weapon.

Porky McTeague, a pot-bellied deputy with three chins, planted himself on a bench in the jail corridor to guard the condemned. He was glum, being forced to miss the preparations for the barbecue that was to precede the hanging; but that evening, slightly after sundown, he brightened; and not entirely because of the pint bottle he had sullenly guzzled.

Heel clicks—woman's heels—sounded in the corridor. Grub for the prisoner; spicy, pungent food, reeking of chili and garlic and cumin seed. However, it was not the marshal's hay-bag wife who brought it, but a girl—slender, with glistening black hair and hazel eyes that were strangely lovely against her cream-colored skin. Even in the face of the hangman, Simon Bolivar Grimes knew a rare armful of feminine flesh when he saw it.

Now that he knew women had legs, his imagination told him what must be above the girl's trim ankles; and though he got but a peep of the lamplight glow reflected from the curves in her bodice, he reckoned that what she carried there would repay further study.

"My mother sent me weeth the supper," she explained to the prisoner.

The marshal's daughter flashed an angry eye at Porky, who chuckled drunkenly and patted the elegant roundness south of her hip, and flared, "Peeg! I weel not give you wan bit of thees chili. Ees for Señor Grimes."

One spoonful made the captive think he had swallowed a volcano in full eruption. He gasped, blinked tears from his eyes; but he couldn't offend that sweet creature, so he said, "M'am, this is sho' good, but lookin' at yo'all jest takes my appetite. I'm a-seein angels a-fore they hangs me."

And that, coming from the damned, touched Catalina's half-Latin heart.

"Do you, really?" She wedged her lovely face between the bars. "Kees me, joost once—"

And that burned Porky to alcoholic fury.

"If you like him, have at it!" he snarled. He had the door unlocked before Grimes, dazzled by hot lips and a cloud of black hair, could sense what was happening. And when the grating swung in, smacking him back and off balance, it was too late. Then the girl pitched head first into the cell, driven by the jailer's paw.

"Yo' low down skunk," roared Grimes, recovering; but Porky's gun drove him back.

He locked the door, then, face to the bars, taunted, "Now see how she likes yuh!"

Grimes, gentleman by instinct, snatched the big bowl of *chili colorado* and hurled it. The stuff, hot from fire and even hotter in its own excoriating right, poured into the piggish eyes and gaping mouth. Porky's gasp drew in a lungful of caustic gravy. It would have raised blisters on a packsaddle.

"Oooow!" howled the tortured jailer. "Hell on the mountain tops—you damn' ____, yuh've killed—"

But the rest was lost as Porky, rubbing his burning eyes and making them infinitely worse, ran screeching into the darkness; and with the rest of the town preparing for the barbecue, he found neither advice nor spectators.

"That peeg 'ave run away weeth your supper," commiserated Catalina. "An' now I cannot get some more. I am lock in the jail, no?"

She eyed him, and had to tilt her head well back to do so. Then she sighed, remembering Grimes' valiant slayings, the dance hall girl's treachery. Her mother's account of the hillbilly had led to her guilefully suggesting that maybe mama was too tired to feed the captive.

The result of that was that Grimes forgot he had a knife that he could now use to chop out enough mortar to make a getaway. The more he saw of Catalina, the more he did get that way. He lifted her up to the bench that he had mounted, attracted anew by Porky's groans and a prodigious splashing.

For a moment, they watched the jailer's vain struggles in a horse trough. Then, as Porky emerged and set out at a full gallop, Catalina laughed, and said, "Ees going to hunt the doctor. For the eyes, no?"

Catalina was nice lifting, if you grabbed her in the right places, and there wasn't a wrong one between her shapely shoulders and her dimpled knees. Even a man facing execution couldn't miss that; and when she remarked that she'd rather never be kissed unless someone other than Porky McTeague did it, Grimes lost no time.

In the meanwhile, he had lifted her from the bench and moved it into a corner. And with a bit of privacy at his disposal, Grimes remembered things he'd learned about women. He was bolder than a nice girl like Catalina approved of, even though she was warm-blooded.

She said, "No." Grimes, a born gentleman, would have stopped, but these greasers, mother and daughter alike, meant yes when they said no. So he didn't stop, and pretty soon, Catalina was warmer than Porky McTeague's eyes, and her little breasts were trying to keep her heart from pounding them out of place. But Grimes held her tight enough to prevent that.

So Catalina sighed and liked it . . . and, anyway, it was sort of romantic, brightening the last hours of a condemned man. . . .

BUT SHE DIDN'T HAVE AS MUCH TIME AS SHE HAD HOPED. THEY DID NOT HEAR THE TRAMP of heavy feet; not until two men stopped at the cell door. It was not Porky returning; that lawman, sobered up by pain, realized how he had mishandled the marshal's daughter, and borrowed a horse to head west. The new arrivals were the marshal himself, and Amos Brunton, the sheriff of Orange County, summoned to take charge of the hanging.

He arrived early, eager for a look at the incredible condemned; but what he saw made him envy the prisoner.

"Porky, dad-bust yore—damn' hide!" roared Ferrell, who saw much more of his daughter's' sleekly curving legs than her skirt was ever meant to display. "What the—damn' tarnation hell's this—yuh gol-blasted skunk—whar air yah, Porky?"

The sheriff stroked his beard and muttered something about seduction as well as murder, and delicately turned his head.

"Seduction, is it?" bellowed the outraged marshal. He drew his gun, but Brunton seized his wrist. "I'll seduct him!"

He stormed out of jail; the sheriff after him. Catalina was hysterically laughing, crying and trying to induce her skirt to meet her ankles. Grimes felt foolish; and then, having succeeded in soothing the distracted girl, he heard a soft, grating sound that startled him.

Something was scraping at the high, barred window of his cell. His first thought was that jealous Porky had returned to kill him secretly. He remembered the Bowie knife in his pocket, but as his fingers closed on the butt, a small hand gripped the bars. Then a woman murmured, "Honey, I've got a file to cut a bar, an' you can bend it open."

"Git away!" cried Grimes, horrified and confused by Lorette's whisper. "Yo'll wake the jailer."

Metal clinked on the floor; a heavy file thrust between the bars. But Catalina had heard enough.

"*Cabron!* You still love her?" she screeched, slapping and clawing him,

Grimes froze as, from without, he caught an incredulous gasp, then the muted *pad-pad* of a horse's muffled hoofs. Worse and more of it! Lorette, he now knew, had slipped out at the marshal's arrival at the saloon the night before, not realizing she could help him by remaining to prove he had not held up the Sabine Palace. Now, having heard Catalina's jealous fury, she had gone. There would be no horse waiting, even if he could file a bar.

"Shut up, woman!" he growled, wrenching the Bowie knife Catalina had snatched from his pocket. "I'm gittin', an' I don't want to throttle you lest I has to."

Grimes, gentleman by instinct, forgot himself so far as to shake her till her teeth rattled. Then he slapped her in the only place women ought to be slapped. That quelled Catalina, and she calmed down; frowned, suddenly brightened as it dawned on her that anyone as popular and deadly as Simon Bolivar Grimes was a man among men.

"That' ees right, *querido mio,*" she fondly murmured. "We weel escape, and leave her here, no?"

"No," agreed Grimes. Oddly enough, that was the wrong answer, but Catalina did not hear, being already busy gouging out mortar.

After what her father had seen, a trip with Grimes would not be so bad. So she plied the knife till her little hands were blistered; and the file rasped valiantly. Maybe he could make it before the marshal found a sober deputy.

But he didn't. Footsteps echoed in the corridor, and his heart sank to his cowhide boots. Ferrell was returning. Grimes snatched Catalina's knife, crept toward the door jamb and whispered, "Yo' file, an' they'll think it's me."

The window, though not entirely out of the line of vision from the door, was not the first thing visible from the dim, lamplit passage.

Two men accompanied the marshal: Sheriff Brunton and a solemn person in a black frock coat.

"Quit that filin' and come out, Grimes!" bellowed Ferrell. "Quick, a-fore I blast yuh!"

A shotgun barrel reached in between the bars. Grimes dared not snatch it, lest the startled marshal jerk the trigger and blow Catalina to ragged bits. He pocketed his knife and answered, "I'm here, and what yo'all want now?"

"Git busy, parson," boomed the marshal, ignoring the defiant query. He opened the door; then, shifting the double-barreled shotgun to point at Grimes' stomach, he added, "Ain't goin' to be no hangin', yuh dad-gummed skunk. Yo're marryin' my daughter, right now, or I'm a-blowing yore belly around yore spine."

Not long ago, that would have been a reprieve; but Lorette's unexpected loyalty had touched him deeply, and anyway, she was his first girl. More than that, Grimes was pig-stubborn, like all his kind. In spite of the pleasant things he had learned about Catalina, he wasn't being herded into a wedding.

"Listen, yo' ornery sculpin," he growled, as parson, witness and father of the bride-to-be entered the cell, "ain't never been a Grimes married with a shotgun, and ain't never goin' to be. Anyhow, I didn't seduct yo' daughter."

"Yuh warn't tellin' her fortune when I come in, yuh dad-blasted scum," raged the marshal. "An' now they *will* be a hangin'. *After the weddin',* yuh ongrateful ruffian."

"Yo'all try it!" challenged Grimes, arms akimbo, fingers almost touching the Bowie knife in his right pants pocket. "Lynchin' an honest man fo' trying to keep what's hisn. Ain't no parson'd have a thing to do with a thievin' disgrace to the law!"

Ferrell's face darkened. Death again commanded silence in the jailhouse; and this time Grimes had no revolver, nor could he hope to duck the double muzzles almost against his stomach.

"Brother Ferrell," quavered the parson, "Miss Catalina—"

"Not even if the priest married us!" shrilled the indignant girl, bounding from her corner. "I weel not marry that peeg!"

From one side, she pounced like a panther to claw Grimes; and the marshal's hair-trigger nerves were ready for anything. He had heard more than enough of the boy desperado that afternoon. The double charge of buckshot, however, only tore the skirt from the parson's long coat, and the flame set it smouldering. Catalina's reckless fury at her lover's repudiation had brought her hip against the gun barrel. Thus she saved the man she tried to claw.

The sheriff's gun danced out, but in the dense cloud of black powder smoke and the fumes of burning cloth, he dared not fire; not without the risk of riddling the horrified man of God or the frenzied girl. And Ferrell, dropping his empty shotgun, had no chance to go for his holsters. The prisoner saw to that.

Grimes, maddened by the gun blast, exploded in a blind rage, great fists hammering, shoulder driving through. In the confusion of descending pistol barrels and the parson's flailing boots, he jerked loose Ferrell's gun belt, bellowed his triumph and broke from the tangle.

The sheriff's gun blazed, but an instant after, Grimes snapped a shot into the overhead lamp. Flaming fuel poured to the floor; and as the enemy ducked, he cleared the angle of the corridor.

Men, drawn by the fusillade, were running toward the square. None knew what it was about, but some poured lead at the lanky fugitive as others, more prudent, flattened behind a watering trough and tried to drop the fugitive as he raced toward a hitching rack packed with horses belonging to visitors from out of town.

A slug nicked Grimes. He dropped; three heads and shoulders cropped up, gun barrels gleaming in the moonglow. Then Grimes' borrowed Colts blazed. A man jerked up, clutching his throat; another howled. The survivors flattened out of sight, deciding, "Ain't our hosses, nohow!"

Then the sheriff burst from the red glare of the jail front, and after him came Ferrell, reloaded shotgun in hand, and daughter trailing him.

"A thousand dollars, dead er alive!" he bellowed, leveling the gun.

Grimes, rounding the cluster of panicky horses, missed the screaming pellets; but a dozen mustangs, rumps riddled, stampeded in every direction. For a moment ,he hesitated. He was on foot, and a price was on his head. He'd better have married the girl. Or could he make the outskirts of the town, capture a horse whose fright had subsided?

Not a chance. They were coming, now. He bounded into the narrow space between two deserted houses, guns ready. Moonlight shooting might be tricky, but they did little else, back home in Gawgia.

Smack-smack-smack! He held them at bay; and then the heavy blast of a .60 caliber Sharps shook the tumult. Half the siding was torn from the shack as the heavy slug spattered him with splinters. Someone was trying to pick him off with an old fashioned buffalo gun.

Some stampeded horses were coming to a halt, but far behind the attackers, not where Grimes could mount up.

A pistol crackled behind him, though he did not hear or feel the bullet. A yell. They were flanking him. He whirled, desperate. A horse was stretching long legs up the narrow space behind him. A familiar horse—his own thoroughbred, and a woman mounting him. Lorette!

"Quick, honey!" she gasped, boosting herself backward over the cantle. "They're chasing me—they caught me hiding—"

He piled the gallant beast that stood fast, though snorting and quivering. Another shot from the rear. A shrill, quavering cry, and the thoroughbred soared incredibly into the moonlight and searching gunfire of the square. Panic nicked his high-strung nerves, and raking lead had stung him; but Grimes, holstering an empty .45, used hand and knee, wheeled and rode for it.

Lorette moaned as she clung to Grimes, hunched low in the saddle. The beast was wounded, overloaded, and he was hampered by clumsily tied hoof-mufflings; yet his whipcord muscles stretched in mighty strides, carrying him westward.

But the respite was brief; and soon they heard from behind the drumming of hoofs on the hard soil. The pursuit was gaining, and the thoroughbred's stride was failing. Grimes wheeled him about.

"Ease up," he panted, trying to shake Lorette's arms a bit looser. She coughed, moaned softly, relaxed. Grimes' borrowed Colt crackled savagely, and before the pursuit came within their firing range.

A saddle emptied; a horse dropped; but Grimes had shot his last shell, and one man charged on alone. It was the marshal, on a racing pinto pony.

"Let's git, boy!" panted Grimes, urging the thoroughbred into action.

He made a valiant effort, but he was losing. His great heart could not carry him much further. The following hoofbeats became stronger, and punctuated with pistol blasts. Lead sang, first wild, then nicking Grimes.

"Oh, Gawd, if I had a gun," he groaned as his horse stumbled, recovered, then reached out with a killing stride. His last effort, and Grimes knew death was gripping that gallant heart.

Lorette tried to say something, but it was lost in blended hoofbeats and a man's hoarse yelling. Then the thoroughbred pitched in a heap, and his riders with him. He had been dead in his last two strides.

"Here's a gun, honey," gasped Lorette, crawling toward Grimes. She fumbled in her bosom. Her hand came out with a little derringer, short, deadly—but now red as her own tiny hand. "Your money's in—the saddle—bags—go back—an' marry—her—"

She crumpled, and Grimes, himself wounded and dazed, lurched to his face, still clawing for the derringer with its two murderous barrels. He heard the snorting mustang, and Ferrell's exclamation. He wondered why the marshal didn't shoot.

"Yuh dad-bloomed scoundrel," rumbled Ferrell, misunderstanding the sobbing gasp and shudder that racked the man who lay near the girl whose blood frothed face smiled at the moonlight.

His drawn pistol drooped. Lack of answering fire proved Grimes was nearly dead, or had no more cartridges. But Ferrell did not know of the derringer, of the slaying wrath and grief that made Grimes thresh and shudder in the dust. Then he did get an instant of understanding.

That was when both barrels coughed lead, driving his nickeled star halfway through his heart. Grimes' feud was settled, and he at last clambered to his knees, weak but intact. Now that it was over, he was sorry for that old man; he'd rather not have shot him, but one of Ferrell's men had killed Lorette. . . .

He took the saddle from the thoroughbred and put it on the pinto; then, gathering Lorette into his arms, he choked, "I got him. An' they wasn't no weddin' after all. . . ."

He had some difficulty in mounting a horse skittish from the smell of blood, but he finally made it, and with a dead woman in his arms.

"Uncle Carter," he half sobbed, spurring his pinto westward, "'ll lambaste me fo' losin' that hoss . . . honey, I didn't really care nuthin' for Catalina, nohow. . . ."

He blinked, swallowed; and a full-grown man rode on, looking for a place to bury his first girl, whose pale face still half smiled up at him.

• • • • •

Treason's Kiss

HE FORKED AN EXHAUSTED PINTO MUSTANG TAKEN FROM A SUDDENLY DECEASED TOWN marshal in east Texas, and the pair of .45s he wore had, until a few days ago, been the pride of the sheriff summoned to hang him. Simon Bolivar Grimes, wanted on an unjust charge of murder and robbery, was not yet sure that he had shaken off pursuit. He was a long way from home, and almost as far from his uncle's ranch in Crockett County.

His coffin-shaped face was drawn with weariness and his gangling body ached from recent wounds. Though his saddlebags contained nearly a thousand dollars of his father's money, he had not dared pause to buy food, nor ask for Texan hospitality. Grimes was lost; he did not know that the moon-silvered stream at which he halted was the Brazos, that he was approaching the route followed by cattle drovers on their way north to Kansas.

He dismounted to drink, rub down his pony; but he paused, perceiving signs he might otherwise have ignored; a distant rumbling and lowing, men's voices, the odor of wood smoke—and a scarcely perceptible tang of bacon fumes and coffee.

Someone was eating! Grimes turned upstream, then checked himself, irresolute. Every man was his enemy.

"But I been eatin' regular nigh onto eighteen year, an' it's dang hard quittin', sudden-like," he finally muttered. His eyes became granite hard, desperate; he tossed the reins over the pinto's head: "Yo'all wait here, jest in case I leaves faster'n I went."

He hefted the elaborately carved bone butts of his borrowed pistols, loosening them in their tooled Mexican leather holsters, though that was a needless precaution. Grimes was a natural gunner. No amount of practice could have given such deadly quickness to those large, awkward-seeming hands; but having in one red night kissed his first girl and killed his first man, the boy had not yet become acquainted with himself.

As Grimes stealthily took advantage of cover, the yipping voices of the cowpokes became plainer, and so did the odor of food. Fresh from Georgia, he could not yet read the signs clearly enough to know that the herd was small, that only a few men watched it.

His advance became more cautious as he perceived the fire and the black bulk of a wagon. The drovers hadn't thus far sensed his approach; but a twig crackled and water splashed close at hand. Grimes dropped to the shelter of a fallen tree; but while sudden danger was almost within arm's reach, it heated his blood instead of chilling him to desperation.

A girl, seated on a log beside the shimmering pool, was slipping out of her next to last garment. Her hair was gilded by the light stealing in through overhanging foliage, and her beauty was ivory barred and mottled with shadow transparent enough to thrill Grimes with fascinations half seen.

She was substantial, with generous hips and full, round breasts; but the first semblance of maturity was illusion. She was young and, while amply formed, every line was clean and firm, from her well muscled legs to those upthrust breasts that challenged Grimes as, still not sensing his presence, she extended her arms to stretch the weariness from her body, inhale the evening fragrance.

It was only a few nights ago that a dance hall girl had convinced him that women have legs, not just feet and skirts; but this was a postgraduate course! He forgot his hunger; but Grimes reddened to his cowhide boots as he realized that he had no business watching.

He had the instincts of a gentleman. To lurk in hiding was taking an unfair advantage of her. He tried to move on, but despite his woodcraft, which was somewhat shaken by that generous display, a twig crackled. She started, hesitated a moment, one hand lingering where the yoke of her garment was so beautifully rounded out.

Just ahead, a dog yipped joyfully. She relaxed—and then the beast scented Grimes, and snarled. He could no longer conceal his presence; better reveal himself before she exposed her reserve fascinations. She *would* let out a scream if she knew a lurker had seen everything!

"Jes' keep yo' shirt on, m'am," Grimes hailed, breaking cover as the dog bristled and growled. "An' tell yo' dawg—"

"Ohhh!" A gasp; she was too self reliant to scream. And while she ignored the animal, she accepted the first suggestion as given.

"I'm Simon Bolivar Grimes, m'am," he added, "An' I didn't know yo'all was . . . gittin' yo'self a drink."

She smiled, appreciating tact; then, eyeing him as he stepped into the moonglow, she read the weariness graven into his young face, recognized the tense, wary shift of his narrowed eyes, the hand lingering at a gun butt.

He read her unspoken query, warmed to her friendliness; and moved by a fugitive's loneliness, he ended by telling her he was lost, hungry and hunted by enemies. And he learned that she was Sally May Pruett, accompanying her father on the long march to Kansas.

"Ma's dead, and pa couldn't leave me alone in San Saba," she concluded; then, though he hadn't told her his enemies wore stars, she patted his arm and added, "You wait here, and I'll get you something from the grub wagon."

Sally May donned one boot, but swayed, half losing her balance as she tried to draw on the other one. Unassisted, she would have regained her footing on the shifting gravel bank; but she depended too much on the fugitive's ready arm.

She was substantial, all the way up, or perhaps he was disconcerted by the handfilling roundness he caught instead of the arm for which he reached. Between scrambling to keep her upright, and tingling from the unintentionally intimate grasp, the fugitive's wobbly feet and uncertain legs betrayed him.

Grimes and the girl landed in a heap, and his efforts to recover made the tangle closer. Sally's instinctively tightened arms improved it; so that hunger was again forgotten. He couldn't keep his mind on food, not with the single garment that separated him from her generous contours.

He misread her soft laugh and felt foolish. Wasn't any woman in the world he couldn't set back on her feet; but his fumbling moves only got him from one embarrassingly pleasant spot to others even more so.

Grimes was red and stuttering before he realized that Sally liked it and was wriggling closer, thrilled by the feel of whipcord muscles and the pawing of blundering hands. He was so delightfully awkward—she'd have resented it, if it had been intentional. So Sally, who still had a lot of curiosity about life, half smothered him with a tentative kiss, and her tangle of free flung hair.

And then Grimes took the initiative. . . .

If he had not been so near exhaustion, her tremulous protests would have been wasted breath; and as it was, her eyes were misty and she was panting when she half wriggled from his arms. But she did not brush away the hand that made her tingle and shiver all over; not until after she had whispered, "you'd better eat something first. . . ."

He tried to detain her, but the effort was too much. He slumped, scarcely heard her add, "You just stay quiet till I get back. . . ."

Grimes, brain whirling, thought of the girl he'd buried after she stopped a bullet meant for him. No one could ever equal her reckless loyalty . . . though Sally was mighty sweet . . . wonder if the sheriff was still on the trail . . . dang them beef critters, lowing that way making a fellow sleepy. . . .

He roused himself, finally, hearing a furtive creeping in the underbrush.

"Here he is, Pruett!" gasped a hoarse voice.

"I'll teach them skulkin' beef thieves tuh spy on us!" growled the other.

Grimes, realizing it wasn't the girl, but her father, tried to tell them that he wasn't a cattle raider; but Pruett and his companion ploughed in, guns drawn. A shot blazed out of the shadows. Grimes flung himself aside, diving for the belt and revolvers he had discarded during the tangle with Sally; but he was slow, and though the move pulled him clear of the bullet, the two were on him with boots and spurs. Arms lashing out, he caught one about the legs toppled him over; and then things became too close packed for gun work.

"Watch out, Gil!" grunted the heavy hulk that ground him into the gravel. "Git that gun—"

Grimes' upward jabbing knee knocked Pruett breathless, but his blood-blinded groping for his lost belt was interrupted by a kick in the wrist; and then blows combined with exhaustion to blot out all but a shred of the boy's consciousness.

"Suppose they's any more?" wondered a distant-seeming voice.

"Kaint be or they'da piled into us," was the answer. "Must be alone, and left his hoss somewhere whilst he sneaked up afoot."

"Mebbe we oughta plug him?" was the next hopeful suggestion. "Be poison, turning him loose."

"Mmmm . . . I don't like that, Gil," rumbled the other. "Sally said he was jest a kid."

And that whipped Grimes to rage that conquered fatigue and battering.

She'd sold him out, played with his outlaw's hunger for human friendliness.

"Ef he's one o' Quentin's gang, he's a murderin' skunk, even ef he is young," snapped Gil.

There was the deadly click of a hammer thumbed back. That prodded Grimes; and Pruett's humane protest gave him the instant he needed to find his belt and a gun butt.

"I tell yah," snarled Gil, jerking from Pruett's grip. "He's a—"

The argument ended in a red haze. Grimes, now armed, tried to cry out a fair warning, but his lips were too thick. Gil whirled, but the glint of blued steel as the barrel shifted into line was drowned in the yellow blaze from the fugitive's gun. The drover lurched back, drilled through the middle. His fall blocked Pruett's draw.

Dying, he saved a life. Grimes, smashing down with his barrel instead of firing, knocked Pruett to his knees, revolver sliding across the gravel.

"Stand fast!" growled the boy. He retrieved his belt, but could not risk groping for the other Colt. "An' I hope they steal every critter yo' got!"

He backed off until he broke through the thicket, then turned and crashed downstream toward his horse. There was no pursuit; and as he piled into the saddle, he heard the renewed and now louder sounds of the camp. Pruett had hurried back to warn his men.

Grimes laughed bitterly. Alarmed by his prowling, they were getting ready for defense, and pressing on with their herd. But what cut the deepest was Sally's treachery.

He swam his mustang across the stream, spurred it into the sparsely wooded, rolling country beyond. The world became a moonlit nightmare. He was lightheaded now, and no longer felt his hunger; he had no feeling other than a corrosive wrath. But, very dimly, he knew that he must soon eat, else his next encounter would find him helpless.

It was sheer luck, seeing that jack rabbit which curiosity had led out into a moonlight clearing. Grimes steadied himself, made the tricky shot. Then, sheltered by a thicket, he kindled a small fire and prepared his meal. He wolfed it half raw; though it was tough as buckskin, it was food.

Grimes presently rode on; but he never knew for how long, nor when he dismounted. It was not until sunrise that he realized he had unsaddled the pinto, then lurched headlong across his equipment and slept sprawled under a scrubby oak. Yet he had gained new strength, and after eating the last bits of cold rabbit, he rode west, following his long shadow.

He had no plan except to get far enough ahead of pursuit to win's a day's rest in some cattle town, regain his bearings and buy a fresh horse. The pinto was on its last legs, limping and exhausted. And then, in mid afternoon, it happened. The weary mustang stumbled, piled headlong down the steep approach to a stream. Horse and rider were stunned by the shock; but Grimes was more fortunate than his mount.

The beast had broken a leg. He had never shot a horse, but he gritted his teeth and forced himself to it. That done, he shouldered the saddlebags and marched on.

"Nuthin' left now to shoot but me!" he somberly muttered, thinking of the trail of destruction in his wake. "An' if I don't git myself some vittles pretty soon, they'll be a-savin' ammunition when they find me!"

Stubbornness, however, carried him on; and toward sunset, he cleared a wooded crest, where he paused to study the rolling expanse below him. To his left, he noted a thin thread of smoke, seemingly rising from unbroken ground; but as he cautiously advanced, planning a raid on the food supply which must be near the fire, he saw that he was approaching a deep, steeply walled depression, apparently formed by the earth's settling into the space left by the cave-in of one of the caverns that honeycombed the underlying limestone.

But for the smoke, he would never have suspected the existence of that deep bowl and the saddled horses at the farther edge of the clearing in the center of the wooded bottom. Men were moving about, cattle were bellowing. The stench of burning hair and hide tainted the air.

"Looks like I done found a ranch," he decided. Then, watching the activity below him, "U-huh—they's brandin' their critters."

He counted the men in sight: half a dozen, and too many to handle in case of trouble. After Sally Pruett's treachery, and her father's hot reception, Grimes was wary of Texan hospitality.

"Better wait till dark. Then, if they's a ruckus, I kin git away better."

But his plan went awry before he had picked out the approach and exit. Crouched, hands parting the clump of vegetation through which he peered, he could only obey when an ironic voice commanded, "Jest raise yore hands an' scrunch around so's I kin git a look at yuh—but don't move sudden-like, or I'll blow yore guts so fur yuh won't never ketch up with 'em."

Grimes slowly turned toward a man with a drooping, tobacco-stained moustache and a face that looked as if its owner had spent most of his life avoiding the hangman. For a moment, his squinty eyes appraised his prisoner; then he demanded, "Who are yuh? What yuh doin' here? Whar yuh goin' to?"

The fugitive swallowed his wrath.

The cocked .45 allowed him no chance to dive for his own gun. He answered, "I'm Simon Bolivar Grimes, I'm goin' to Crockett County, an' I'm lookin' fo' vittles."

"Hhhmp! Yuh do look hongry," admitted the gunner. Then, suspiciously, "Whar's yore hoss?"

"I done shot him."

"Yuh did, eh?" The pudgy face tightened into a frown. "Yuh'd better stayed an' et him, too. Git along, boy. But fust, drap yore guns. *After I'm behind yuh.*"

That last amendment stole Grimes' chance for a desperate break. He unbuckled his belt; and when his captor scooped it up, he marched on, pistol jammed to the small of his back.

TWENTY YARDS FURTHER, GRIMES WAS PRODDED DOWN A NARROW PATH THAT LED INTO the bowl; but they had scarcely reached the floor when a red-bearded hulk hailed his captor: "What yuh got there, Sam?"

Grimes' pie-faced captor snorted derisively, then answered, "Looks like some jasper, but yah kain't never tell, so I brung him along 'stead o' pluggin' him whilst he was snoopin' around."

"Shootin' strangers," Grimes bitterly interpolated, "is a unpleasant custom yo'all have out this way. All I want is some yittles, and a hoss."

But the face above the red beard told him he'd picked a tough place for finding either necessity; yet, marching across the clearing, Grimes resumed, "Listen, yo'all, I'll work fo' my vittles. Shucks. I kin handle that there iron. But I sho' kain't figure out why yo' got so many different brands on them critters already."

Red and Sam laughed gustily; then the latter hailed a burly, evil faced giant who wore a silver adorned Mexican sombrero: "Yuh, Carver! Lookit what we got! He says he's hongry, an' walkin' tuh Crockett County. An' why is they so many diffrunt brands on them critters?"

Carver had no sense of humor. "Yuh jugheads been keepin' a hell of a watch, lettin' a jaybird like this sneak right up on yuh! Fust thing we know, we'll have—"

But he didn't bother with somber prophecy; he drew a Colt the size of a siege gun. Sam yelped, "Hey, yuh damn' fool! Lemme git clear, afore yuh plug him!"

Grimes made the most of that distraction. He flung himself sidewise during Carver's instant of hesitation and ploughed into Sam, whose smoke pole was now out of line. As they crashed headlong to the hard earth, he snatched at the butt of his own holstered gun, which Sam had dropped in the tangle. For a moment, the fugitive had the advantage. Neither Red nor Carver dared shoot, but every man was fair game for Grimes; and there were three saddled horses closer to him than to the men at work with the branding irons. Get his gun, shoot his way through, ride for it!

He had it—had Carver sky-lined; but as the gun roared, Red's boot kicked the weapon from his fingers. The slug went wild and then Grimes had his hands full. Though they couldn't shoot, they could pistol whip his head to a pulp; and the cow-pokers, alarmed by the shot, were charging in with running irons.

One more blow, and he was through; but Carver intervened: "Hold yore hosses! Wait til I asks this jaybird something!"

They booted him to his feet; and as the world whirled in a dizzy circle, Grimes wondered at his respite. Carver was facing him. He held the captive's gun by the barrel, stared curiously at the carved butt.

"Whar'd yuh git this pepper box?" he demanded, eyes narrowed.

Worse and worse! That was one of Sheriff Amos Brunton's .45s; but Grimes stoutly insisted, "I done bought it offen a man that didn't need it."

Carver slapped his thigh and laughed till the silver *conchas* on his bull hide chaps rattled. "He done *bought* this here weepon with the hand-fancied butt from that damn' skunk, Brunton! Boy, I dunno how yuh done it, but thar she is, and it's his'n! An' Brunton's belt an' holsters! Let go, an' give him some grub and a drink."

There must, Grimes reasoned, be a feud between Carver and the sheriff of Orange County; which automatically made this ranch boss his ally.

"Thank yo' very kindly, suh," he acknowledged. "An' I'll sho' be tickled to death to help yo'all mark those cow critters."

"Sufferin' horn toads!" Red cut in as he arose from his inspection of the scattered contents of Grimes' saddlebag. He hefted the buckskin pouch of gold pieces. "He got more'n yore friend's artillery!"

"Yuh'll do," admitted Carver; but the speculative glance which followed the returned pouch on its way to Grimes' pocket made the boy wonder how things were going to work out.

Still, they hadn't murdered him yet; and with his gun belted on again, the smell of grub in his nostrils, he allowed that maybe it wasn't so bad, this chance to learn a bit about the cattle business before he reached his uncle's ranch.

GRIMES, DESPITE FATIGUE AND A WELL-FILLED STOMACH, SLEPT LIGHTLY. IF CARVER HAD a feud with the folks in Orange, no telling what might crop up. And just for luck, he had before darkness found the gulley cut into the lip of the bowl by rainfall running from the upper level. That was the exit, and the route through which the beef critters came from the open range. . . .

What woke him was the voiceless rumble of cattle, and the oaths of the waddies driving them into the bowl. He stirred, sleepily, allowed he ought to help them. But he drowsed on, comfortably bedded under the chuck wagon, until again aroused, this time by muttering voices, a hoarse, drunken laugh, the spatter of breaking glass.

Grimes felt the tension in the air. Small shivers twitched in his legs and his heart hammered. Instinct, keener than his half-drugged senses, told him that things had happened, that more was coming.

He crept clear of the wagon in which the cook was snoring. By the half glow of a dying fire—the moon had not yet risen—he saw that the incoming cattle were agleam with sweat, which made their brands stand out.

"Dawggone . . . that's a new one," he frowned. "Only, these critters is marked all alike!"

And wits now sharper than they had been when he arrived, drugged with exhaustion, he began to put things together. Old Man Pruett's waddy had nearly shot him as a suspected cattle thief, had muttered about Quentin's gang. . . . No, that wasn't the answer; Carver was the name of the man who had a feud with Sheriff Brunton. . . .

It was time to leave, and farewells would be out of order. He took some gold pieces out of his pouch, wrapped them in a scrap torn from his shirt tail, and hung the parcel to a nail projecting from the chuck wagon door. With a piece of charcoal he laboriously scrawled beneath it, *"This is for the hoss I borrowed."*

Now to select the cayuse; though he'd have to wait until the rest of the incoming cattle cleared the narrow passage to the north.

As he crept from cover, he heard a sobbing, scarcely audible above the dull confusion at the further side of the bowl. Grimes' mouth hardened. A woman—and the more she wept, the better! Anyway, that was a strictly family affair, he told himself as he skirted the shadows, passing not far from the darkened cabin, half buried in the timber, from which the sound came.

Then he halted, motionless, blending into the gloom. Spurs jingled and a pudgy man, preceded by whiskey fumes, came toward him. It was Sam. Grimes' fingers quivered near his pistol butt. Had someone checked up on him?

A spine-chilling instant, and then he relaxed, trembling. Sam passed on, and there was neither struggle nor pistol shot to betray Grimes. He was now certain that, but for Sheriff Brunton's pistol, he would have been shot in his tracks, just to keep him from ever speaking of a place where cattle had such an assortment of brands.

All his native woodcraft then came into play. He found a saddled mustang, still wet with sweat, but it would do. He led the beast almost under the noses of a pair of waddies heading for the fire on which someone had heaped fresh fuel. And the snatch of conversation he picked in passing was a revelation: ". . . don't be so skittish, yuh jughaid! Ef yuh think ary a sod-bustin' law man's go'n' to sneak up on Carver Quentin, yo're plumb full o' loco weed."

Carver Quentin! No doubt now that he was leaving the company of desperate thieves, each of which—like himself, he bitterly reflected—had a price on his head.

He finally reached the narrow passageway. For some moments, he waited, trying to plumb its darkness, shut out the sounds of the camp behind and detect the advance of any laggards still on their way to the bowl. Then, certain that the way was clear, he mounted and cautiously reined his cayuse up the incline.

Suddenly, the beast whinnied, and before Grimes, leaning forward, could seize its nostrils to cut off the betraying sound, a rider lurched from the concealing gloom at his left, exclaiming, "Yuh, Baldy, what the hell—"

The answering horse talk blotted out the query; and then, sensing the purpose of Grimes' belated gesture toward the mustang's muzzle, he knew that it was not the man he had expected. He spurred forward, though still not certain that trouble was riding from camp; not until, in the level shafts of moonrise, he saw the strange face.

His hand whipped to his belt. Grimes could have beaten him to the draw, but he dared not risk a shot. Instead, he hurled himself from the saddle, shoulder catching Baldy's friend squarely in the stomach, long arms locking his assailant's. They crashed clear of the other horse, grunting and threshing. The stranger's gun clattered to the rocks.

There was a moment of snarling struggle, flailing spurs roweling the rocks. A dislodged fragment clipped one of the mustangs on the fetlocks; and as Grimes pounded his enemy's head against a boulder, both beasts squealed, snorted and clattered back into camp.

"I oughta cut yo' danged throat," muttered Grimes, booting his unconscious assailant for luck. "But yo'll keep till I finds myself another hoss."

And this time, as he passed the cabin in the timber, it was not a sob, but a woman's tense, vibrant cry of wrath and terror that caught his ear; that and a man's drunken chuckling, inarticulate sounds that Grimes could not misunderstand.

"Tain't none o' my business," he told himself; but despite feminine treachery, despite his peril, he could not ignore what was happening. Those primitive sounds, now reminded him of a girl who had not struggled. . . .

Grimes ploughed through the underbrush, lurched against the cabin door. It was barred, and the man inside growled, "Keep out, or—"

An oath and a slap broke the threat; but he recognized Sam's voice. Then a wavering yellow glow guided him to the window, and what he saw by candlelight was eyefilling.

What little the girl wore was in tatters, but Grimes was denied more than a fleeting glimpse of her breasts and white, shapely legs and substantial hips. Sam blocked the view, despite the clawing that she was giving him. Her yellow hair was streaming and her breath came in gasping sobs. She couldn't hold out much longer. She was now done in, quivering, helpless.

Grimes had his own hide to consider. No one had paid any attention to the girl's struggles; yet a shot or a man-to-man battle would bring the pack down on him.

It was none of his business, he told himself, even as his fascinated gaze clung to those well muscled, shapely legs; whoever she belonged to ought to look out for her, and if she was Sam's, why, let him handle her rough.

And then Sam, panting from more than his exertion, straightened up for a breath before clinching his victory. That gave Grimes his first glimpse of the girl: Sally May Pruett, her firm, generous body clawed and almost bare. Her long hair veiled her quivering breasts, but they would soon be denied even that shelter—

"Serves her right," Grimes gritted through clenched teeth, remembering the treachery that had given him lead instead of bread; but as Sam paused to pull at a whiskey bottle, the boy remembered other things—that moonlit pool of the Brazos, that white body he had fondled, the rise of her breasts and the clinging of her arms as she had kissed him.

A Judas kiss, but the memory choked him and his anger. And then, as Sam resumed his pawing, Grimes' brain became a red haze. Pulling himself to the sill, he lurched headlong through sash and glass, moving so fast that he landed ahead of the shattered panes.

Sam whirled, reaching for the gun on the adjoining table; but the hillbilly's fury overwhelmed him. They landed in a kicking, slumping heap beneath the table, and the savage pinwheel of fists spun over everything but the ceiling. Food, rest and wrath brought back Grimes' strength, and he passed it on to Sam.

The exhausted ruffian, groveling near the overturned table, had had no chance to yell; but as Grimes' slaying frenzy subsided, Sam found a comeback—his pistol, lying near the leg of the bunk in the corner.

"Drop it!" snarled Grimes, hand flashing to his belt; but his gun had fallen clear in the struggle.

Time ceased for an instant; yet shaky legs were better than fumbling trigger fingers. The boy leaped straight forward, landing before the battered gunner could make his sweat-slippery thumb and hand obey. His full weight and heavy boots caught Sam's forehead, and as Grimes rolled on to crash against the wall, he heard a sharp snap, and the skating of a gun across the planks.

He whirled, but the move was wasted. Sam lay twitching on the floor, and his head lolled at a crazy angle. His neck had been broken neatly as though done by the hangman's noose he had so long dodged.

And then Grimes saw Sally, unsteadily regaining her feet. She made helpless gestures to rearrange the scraps that scarcely hid her; but the flush left her face dead white when she recognized him.

"So you are one of them?" she said, voice low and bitter. "That makes me feel a little better. *But* if you saved me for yourself—"

She made a desperate lunge for Sam's abandoned gun.

Grimes did not block her. He said, "M'am, I wouldn't touch yo' with a running iron—not after sellin' me down the river. Yo' suppose I'da interfered if I was one o' these thieves?"

It was his scorn, not his logic, that convinced her. Sally's face changed, then she said, "Pa caught me getting some food, and he made me tell. I couldn't help it. I told him—that you were just a kid—in hard luck—but—"

She came closer, eyes wide and appealing; and Grimes a second time believed her. It was easy, now that she was again in his arms, telling him how rustlers had attacked the camp, captured her, dispersed the waddies that had not been shot down.

"And I don't know if pa and the sheriff escaped or not," she concluded.

"Sheriff?" Grimes became tense; then, pinching out the candle flame, he demanded, "Brunton?"

"Yes. And he was looking for you. Just before the raid, pa found Brunton's gun, down there, where you . . . dropped it."

"Git yo' boots, Sally," he cut in. "We got to git befo' someone misses Sam."

"They're too busy with stolen cattle to watch me," she whispered, drawing away. "They—Carver Quentin—tied me. And at first I thought Sam was going to let me loose. But that wasn't why he cut my feet loose—"

He felt her shudder as they went toward the door; and then Grimes recoiled, catching her arm. More cattle were being driven into the bowl. The passage was blocked.

"That's the rest of our herd," whispered Sally. "I was with the first lot."

"Can't never git a hoss up the steep wall," muttered Grimes. "They got us bottled up."

Hours might pass before they could slip out that narrow gulley. And before then, the lookout he had laid out would recover. Grimes drew his Colt, intending to risk escape on foot; but Sally restrained him: "If he was unconscious, those cattle trampled him to mush. They'll never suspect you when they find him in the morning."

"But they'll find Sam," he somberly reminded her. "We got to move."

"Wait," she urged, drawing him toward the door. "They're all too dog tired to remember me. We're safe here, for a while, and—"

She clung closely to him, and he sensed her thought before she added, "We've not got much chance at the best, Simon—and somehow—after last night—don't you understand?"

Her close-pressed warmth inflamed him, despite reason and peril. Life had become a succession of blazing guns; and the desire that had almost fought off hunger, that night by the Brazos, became stronger because of desperation. He was too young to die before he had another woman in his arms.

Neither had tasted enough of life to be other than eager, and yesterday's interrupted moments were clamorous. He felt the sudden rise of her breast, and the hot breath that fanned his cheek in the darkness just past the threshold.

"Now maybe you'll believe me," she sighed, her lips finding his.

But that kiss was short. Not even love can blaze in the flame of pistols. He thrust her aside as a fusillade crackled at the farther edge of the clearing. Men were yelling, horses snorted, the lumbering cattle had begun to bellow as they stampeded into the bowl.

Grimes caught it all at a glance. Pistol fire and rifle flame were pouring from the upper level; lead sang defiance to the answering shots from camp. And while the wooded belt of the bowl would break the stampede, the fast developing battle would envelope them. He thrust Sam's pistol into Sally's hand and said, "There's a hoss by the chuck wagon—"

"You can't make it!" she gasped, catching his arm; and as she spoke, the beast, stung by a ricochet bullet, broke loose and raced madly across the lead-swept clearing.

Carver Quentin's voice boomed above the confusion, and flame now spurted from the lower levels of the wall. The raiders were stubbornly advancing. Then the chuck wagon burst into flame, and the defenders surged back toward the timber.

Whichever way Grimes turned, he had not a chance, hampered by Sally. The further flank of the retiring defenders had now cut off their retreat; and Quentin, rallying his men, recognized Grimes and the girl as they ducked for cover. Red, at his side, jerked about, smoking Colt leveled.

"That's the snake in the grass—he brung the law—"

A slug from across the clearing dropped him as he fired; and then the confusion centered on Grimes and the leader. For once, the boy's speed was matched. Though his own gun blotted out the blaze of Quentin's, he did not see his enemy drop. Blood blinded him and he fell, scalp furrowed by a dead man's bullet.

Sally's scream, the insane bellow of the Colt she fired past him were blended in the ringing of his jarred skull. And when his wits assembled, he knew that, though he had been out only a few minutes, the raid was over. A strong hand was jerking him to his feet.

"Here's one of 'em, an' he ain't dead . . . they's plenty o' rope for all—" A woman's voice cut into the blurr of voices: "That's Simon—I—I tell you he helped me—Oh, pa, they didn't kill you—how'd you find this place—"

Old man Pruett's grim face relaxed and as his daughter clung to him, he thrust aside one of the posse who was coming forward with a *riata*.

"We found the pinto hoss he stole from that marshall he shot, an' followed him from whar he'd gone a-foot—"

"But, pa, I tell you, he's not one of these rustlers—"

GRIMES, STILL DAZED, HAD NO CHANCE TO ARGUE. A WHITE-HAIRED LITTLE MAN WITH A star on his chest approached; the sheriff who had organized a posse after the raid on Pruett's camp. He listened, and for a moment Grimes and Sally exchanged a hopeful glance. Drawn weapons were lowered—

But that respite was only for an instant. Brunton, who had pursued him all the way from Orange, shouldered into the group. He was far out of his jurisdiction, but vengeance and wrath drove him.

"I'm a-takin' that young skunk," he declared, reaching for the recovered Colt that had led him to the rustler's bowl. "Hist—"

Grimes, however, had expected trouble. Though he had not reloaded his gun, his legs served. He lunged, shouldering Pruett against Brunton. His unexpected move, made in the face of his vindication by Sally, caught the posse off guard. Before they could realize what was happening, Grimes was stretching long legs into the timber.

"Simon!" screamed Sally. "Come back—it'll be all right—"

She might be right; but there was a feud between him and Brunton. He raced on, in a curve; and somehow, the pursuit headed for the passage, in the opposite direction. He allowed that Pruett had deliberately led the rush astray to give him his chance.

Scrambling up the steep wall, Grimes reached into his pocket for cartridges, but when he cleared the lip, he had no use for his reloaded Colt. Intent on their surprise attack, the posse of irate cattlemen had left no horse guards. He had his choice, and he picked a good one.

But as he galloped west, with no hoofbeats drumming behind him, he smiled ruefully, and muttered, "Dang that posse . . . if they'd only waited a spell . . . that last wasn't no Judas kiss!"

• • • • •

Grimes, Outlaw!

FOR SOME TIME, THERE HAD BEEN NO PURSUING HOOFBEATS; BUT, AS THE YOUNG FUGITIVE pulled up to wind his exhausted horse, the beast collapsed. The tall, gangling rider flung himself clear, staggered drunkenly in the gloom, regained his balance. Though he had won distance, he had killed his mount. The sheriff who had chased him halfway across Texas would finally track him down.

He fumbled in his pockets and saddlebags, but found no cartridges for his single action .45; and his belt loops were empty.

"Gawd," he groaned, his coffin-shaped face twisting in a pained grimace, "here's one time pap won't git a chanct to lambaste me. I'll be gittin' hanged fust, on-less I find me a hoss."

Simon Bolivar Grimes was exhausted, but he shouldered his saddlebags, stumbled along; and then, as the riding stiffness left his muscles, his long legs stretched out in the space-eating stride of a Georgia hillbilly.

Finally, a light beckoned, far to his left front. Someone was up mighty late. Moonrise would soon expose him; so he hurried toward the lamp glow, hoping to raid a barn and get a good horse.

Presently, barbed wire and ploughed soil hampered him. This was some sod-buster's place, not a ranch. His heart sank; instead of an agile cow pony, there'd be a lumbering draft animal. But as he neared the house, a shaft of light from the corner room revealed a horse at the hitching post, brought out the pale golden mane and tail, the strawberry roan coat of a sleek, slim legged palomino, saddled and ready to ride!

And then the light winked out. That alarmed Grimes. Someone must have sensed his approach. The farmers certainly would not be going to bed and leaving the horse at the hitching post. Grimes had to strike first.

He found a rock and crept closer. There was a chance of tossing the missile so as to make a disturbance some distance from the house; then, as the unwary watchers took the bait and rushed out, he could pistol whip them, mount up and ride.

Indian stealth brought him to a clump of shrubbery beneath the sill. There was a stirring and a murmuring within; and a vagrant shaft of moonlight, coming in through a window on the exposed side of the corner room, thinned the gloom just enough to make Grimes change his plan. The man was scarcely more than a splotch of darkness, but the woman was more clearly revealed.

She wore a light slip, and the whiteness of her shapely legs, the thinly covered roundnesses and the generous curves of her figure straining at the confines of her garment for a moment were ivory-tinted luxuries; then they were partially blotted out as her companion caught her in his arms, drew her toward him, avidly kissing, embracing her buxom curves.

She was half protesting, half yielding; then her arms closed about his neck, and the lurker outside felt thrills racing through his veins as he saw the movement, heard her ecstatic sigh. . . .

Grimes, blood boiling, turned away, convinced that the lovers would not hear him if he moved cautiously; but the next instant froze him. That was when the palomino impatiently pawed.

"Sam!" gasped the woman, the ardor drained from her voice, "You shouldn't of left your hoss out in front. Suppose Hillis came home, an' you had to duck out the back—"

Grimes edged toward the steps to bushwhack Sam when he emerged; but that tense moment ended when Sam assured her, "Don't yuh worry, honey. Hillis was so drunk he won't know his name fer two-three days."

The fugitive wiped the sweat from his forehead; and when Sam and Honey uncorked their next clinging kiss, Grimes set to work cutting up his extra shirt to muffle the palomino's hoofs. Then he wrapped up several gold pieces in a shirt scrap and tied it on the hitching post, where Sam would find it when he sought his hoss. He believed in paying for borrowed mounts.

As he swung to the saddle, he noted that there was a Winchester carbine slung from the saddle. Life, and freedom were ahead!

He rode south, heading away from the lights of a distant settlement; then, by moonlight, he saw that the rolling range was becoming rocky wasteland, broken by monstrous masses of towering stone. The sheriff, far from his bailiwick, had no posse, nor could he organize one among people who had troubles of their own. This was almost a feud, private vengeance for Grimes' jailbreak; and these wastelands offered a chance to ambush his pursuer.

AT DAWN, AS HE HEADED FOR A BUTTE THAT COMMANDED THE COUNTRY FOR MILES AROUND, Grimes saw a familiar, hunched figure, now on a white horse.

The sheriff, getting a fresh mount, had reasoned that Grimes would head for the wastelands. The tow-headed fugitive halted, waved a derisive arm. The distance was far too great even for rifle fire; but Grimes caught a sudden gleam, for an instant almost blinding. Then the horseman spurred forward.

"He was usin' a spy glass," the boy told himself. "That's whut made that glitter. An' my eyes bein' better'n his'n, I reckonized him fust."

He held the sturdy mare to a moderate pace, letting her out only as Brunton gained. The sun became blistering hot, and there was no water; but Grimes' heart leaped as the lawman's wrath made him snap at the bait.

Brunton had to catch Grimes. The boy's jailbreak to avoid hanging on an unjust charge had made a fool of the sheriff; so he rode on, vengeful.

"An' heah it is," muttered Grimes, through thirst-baked lips.

A small whirlwind was freakishly marching ahead, like dust kicked up by a running horse. Grimes rounded a towering rock, concealed the palomino in the sparse brush. He jerked the carbine from its boot, took cover just as the sheriff, a quarter of a mile behind, came into view. The treacherous little whirlwind had skittered around a further rock, leaving only lingering dust.

Brunton pulled up. It didn't make sense, entirely; but he was reckless.

Grimes ducked as the glasses swept the further cleft. Brunton, assuming that the fugitive carried only a pistol, had a four hundred yard margin of safety. He was in the open, and no one could sneak up on him; he was wary only of the approach to the pinnacle beyond.

Yet Grimes hesitated, and his hand trembled. This was a feud, and generations of Georgia tradition made Brunton fair meat; but while the boy's dancing pistol had blotted out two ruffians in a brace of seconds, they had been reaching for their own guns. This was different.

"I got to plug him, or I'll never git to Uncle Carter's ranch," he said through gritted teeth; then his trigger finger contracted.

The rifle blast echoed savagely among the rocks; but as he leveled home another .45-70, Grimes knew that the stubby carbine had tricked him. At that range, it didn't throw slugs as flat as his long-barreled rifle back home. The shot was low.

Brunton's horse pitched in a kicking heap, throwing its rider. He tried to creep to the shelter of the dead beast; but Grimes' next shots kicked dust in his eyes, blinding him. And then, rifle at the ready, the boy broke cover.

Well beyond revolver range, he halted; but though one slug from the carbine would now settle it, he couldn't cut down a man who was virtually unarmed. He was too young to be practical, cold-blooded.

"Git up!" Grimes bellowed, rifle leveled.

"Shoot, yah long-legged sidewinder!" the sheriff challenged.

"Shuck yo' guns an' star, take off yo' boots, an' start foggin'!" commanded Grimes. "I'm a-givin' yo' that chanct. Now move smart!"

The grim old sheriff, dazed by unexpected mercy, obeyed. As he retreated, barefooted, across blistering earth and rock, Grimes scooped up the loot. Then he ran back, mounted up and galloped south.

But somber thoughts haunted the boy as he rode; even though he finally killed Brunton, that remorseless man would first have plastered all Texas with reward notices for Grimes, dead or alive. Not even his uncle's ranch on the bank of the Pecos could long shelter him.

He kain't go back home 'thout me. Onless he starves on foot. Some time he'll git to me, an' I'll have to kill him, toe to toe. I jest ain't made fo' bush-whackin' or I'd not missed him that fust chanct, he told himself; and that shaped his decision to go south, into Mexico.

AT SUNSET, SEVERAL DAYS LATER, HE HEADED FOR A TOWN INSTEAD OF AVOIDING IT. HE was far ahead of pursuit, and he needed rest and some square meals. Though he did not know it, this was El Aguila, whose dusty main street was flanked by squat,square 'dobe houses, and crowded with yapping dogs and half naked, brown children. And as he reached the plaza at the heart of the town, his haggard blue eyes became speculative.

Half the population seemed to be Mexican. He could not be far from the Rio Grande. This was the place to join some outlaw who operated along the border. Meeting one should not be difficult. They defied sheriffs, came and went openly, secure in the tolerance of the common people—an advantage denied a lone fugitive. Grimes, Georgia hillbilly, had elected his destiny before dismounting at the livery stable adjoining a hotel that faced the plaza: he would be an outlaw.

Grimes fished a gold piece from his heavy buckskin poke, tossed it to the squint-eyed hostler, and surrendered the reins; but before turning to the hotel, he paused to listen to Spanish voices singing *La Paloma,* to laughter and the *click-click* of castanets. The sound came from a 'dobe building nearby. That would be the place to make contact with people who knew the border.

Intent on his plans, he did not notice that the swarthy hostler was thoughtfully regarding the pocket in which Grimes had buried his initialed buckskin pouch.

It was good to be where people could sing and laugh at sunset. The loneliness of flight cuts deeper than the peril.

"Verree nize place, *señor.*" The hostler's smile was ingratiating, and he suggested, "You try heem. Verree fine girl, no?"

"Mebbe later," compromised Grimes, stepping toward the inn with his saddlebags.

A Mexican woman whose age and plumpness had not quite blotted out all her former beauty showed him to his room. She had a pleasant face, and like most of her kind, splendid eyes. Her feet were small, and her legs, Grimes observed as she bustled about the room, were shapely. And after the burning memories of the farmhouse a few nights past, Grimes had an aching interest in feminine contours—of which this not-too-plump Mexicana had plenty.

She sensed his scrutiny, and her eyes had an expectant sparkle as she finally left, leaving him to wash off the dust of travel and shave the fuzz from his chin.

Glancing about the room, he observed that the partition dividing his from the one adjacent was fully a yard short of the beamed ceiling; but he did not notice that the bars of the unglazed window, instead of being of iron, were wooden rods set in a thin frame: dummy substitutes to conform to tradition. Music and the fumes of cookery were reminding him of the hostler's suggestion; but as he opened his door, the plump Mexicana barged in.

"Eef you are hongry, I 'ave some tamale," she suggested.

But Grimes, despite the friendly smile and the caressing hand on his arm, answered, "Thank yo' kindly, m'am, but I got to see a gent down theah wheah they got all thet music."

"No, you mus' not," she protested. "Ees no good. Me, Tula, I run the honest place. Don' go in those bandit den. An' those girl—*muy malo!"*

Tula, detaining him, almost smothered Grimes with her generous curves. Her dark eyes had an eager gleam; her lips, scarlet and full, were tantalizingly close to his in her insistence.

She was no prize beauty, but she was pleasant, and trying to extricate himself from detention was warming Grimes' blood. It was becoming much easier to hold her closer than to break away, but he resolutely downed his urge, and stuttered, "M'am, I sho' love this, but I jest got to see a gent on impo'tant business fust."

He broke clear and dashed down stairs to meet his future.

MUSIC AND LIGHTS GUIDED HIM TO A SPACIOUS HALL CROWDED WITH COWPUNCHERS, traders in fringed buckskin, arrogant Mexicans swaggering about in velvet trousers and jackets agleam with silver conchas. The blue-jowled bartender kept a sawed-off shotgun on the back bar, ready to quell riots. Every man was heavily armed.

Most of these gents must be outlaws, pondered Grimes as he downed a slug of whiskey, then wolfed a bowl of savory stew from the lunch counter.

He overrated the crowd; but that was natural. Here, close to that no-man's land not far from the Rio Grande, life was more flamboyant than further north.

Then the musicians again struck up; an incredible girl came dancing into view, high-piled black hair agleam with jeweled combs.

As she whirled and postured, her voluminous scarlet skirt swirled out and upward, giving Grimes inflaming glimpses beyond the little bells on her garters. Castanets clicking, she swayed lightly, making her brocaded silks cling to her supple body, shape to the splendor of her lithe curves; and as she bent back, there were dazzling instants when he could see more of that ivory-tinted skin than the costume was meant to show.

"Olé! Olé! Paquita!" the spectators shouted when a crashing chord ended her dance. Even the squint-eyed hostler, now crowded to Grimes' side, had come to see Paquita.

Grimes' gold piece was the first to tinkle to her dainty feet, and as the rain of coins subsided, her magnificent black eyes invited him. And the hostler, nudging him, said, "She likes you, *señor.* See—"

That was when she plucked the only gold piece from the collection and touched it to her lips. They were red and promising. Heart hammering, Grimes advanced. She caught his hand, and, undulant hip brushing against him, led him to the alcove from which she had emerged.

"M'am," he groped, dizzied by her fragrance, "watchin' yo' dance made me fo'git I ain't et sence this mo'ning."

"You are too sweet," she murmured, her throaty tones making his blood race; and then she wondered if he had relatives in town, or if he was passing on.

"I hope you're staying," she hopefully added, eyes suddenly somber. "There's always someone wanting to go home with me, only I care for none of those bandits!"

The curtained alcove was furnished with a chair, a lounge and a small table on which stood a bottle of tequila and a single glass. It never occurred to Grimes to wonder why that glamorous girl had been drinking alone, or why she had picked him from the crowd. Such things just happened, he reckoned.

And as she snuggled closer, another gust of that heady fragrance exhaled from the soft mystery of her bodice made him feel as though he'd swallowed a prairie fire. He was half afraid to touch her, but those black, half veiled eyes invited him, and when little tendrils of hair brushed his cheek, he began to realize that even such beauty can be human.

Grimes' arms closed about that slim length of scarlet and ivory, and his lips smothered her protesting murmur. She was clinging to him, murmuring endearments in Spanish; and the throb of heart close pressed against his own made him as reckless as he had been shy. His awkwardness was displaced by aggression that ignored both time and place; and every touch of that shapely form further inflamed him.

But Paquita, restraining him, said in a tremulous whisper, "Don't, *querido*—please—there ees only a curtain for a door—an' I mus' soon dance again—but I live just around the corner from the cathedral—and father won't be home to-night—"

And before he could fairly realize it, she was out of his arms.

"What's yo' pappy do?" he demanded, again aware of her lavish jewelry. Her father must follow some unusually profitable occupation to keep her so glittering; and if she had any lovers, Grimes would now be fighting for his life. "Yo' sure he won't be back?"

"Oh . . . he's often gone . . . two-three days at a time," she answered, ignoring the reference to her father's business.

No, he didn't make whiskey; and Paquita's continued evasions were a dead giveaway, here in a border town crowded with elegantly dressed and heavily armed men. And Tula's hints about bandits clinched it.

"Ef he's a outlaw," he at last said, coming to the point, "I'd sho' like to meet him, some time. I'm aimin' to be one myself."

Paquita's smile became cryptic; then she confidentially whispered, "You're awfully clever, guessing that way. But we'll talk about that tonight. I know he could find a place for you."

Her glance lingered knowingly on the red weal a bullet had traced on his cheek; and then, when Paquita had to put on her next dance, he left, with the address and the hour burned into his mind.

HALFWAY ACROSS THE PLAZA, HE HALTED, HEFTED HIS BUCKSKIN POKE. A STAGECOACH was just pulling out; the express office was still open. He stepped to the counter, emptied the pouch of gold, pocketed a few pieces and then addressed the hatchet faced clerk: "I'm Simon Bolivar Grimes, suh, an' I'd like to ship this here money to Mistah Carter Grimes, in Crockett County."

While the clerk set about making the receipt, Grimes hunched over the counter and laboriously scrawled a letter.

Dear Unkel Carter,
    I ain't coming to your ranch, so I'm shipping you $500, which is all what's left of the money Pap give me to give you.

He owed his uncle some explanation, but he couldn't tell him anything like the truth; so he finally improvised,

> I'm going to Mexico to be a outlaw, because I done killed a revenue man named Brunton and got myself into a feud with his folks.
>
> Hoping you are the same, yours truley,
>
> Simon Bolivar Grimes

That put no stain on an honored name; and if the sheriff, who knew the fugitive's destination, did survive and reach the Box A Ranch, he'd get his gizzard shot out before he could begin to give the details of Grimes' affair with the jailer's daughter, just before his escape from Orange.

PRESENTLY, HE WAS BACK IN HIS ROOM. TULA, WHO APPARENTLY HAD MISSED HIS RETURN, certainly had been way off the track in her warning; though, of course, she had not known that he was looking for a bandit rendezvous.

Grimes, weary from hard riding, dozed as he waited. He awoke with a start, chilled at the thought of having perhaps missed the cathedral bell; then he heard a key turning in his lock. Silent as a cougar, he was on his feet, pistol drawn, creeping toward the door jamb to reverse the game.

The prowler was now very stealthily swinging the door inward. Grimes jerked it open. He came within a hair of firing before he saw that it was Tula, and barely caught her in time to keep her from pitching headlong into the room. But while she gasped, she recovered, and still hanging on, she whispered, "I deed not want no wan to hear w'en I come in, *verdad?"*

Her eyes were eloquent; and significantly enough, she had not brought any food. Grimes, however, had an important engagement, so that Tula's draping herself on him was now not as blood-stirring as it had been earlier that evening, when she spoke of groceries and wild women.

He couldn't understand her Spanish endearments, but her caresses needed no interpreter. Grimes was embarrassed; he didn't want to dally with Tula, but neither did he want to hurt her feelings. He was red and bewildered as he watched her carefully closing the door. And then Tula fairly swamped him.

There was no retreat. He was half horrified now by her advances; comparing her substantial though passably shapely contours with Paquita's exquisite beauty was too much. But as he vainly tried to thrust her aside, her ripe curves began to overcome his revulsion.

That abundance of feminine flesh began to stir and inflame him. Her hot lips and soft arms began to claim their due from a lonely fugitive. There was no resisting a woman like this! And the prospective outlaw tried not to think of Paquita, and the cathedral bell. . . .

But it was Spanish architecture as much as ardor that caught Grimes wholly off guard. A scraping and a thumping against the dividing partition warned him, and Tula cried out; but before he could reach for the gunbelt hanging over a chair back, a stern voice commanded, "Leggo an' hist yore paws!"

Sheriff Brunton, mustache and iron-gray, horseshoe face, mummy thin from hardship, was straddling the partition, gun leveled, eyes frantically blazing as he snarled, "Yuh never reckoned they was a stagecoach trail I could git afore the buzzards et me? Never figgered I'd guess yuh'd head fer Mexico, an' that a palomino is a conspicyus hoss!"

Intuition, and that spyglass glimpse of the golden-maned mare had damned Grimes. His hands rose, and Brunton growled, "Turn roun' an' belly up agin the wall while I git down. That's whut yuh git fer foolin' with bad women!"

He dropped when Grimes was well out of reach of the gunbelt; but it did not occur to Brunton that he had misjudged Tula, that she was interested in more than Grimes' money. He entirely missed the hand that had a pillow by the edge; his scornful glance at the shameless hussy was a shade too late. The hurled pillow plopped him in the face, muffling his gun. The shot he instinctively jerked went wild.

Grimes whirled, ducked as a second slug blasted the wall. Tula's reckless wrath and the boy's desperate whirl sent all three into a kicking tangle. He seized the sheriff's wrist, his other hand hammering home. There was another wild shot, and as Tula impartially squashed both Grimes and the invader, there were shouts in the hall, pounding feet, shoulders crashing against the door. The lock yielded before Grimes could get a weapon into line.

The town marshal and a deputy were in control, guns leveled.

"Git that sidewinder!" yelled Brunton. "I been chasin' him all over hell's half acre. I'm the sheriff from Orange—"

"He ees crazy!" screamed Tula. "Where ees the star? I saw heem get off the stage. I hear the driver say he 'ave pick heem up barehead, barefoot, *loco* weeth the heat. An' now he 'ave buy the gun and break into my hotel."

That gave Grimes a chance to play it up: "This po' old man is tetched in the haid. Wheah's his warrant fo' me?"

Half an hour's investigation clinched it. Brunton actually was half delirious and on the verge of collapse. Having taken the trail without a warrant, he was only a discredited stranger in El Aguila. They flung him into jail to keep him from hurting someone. And long before he could establish his identity, Grimes would be an outlaw.

His bulky benefactress, in the meanwhile, was at the hotel, hopefully awaiting an encore; but it was too close to Paquita's appointed hour for Grimes to risk getting within reach of Tula. . . .

He loitered in the plaza, drinking in the crisp night air, which but, for Tula's quick wit, he would be breathing in a cell. Only her claim that he was sunstruck had kept Brunton from making it stick; yet, once a man is plausibly called *loco,* he can talk sense and still get no credence.

But time dragged. To go back to the cabaret would make Paquita too conspicuous. And his room was now off limits. So he headed for the stable to see if the solicitous hostler had taken good care of the palomino mare.

He wondered at the cluster of men gathered about her stall. There was Landers, the red-headed marshal, and a burly, round-faced fellow all covered with dust. Pride warmed Grimes as, barging toward the group, he caught a few words: "... ain't another hoss like her in south Texas ... *si, señor,* the young gentleman tol' me to feex her up nice...."

An instant later, Grimes realized his mistake. That was when one rasped above the murmur, "Besides, thar's Sam's brand—tain't plain, but yuh kin see it."

He moved fast, and just a split second before the hostler's gesture and recognition. His guns were out as the group whirled. The marshal cursed, raised his hands at Grimes' command.

"Back up, yo'all! An' yo', theah, saddle up that hoss!"

One move, and some of them would die, even though a cross flame of guns would cut Grimes down. He had them nailed; and the trembling hostler seizing the saddle, passed behind the wrathful group.

"One at a time, shuck yo' belts," he ordered, "Startin' from the left!"

There were hard men among them, but they read from the long, tense face that valor and suicide meant the same that night. They reached for buckles, not pistol butts. And then, as Grimes took the reins, he backed with the palomino toward the door, unwavering gun enforcing his command: "Come forward slow-like, an' don't try trippin' over my iron!"

A pace ... another ... and again, step by step, he drew them from their abandoned artillery. Then, once at the door, mount and ride as they scrambled for weapons, gave the alarm. Deadly, but he had a chance.

The sense of power thrilled him. Not a man of them had ever witnessed his deadly gunwork, yet their instinct had warned them. He was a man among men now. That knowledge was almost worth flight, and the loss of Paquita. But, once established, he'd return for her.

He cleared the door. It was perfect—perfect, until a shotgun muzzle prodded his side.

"Drap it, hoss thief!" boomed a voice from the door jamb. "Git him, yuh statues. Landers, looks like I picked the lucky time tuh come from his room whar yuh figgered on findin' him."

Once disarmed, Grimes learned that he had run in with hard men. Killing, within reason, was tolerated in El Aguila, but not stealing horses. Yet there would be no summary execution, despite the indignation of the palomino's owner. The red-handed culprit was hustled to jail, safe from a population that believed in the sanctity of horseflesh.

An early hanging, Grimes bitterly rejected, was bad enough; but what burned him to the marrow was being flung into the cell occupied by Brunton, who still vainly swore to the night and the world that he was a sheriff.

"Shut up, yo' old coot!" snarled Grimes as they glared at each other, for the first time meeting empty-handed. "Y'oughta be happy, me gittin' hanged. Though I guess yo'll bust a gut, knowin' it's fo' somepin I did do, instead of fo' what I'm innocent of."

Even if there had not been a guard, Grimes' sudden downfall left him without the heart to use his bare hands to slay the man who had hounded him into this fatal mess.

"Innocent?" flared Brunton, eyes blazing. "Yuh coyote, it's yore fault they claims I'm loco! Innocent—dad blame yuh, yuh held up that saloon, yuh killed the marshal that was chasin' yuh after yuh'd busted outa jail—"

"Bein' as I didn't hold up that saloon," Grimes cut in, "that shootin' an' jail breakin' was jest self defense to keep from gittin' hanged. Wall, wasn't it, ye' old sculpin'?'"

Misery broke down barriers; Brunton finally conceded, "Yuh convince me they warn't no robbery, an' I'll say yuh was right, smokin' yore way out."

And then, though his neck was in jeopardy for horse theft, Grimes attacked the perjured witnesses who had set Brunton on the trail.

"That saloon keeper back in Orange," he concluded, "wanted my money. So he says the money I had was his'n, not knowin' I'd left it in that gal's room. And when I says, git the poke and look at my pap's initials on it, it'd made it bad fo' him, only the gal, when she saw me arrested, had run out with my hoss and money. She was 'lowing she'd come back and help me, later, which she did, with a file fo' me to cut my way out. But, by then, everyone was agin' me, so they wasn't no time to argue.

"But ef I'd had a chanct to show this poke to the court—" He drew the empty pouch from his pocket. "I coulda cleared myself. *An'* I could, now, by the express company, an' a letter I wrote my uncle."

Bit by bit, Brunton digested the argument, realized that circumstances and incomplete evidence had played into the hands of an avaricious divekeeper.

"Bub, gimme that pouch," he finally said, "so I kin account fer not bringin' yuh back with me. I'm lookin' into all this. I'm shore sorry they's hangin' yuh. I'd be proud of a fightin' son like yuh, yuh gol-danged, onery critter!"

Long silence. At last, Grimes said, "Mebbe yo' kin take me back an' break up this hanging?"

"Son," sighed the old sheriff, shaking his head, "they ain't a chanct. Yuh made too good a job of provin' I was crazy."

And before Grimes could fairly absorb that grim irony, voices echoed, feet tramped down the corridor toward the cell. Landers, the red-headed marshal; an out-of-town lawman and his dusty, round-faced companion appeared.

Brunton extended his hand and said, "Good luck, kid."

Grimes gripped the gnarled paw, swallowed, and answered, "'Bye, sheriff. *I'd* ruther you and me'd had a chanct to shoot it out."

"Aw right, Grimes!" rumbled Landers, "We're goin'."

"Come on, yuh lowdown thief!" snarled the round-faced man. "Ef I had my way 'bout it, yuh'd be strung up here, 'stead of bein' taken back fer trial."

"Fer god's sake, Sam," snorted the out-of-town lawman, "he'll git it soon enough. An' he's jest a kid, anyway."

Grimes stared, blinked. Sam—that name was familiar. Sam owned the palomino. They eyed him, wondering at his sudden change of expression. Even the jailer ceased fumbling for the right key.

"Yo'all mean I ain't hangin' right here an' now?" Grimes queried. "An' that I gits a legal trial, *wheah I stole the hoss?"*

"That's right, kid," said the law man.

"An' I gits a chanct to explain everything?" persisted Grimes.

"Come on, cut it short!" snarled Sam. But his face lengthened, then tightened when he heard Grimes say, "Mistah Sam, I reckon the court's goin' to enjoy this when I tells how Mrs. Hillis sort of moaned an' says to you, *'yo' hurtin' me, Sam,'* and then later, yo' said something about her not worryin' bout yo' hoss at the hitchin' rack, because Mistah Hillis was so drunk he'd not know his own name fo' couple days, much less come home and ketch yo'all—"

Sam jerked a gun; but the lawman knocked his hand aside and said, "Come on, kid—tell that to the court—"

"Like hell, he tells that to the court!" raged Sam. "Yuh lyin' scoundrel—slanderin' Mrs. Hillis—"

"I done forgot all about the money I tied to the hitchin' post," Grimes cut in, hammering home his advantage. "Mebbe someone in yo' town remembers Mrs. Hillis spendin' some pin money, or mebbe her old man foun' it and got drunk agin—"

Landers and the lawman choked, then burst out laughing. Sam, red and raging, was eating his own smoke.

"Sam," roared the lawman, still half doubled up, "The whole damn' county's comin' tuh this trial. I been wonderin' how come Hillis was buyin' drinks fer the town, jest afore we started trailing this kid. Ef yuh want tuh see him hang, all yuh got tuh do is appear agin' him. Otherwise, yuh better give him the hoss and shut up! He'll be glad tuh ride west an' call it quits—but not as glad as yuh!"

SO GRIMES GOT THE HORSE; WHICH, WHILE NOT LEGAL, WAS THE LAWMAN'S IRONIC WAY at giving a spunky kid a break, and penalizing an unpopular citizen who consoled lonesome wives of drunken husbands. . . .

Presently, Grimes was in the plaza again, more than ever a man among men; free, and the cathedral bell about to call him to Paquita's arms; Simon Bolivar Grimes, outlaw; latest score, one sheriff jailed, another lawman made into an ally. But he'd be modest about it; jest let Paquita and her father find out about it, natural-like.

He wondered, for a moment, whether Paquita's father really was a first-class outlaw.

The cathedral bell tolled. At its last peal, Grimes was tapping at a massive door. Heels *click-clicked* across an inner court. A bolt slid and a slender, half-outlined form in the darkness became a fragrant reality. He could just catch the gleam of Paquita's dark eyes, the white blur of her upturned face; but senses more ancient than sight pictured the exquisite body for a moment pressed against him.

He seemed to walk on air as he followed her into a hall and up a narrow staircase.

46

What followed was more than ecstasy. Paquita had become more than a woman; she was now a reward of valor and tried manhood. Entranced, his hungry eyes watched her in the moonglow filtered through window bars, heard the intimate, silken rustlings of her gown.

She moved like a lazy serpent toward him while time stood still, and it seemed an exquisite eternity before she slipped into his eager arms . . . arms that savored the luscious modeling of her slim, soft body, for the first time embracing all that loveliness which, furtively glimpsed, furtively caressed, had for hours whetted anticipation to flame.

Strangely, now that they were alone, Paquita became an amazing blend of ardor and maidenly reticence; half yielding, but tremulously protesting, maddeningly contriving to evade the caresses she invited.

Her surrender, however, was dizzying; she leaned back, drawing him to her, arms twining about him. He scarcely heard the sudden rush of feet behind him; and the lantern glare that flooded the room exploded in a whirl of shooting lights as a club smacked down on his head.

The blow should have laid him out cold, but his assailant had not reckoned on a super-solid skull. He dimly felt Paquita wriggling clear, heard the hostler's familiar voice saying, "You are weetnesses—he ees attacking my wife—I weel get the damages—queek, get the money pouch!"

If an irate husband wanted cash instead of blood, well and good; but the badger artists did not know the express company had all but a few dollars. Their search gave Grimes his chance to recover.

He heaved to his knees, his sudden move shaking them loose. Eagerness had made him forget to reclaim his guns when released from jail, but he needed only his hard fists.

"I'll give yo' money!" he roared, ducking a knife thrust and knocking out an acre of teeth. "Come an' git it, yo' sidewinders!"

"Search heem!" howled the hostler. "He 'as the money hidden—"

The door was barred; the odds were three to one, not counting Paquita; and disappointment made the looters reckless. Grimes dodged a hurled blade, flailed a chair. Paquita tripped him; but he regained his feet as the pack closed in. He couldn't escape, and they'd whittle him down. Growling wrathfully, he charged to get one more scalp—

Smack! The impact slammed Paquita's husband against the window bars. Had they been iron, they would have bent; but they were wooden dummies and they splintered. The hostler, out on his feet, crashed through; and Grimes, despite his amazement, flung Paquita athwart his remaining assailants and cleared the sill. Though he missed a rare view as her legs reached skyward, he gained the ground, and a head start.

He stretched long legs across the plaza, and to the stable, where the saddled palomino was waiting. He did not pause to find out how much drag the shakedown experts had in El Aguila; and neither could he risk stopping at the jail for his guns. Humiliation, as well as prudence, deterred him.

The clattering hoofs of the palomino drowned the yelling in the plaza. Later, clear of the town, he remembered having heard raucous laughter as well.

"Bet Paquita ain't even got any pap, or he'd lambaste her f' sech goings on!" he muttered, reddening and grimacing. "Outlaw, hell! I'm jest too pig-dumb fo' that." Then, brightening as a sudden light overwhelmed him, he chuckled: "Dad-blame it, ain't no use me bein' a outlaw—now that I got Sheriff Brunton sort of unriled fo' a change!"

• • • • •

Reward of Valor

SIMON BOLIVAR GRIMES RODE HIS PALOMINO MARE AT AN EASY TROT, NOT A BULLET-hastened gallop. This was a pleasant novelty to that gangling boy who was so much younger than his granite colored eyes and long, coffin shaped face; but although he had finally made his peace with the sheriff who had hunted him half-way across Texas on an unjust charge, Grimes was worried.

Sooner or later, Uncle Carter would hear of that red hour in which he had kissed his first girl, killed three ruffians and escaped in a hail of slugs.

"An' ef Uncle Ca'tah ever larns about me drinkin' red likker an' consortin' with loose women, he'll lambaste me till my backside looks lak a checkerboard."

Neither could Grimes go back home to Georgia; not with the way his pappy wielded a harness tug! Despite his uncanny skill with a Colt .45, Grimes did not yet realize that though his voice at times treacherously rose from a bull roar to a piping treble, he nevertheless was entirely grown up.

"Facin' Uncle Ca'tah's goin' to be wuss'n bein' a outlaw," he somberly muttered. "Dad gum it, an' they's not a chanct of me becomin' a hero or suthin, not betwixt here an' Crockett County."

Then a more urgent problem confronted him. The palomino developed a decided limp; but the distant gleam of lights, as he cleared the next knoll, indicated a town. An hour later, he was leading the palomino down the main street.

Scouting about for a new horse, however, was interrupted by the arrival of the west-bound stage. His best bet was to get a ticket and reach his destination before the tale of his doings came to his uncle's ears.

In the saloon adjoining the express station, he sold the palomino for twenty dollars, shouldered saddle, bridle and saddlebags, and bounded toward the stage. His haste, however, was needless. Departure was delayed as a massive chest was set up beside the driver. A shotgun messenger, who likewise wore a pair of belted .45s, followed it to the driver's box.

Grimes allowed that this was a gold shipment; but what interested him a good deal more was his fellow passenger.

She had small feet and shapely legs. They were carelessly crossed, and with Grimes on the ground level, he caught glimpses of soft, white curves beyond her hose tops. The shadows that obscured the finer details only made the vista more entrancing; and when he lurched into the stage, he saw that the rest of her was just as blood-stirring.

Slim waist—full breasts—a wanton mouth that was red as a saber slash against her white skin; and her generous smile and appraising dark eyes warmed him all the way down to his cowhide boots.

"I'm Simon Bolivar Grimes, m'am," he began, boosting his luggage on ahead of him. "An' I beg yo' pardon fo' in-trudin' with this hoss-gear."

She laughed, told him she was Leila Graves, and assured him that to anyone who came from her part of the country, the tang of horse trappings was neither offensive nor a novelty.

"Simon Bolivar Grimes?" she repeated, smiling bewitchingly. "Oh, how thrilling! I heard of you back in El Aguila."

Grimes choked and swallowed. He might have known she'd heard of how the town marshal had caught him with an armful of Tula, the two hundred pounds of dusky ardor who ran the hotel in El Aguila.

"Er—am—um—" he groped reddening.

But Leila went on, "The way you got out of jail there was just marvelous! There'll only be you and me from here to the next town. So you'll tell me all about it, won't you?"

"Ain't nuthin to tell," protested Grimes; but his embarrassment dissolved in the sweetness of her caressing voice.

Leila was snuggling closer; and while he was wondering if he'd dare put his arm about her, the jouncing of the stage flung her against him. She gasped, tried to recover, but slipped and wedged him into the corner.

It was dark, but that did not keep him from being certain that Leila was shapely all over; supple in some places, firm and quivering in others. She gasped as he inadvertently brushed the base of one trembling breast with his wrist in his efforts to restore her balance; but she laughed softly and murmured, "Oh, you're awfully strong! I'm not a bit worried, now, even though it's dangerous, out here."

"Dangerous?"

"Terrible. Black Bart has been holding up the express. Killing the drivers and—" She was too nice to say right out what Black Bart did to the women. "But what'd you do if we were held up?"

"This!" That one word had scarcely left his lips when, by some uncanny magic, a .45 was in his hand, barrel cold against her cheek. "An' long afore now, yo' haid'd be lifted right off, ef yo' was a road agent, m'am."

The gun faded out of sight with equally incredible speed. It was gone before Leila could gasp, "Now I know I needn't worry."

For a moment, she leaned across him, and he could feel the throb of her heart beneath the luscious roundness that swelled her blouse. She looked out the window, then cried out to the driver, "Oh, please stop! I thought this was the stage to Rock Springs! This isn't the road."

"'Tis too, m'am!" shouted the man at the reins. "We're jest takin' diffrunt route, account we might git held up betwixt here an' Kerville."

"Ohhh—!" she sighed, sinking back against Grimes. "I was so startled."

That last bit was too much even for a gentleman from Georgia. Before Leila half recovered from her momentary alarm, she was being thoroughly kissed.

She made inarticulate, protesting sounds. She even threatened—in a very small, low voice—to call to the driver. Then she squirmed closer, gasping and murmuring, face upturned for another kiss.

She got it, and Grimes gave her everything he had learned from the several young ladies who had enlivened his flight across Texas. Leila first became tense and rigid, then lay limp in his arms, gasping. He couldn't quite understand what she was saying, so he did some guessing.

Leila did not contradict, so he must have been right. . . .

AS THEY PULLED INTO KERVILLE, SHE HASTILY PATTED HER DISHEVELED HAIR INTO SHAPE, pulled her skirt down over sleek knees and hitched over to the further corner of the stage. Grimes slid to the opposite corner, studiously looking away from Leila, and pretending to ignore her carefully casual inquiries of a hanger-on at the stage depot.

He did not hear the end of the exchange. What caught his eye was a young, sweet-faced girl with sombre eyes whose beauty was tainted by the redness of recent tears. Grimes caught her carpetbag as the clerk helped her to the stage.

"Thank yo', suh," she murmured; and something about that soft voice wrenched Grimes' heart. "If you don't mind, could I sit by the window, facing to the front?"

He lifted his slouch hat, stepped aside to make room for her. She was probably not yet out of her teens; a shy, demure bit of loveliness whose budding breasts and slim, scarcely ripened figure promised rounded and voluptuous maturity. Somehow, she was so very different from Leila.

He seated himself between the two girls, then noticed that the man who had chatted with Leila was mounting a sweating horse. Grimes scarcely got a glimpse of him before the stage was rolling down the deserted street, harness jingling, whip cracking, and the local clerk yelling his farewell.

The newcomer was Sabina Brent. Grimes was glad that she had never heard of him. But, being practical, he presently was discreetly but effectively caressing Leila's more accessible fascinations. Once, in a moment of boldness, he leaned too close to the source of the lusty fragrance that was exhaled from the low yoke of her blouse; and Leila promptly turned away.

Such sudden skittishness puzzled Grimes. Women were funny critters. She might know Sabina wouldn't be watching. . . .

And then, without warning, hell blazed from the darkness of the pass through which the stage was rumbling. Road agents! A rattling volley raked the driver's box and the top of the coach.

Oddly enough, the methodically murderous bandits weren't bothering to kill the passengers, some of whom would reasonably enough be armed. But that did not occur to Grimes as he reached for his plough handle and leaped to the door.

"Git down, woman!" he warned, arm lashing out against Sabina as terror brought her to her feet. The contact was only momentary, but it told him that the little blonde girl was not as immature as she looked.

The stage had come to a halt. The lead horses, shot down, blocked the wheel team, which was snorting, screaming, frantically kicking. The shotgun messenger's weapon boomed defiance. The driver's .45s were rattling, and he yelled, "I got the ______! Watch it, Red!"

In the midst of the uproar, Grimes hit the ground, confident that Sabina was safe on the floor, where he had thrust her. The road agents were breaking from cover, pistols blazing. Grimes, eyes narrowed, face suddenly tight, leveled the weapon that should have been notched from the butt to hammer; but there was no answering blast; just a dry *click-click-click.* He cursed heaven and knew that he had an empty gun.

Dark forms were closing in. Spurts of flame marked their position. Lead raked Grimes where he crouched, fumbling for cartridges. The driver was now groaning, instead of firing. Red, the messenger, yelled in agony, pitched headlong from the driver's box.

And then Grimes seized Red's shotgun.

Boom! Flame and whistling pellets and blazing wads poured athwart the triumphant raiders. One was blown in half; another was knocked sprawling by the concussion; and others were savagely stung by the scattering shot.

That dead man's gun gave Grimes an instant's grace. He snatched a pistol from the bandit who had toppled nearest him. He met the charge; they were coming so fast that even the buckshot blast had not stopped the whole pack. Neither party could retreat; they were too close.

This was gunfighting; shoot till one side is wiped out. Grimes, twisting like a snake heading for a hole, made that salvaged gun play a tune.

To have stood fast would have been suicide. Advancing behind a solid wall of flame, he swept the field, then hurled himself at the one survivor. Both now had empty weapons—but it was not Grimes who was brained by a pistol barrel.

The deck was clear. Grimes retrieved his unaccountably unloaded .45, then boosted the dead messenger to the top of the coach and cut loose the dead lead team. But as he was making awkward attempts to staunch the flow of blood from the wounds of the driver, who seemed to have a chance in a hundred of surviving, Grimes knew that he had gotten out of one mess and into something worse.

"Reach fur yore ears, er I'll cut yuh off at yore pants pockets!" rasped a voice like a buzz saw.

In his haste to attend to the wounded driver and get the stage under way again, Grimes had not reloaded his hog-leg. His hands rose, and he turned about to face the dully-glinting barrel of a shotgun, the one weapon that made the toughest *hombre* refrain from sleight of hand.

He could see only a drooping white moustache, shoulder-length white hair, and a silver star, big as a dinner plate, gleaming from the lawman's vest. That relieved Grimes' frosty apprehensions.

"Ef yo' don't mind, suh, yo' might put up that there gun," he said. "I ain't a road agent. I'm jest a passenger, along with a couple of ladies that's scrunched on the flo', inside the stage."

The lawman snorted, "Come down keerful, or yuh gits it."

Grimes was careful. For a moment, the grizzled old fellow glared at him over the shotgun barrel; then, after a final squint, he admitted, "Seems like I did see yuh at Kerville. Yeah, guess yore a passenger."

And then Leila cut in from the coach window: "He rode with us, but he's one of the road agents. He done shot the driver with a stingy gun—blasted right through the coach and picked him from the box while he was fighting off the raid."

"I didn't neither!" croaked Grimes, appalled at Leila's accusation. "I piled right in an' fit the bandits."

Half a dozen riders came clattering up, cutting into the discussion. This was the posse that had ridden with the sheriff to overtake the stage. A citizen had recognized the man who had in Kerville walked from the stage and mounted up a lathered horse; and the presence of that suspicious character had led to the organizing of the posse. A good hunch, but tough for the boy from Georgia!

Grimes now understood Leila's earlier inquiries as to the route of the coach, and her supposedly casual words with the stranger; but he had not a chance. Not after she laughed off his counter-accusation and said, "Sheriff, this is Simon Bolivar Grimes, the gunslinger that shot up Orange and El Aguila and Lawd knows what other towns."

What clinched it was a deadly little .41 derringer which fell out of Grimes' saddle bags: the weapon which had blasted through the front of the coach and dangerously wounded the driver whose deadly fire was holding the road agents in check. That planted weapon was the last touch.

"No, suh," Sabina finally had to admit, "I didn't see anything. Mistah Grimes flattened me to the floor when the shooting started, so I wouldn't get hurt."

From hero to hanging, all in a few minutes: that was Grimes' prospect when the posse headed for Rock Springs.

UPON HIS ARRIVAL WITH THE ALMOST LOOTED STAGE, THE TOWN TURNED OUT IN FORCE. Rock Springs was all agog at the capture of the notorious Simon Bolivar Grimes, who promised to make the records of John Wesley Hardin and Billy the Kid read like a Mother Goose rhyme!

Grimes, shooting and flirting his way across Texas, was bound to draw a crowd. The story increased with the telling, and a good many women, interested mainly in the last-named phase of his activities, thronged with the men to get a look at the captive.

One, a red haired girl with audacious, greenish eyes and full lips that fairly twitched to be kissed, crowded up to the bars. Despite his desperate plight, Grimes could not help but be intrigued by the way the iron rods betrayed the resilience of her breasts and brought out the roundness of her thighs.

She cast a furtive glance over her shoulder; then, as the crowd shuffled and surged along, pushed by later arrivals, she lingered long enough to whisper, "Hang on, Simon. Maybe I can do something for you. Shame a good man like you is going to—"

She didn't have time to say, "hang." A gnarled paw caught her shoulder and a buzz-saw voice cut in, "You git home, Esmerelda, er I'll whale yuh till yuh kain't sit down fer a week! Tain't fit fer decent gals tuh be gawkin' at sich a desperado."

It was Simms, the sheriff, clearing the jail.

Grimes' cellmate was a lean, handsome old fellow who had been nailed for horse theft. He listened to the boy's attempts at denial, shook his head, and said, "Bub, that's the way this yere law and order stuff goes these days. Now me—I usta swing a sticky rope, years ago. Got me a bad name, jest like you done. Last week, I did take a hoss. Didn't intend tuh keep it, but I needed it bad. Ef I hadn't had sech a record from years ago, they'd believed I was riding hell bent tuh git a doctor. Only, they didn't believe me, an' they larned I was going tuh warn a old pardner tuh head fur Mexico afore the law got him. Which ain't no crime, but borrying a hoss is. So they's goin' tuh hang me on genrul principles."

He offered the boy a chaw of tobacco, then lapsed into a stoic silence. And Grimes, betrayed by his moment of boasting to Leila, could do no better than display his cellmate's fortitude.

Try breaking out of this jail! Grimes somberly debated whether to make a gallant speech from the gallows, or whether to cuss them all out as murderin' sidewinders. Then he settled down to target practice—sniping cockroaches with jets of tobacco juice.

He had scarcely bagged the sixth one when heavy footfalls, a woman's angry protests, and Sheriff Simms' voice cut into his ponderings on Esmerelda's slim chances of helping him.

Two deputies were dragging Leila toward Grimes' cell. She was bedraggled, and her dress was half torn from her. The lawmen, embarrassed by the display of feminine flesh, and the force they had to exercise in the performance of their duty, were begging her not to make a scene.

"I didn't—I tell you, I didn't!" she screeched. Then, seeing Grimes, "He did it! He shot the driver!"

"Shet up, afore I whop yuh!" rasped the salty old sheriff. "Dump her intuh a cell by herself—kain't put a wench like that in with a decent hoss thief."

Grimes, blinking and bewildered, stared as Simms fumbled with the keys.

"C'mon out, Bud!" he rumbled. "That there driver didn't die. He mumbled fer a drink of likker, and then he sot right up and says he warn't shot in the back ontil yuh was on the ground, hosin' the road agents with Red's scatter gun. Musta been someone else what plugged him jest above the pants pocket.

"An' yore gun bein' clean, and a fistful of .45 shells lying on the floor of the coach kind of made me smell a skunk. Was she gittin' familiar with yuh, any time durin' the drive?"

"I told you, he was makin' improper advances to me!" protested Leila.

"I warn't neither!" contradicted Grimes. Then, remembering one caress she had unaccountably repulsed, he amended, "Well, onct I sort of reached fer—"

He reddened until his tow-colored hair seemed to crop out of a harvest moon, choked, and went on, "Anyway, I bet that's wheah she had that stingy gun concealed, or she'd nevah objected. But they wasn't nutin' really improper, suh!"

"Git out of that cell!" boomed Simms. "We're convinced yuh saved the gold shipment. Yo're a hero, by damn!—an' Rock Springs is proud of yuh. And tomorrow, the boys'd admire tuh present yuh with a brace of bone-handled guns as a token of esteem fer valor and sich like. Tuh say nuthing of the keys of the city."

As Grimes strode across the plaza toward the Alamo Hotel, the world looked bright again. He was a hero now, and Uncle Carter would welcome him. So he ordered the best room in the house and followed the clerk to the second floor with horse gear and saddlebags. Too bad he couldn't help his cellmate.

He'd buy a mount in the morning and ride the remainder of the distance. To hell with the stagecoach. A fellow got tangled up with too many loose women and road agents. . . .

GRIMES, HALF ASLEEP, WAS AROUSED BY A SOUND FROM THE ADJOINING ROOM. HIS neighbor was sobbing, though the plaintive sound seemed half choked by a pillow.

"Po' little gal," he sympathized, catching just enough to tell him that she was worried about her father.

The sounds were distorted enough to puzzle him. She might be stranded because of her parent's sudden death on the road. Maybe he could help her.

He stepped into the hall. His diffident tap did not catch her attention; but it sent the door swinging inward a hand's-breath. The po' little gal was no child. He could see only pale golden hair, the soft white shoulders that shook from sobbing. She wore a thin slip and her restless tossing had worked it fairly well toward her hips; but if her face matched the rest of her, she must be a beauty.

Only the distraction of grief could account for her failure to lock the door; but that never occurred to Grimes. Not after a glimpse of those entrancing legs.

His breathing now was interfering with thought.

The curve of her hips was far from childish, and as she shifted, he caught a ripe flash of pert little breasts; but though Grimes' accelerated pulse and breathing interfered with thought, he realized that the only decent thing to do was to retreat, then tap again, more loudly.

But his admiration betrayed him. The girl, sensing his intent gaze, started and sat up. It was Sabina Brent, the girl who had boarded the stage at Kerville.

Her reddened eyes widened. Her lips parted soundlessly; she scrambled to protect her exposed charms from his eye.

"M'am," he stuttered, "I sho' didn't mean to be pry-in', but I heerd yo'all weepin' fo' yo' pappy, an'—"

"I never heard of such insolence!" she flared, for a moment forgetting that the hastily clutched corner of the sheet was still quite a way below her shoulders, and well above her hips. "If my father—"

She choked, and a tear rolled down her cheek. Grimes, brick red, fumbled and cut in, "That's jest it, m'am. I sort of 'lowed I might help—honest, I didn't mean to be snoopin'."

She relaxed, seeing that he was by far the more embarrassed of the two. His long face was now as boyish as it had been when he left Georgia. She smiled sadly, sighed, then said. "I'm afraid you couldn't help my father. They arrested—"

"M'am," he cut in, "I'm Simon Bolivar Grimes, an' maybe I kin help. I jest busted out of jail two weeks ago, myself."

His naive earnestness made her smile fade; her blue eyes narrowed, noting the sudden grimness of his face. In that wild country, gangling boys often did a man's work.

"Come in," she invited, "though there's not a chance. Just wait—"

Grimes was at her side while she was still trying to make a counterpane take the place of the garments heaped on a chair.

"Oh—! You do move fast!" she gasped, seating herself on the edge of the bed; and then, squatting on the floor at her feet, he learned that Sabina's father was in the local jail, awaiting execution for horse theft. Brent was Grimes' former cellmate. She had come to town for a farewell visit.

Sympathy brought him to her side; and as Sabina's voice broke, she sobbed the story into his shirt front.

"I came on the stagecoach—to get a new lawyer—but—there's just—not a chance. Good God, Simon, you can't help—"

She clung to him, sweet, vibrant, grief making her unreserved. Her racking sobs pressed every curve against him; and though he swallowed, and his own voice became unmanfully husky, her warmth and closeness inflamed him. He felt lower than an angle worm's stepchild, and struggled desperately to confine his caresses to her disheveled curls.

Yet, despite his damning impulse, Grimes wracked his whirling brain and assured her, "Honey, I'll bust into jail, shoot their gizzards out, an' turn yo' old man loose."

The iron in his voice steadied her. She regarded him through tears; she had sensed that more than resolution made his voice and body tremble.

"Simon," she said, very slowly, "you'll get yourself killed trying. You're crazy, but I love you for it. And before you go—"

A flush invaded the pallor of her face, crept down to the white flesh of her partially concealed breasts. She didn't quite know how to say it; but he understood. There was no passion in her heart now. Their lips met, flame pressed to gratitude—her fanatic resolve to risk as much as he was staking—

Esmerelda might have helped him escape from her father's jail; but now that Grimes was free, she'd certainly not assist him in liberating a horse thief who had a lovely daughter!

LATER THAT NIGHT, GRIMES WENT TO A GENERAL STORE, BOUGHT CARTRIDGES AND A Bowie knife, neither of which he needed; but it gave him a chance to steal a pair of files and a hank of clothesline when the proprietor's back was turned. He laid a coin on the counter where it would in due course be observed and pocketed. Then he went on the prowl, finally halting at the rear of the jail.

Grimes whipped the end of the cord up and between the bars of the window. He dared not risk even a whisper. But he gently played the line so that the inside end worked down into the cell. Finally there was an answering tug.

He responded with a stronger pull, and in a moment he and the prisoner were of one mind. The man inside held the cord, and Grimes, supporting himself with it, "walked" up the masonry face of the building.

"Mistah Brent," he whispered, pulling himself to the sill and drawing the cord after him, "I done got a couple files, so we kin git to work on two bars at onct. An' yo' all pertend yo'ah snorin', so they won't be no scrapin' to be heard."

He looped his end of the cord about a bar; then, with the bight to support his weight, Brent scrambled up the inside wall, snatched a file.

"An' he'ah's my gun," whispered Grimes. "But we bettah cut yo' way out."

"That's right, Bub," agreed Brent. "Don't believe in onnecessary shootin'. Mebbe you better tell my daughter tub quit worrying."

"I done seen Sabina," answered Grimes.

But the jailbreak was abruptly interrupted. Sheriff Simms was on the job, right beneath the window at whose sill Grimes was crouching.

"Come down from thar, er I'll blast yore pants pocket acrost yore gizzard!" he rasped. "An' come down thout anything in yore paws."

Grimes, blazing with fury, thudded to the ground. Simms chuckled grimly, and said, "Yo're a purty smart lad, but in some respecks, yo're pig dumb. Old Si Walsh found that five dollars yuh left an' he missed the last two files you took ouffen the shelf, so he put two an' two together.

"An' I figured that hoss thief's gal mighta tempted yuh by playing up tuh *yore* young-buck notions." He sighed, regretting his own age, then booted Grimes and added, "Now git! Since yore a damn hero, I ain't putting yuh in the jug, but ef I ketch yuh in Rock Springs a hour after sunrise, yuh gits shot on sight fer aidin' and abettin' hoss thieves!"

Once he saw Grimes heading in the general direction of the hotel, Simms stamped back into his office. But the long-haired old sheriff did not yet realize that Grimes was of a persistent, pig-stubborn breed. Neither did he know what his daughter, Esmerelda, had whispered through the bars of the cell.

GRIMES, HOWEVER, HAD NOT FORGOTTEN THE REDHEAD AND HER TAKING SMILE; AND having already heard that the sheriff lived in the white house across from the stage depot, he did a bit of back alley stalking, cleared a fence and landed in a yard crisscrossed with clotheslines. With Indian stealth, he skirted the rambling residence.

The light in the window just above the side porch was worth investigation. He silently scaled a column, drew himself to the shingles of the canopy and bellied along the gentle slope until he could peep in and make sure it was not Mrs. Sheriff's room he was investigating.

He made sure—and he spent the next few moments blinking. Esmerelda was sitting before a cracked mirror. What made the view entrancing was the thin night-gown that was drawn taut in just the right places as she leaned back, arms uplifted, to pick the pins out of the coils of shimmering red hair that crowned her partly tilted head.

The glow of the kerosene lamp played tricks with the frail fabric, brought golden highlights out of the plump white hemispheres that promised to pop over the edge of that low cut gown.

"You, Esmerelda!" he whispered. "Quit lettin' down yo' hair an' listen to me!"

She started, faced about, and the sudden motion revealed further details. Before she could quite decide whether to yeep or not, he added, "Now that I done got out of jail, yo' don't need to help me, but they's a few things we kin talk about."

"Oh, Mister Grimes!" she cooed, having by that time recognized him. "You sure startled me!"

Then, as he hurdled the sill, she had presence of mind enough to blow out the lamp.

"I been hearing a lot about you," she began; but he caught her arm and countered, "Ain't nothin' to what yo' going to hear. Yo' pap jest ordered me to git out of town by sunrise—I guess he musta heard whut yo' said to me—"

"He would!" she bitterly exclaimed, snuggling closer. "And so you came to say goodbye? Guess he reckoned you was too notorious, even if innocent."

"Goodbye? Hell, no! M'am, mebbe you could fix me up with some place to hide fo' a day or so, an' then when I slip out, I kin pertend I *jest come back,* an' by then he might be calmed down a bit."

Esmerelda was entirely too thrilled by her notorious visitor's strategy to see that his story had more holes in it than a sieve. Grimes had no intention of lingering in Rock Springs; all he wanted was a good place to waylay the sheriff without resorting to gunplay. Liberating Sabina's father would be easy.

To keep Esmerelda from reckoning the score, he drew her close and kissed her until she squirmed like a basket of angleworms. Her greedy lips clung as tightly as her arms, and she panted, "Maybe I can hide you in a clothes closet—"

"Ain't they no other place?" temporized Grimes, following her to a lounge near the door.

"Quit talking so much, and kiss me," Esmerelda gasped.

And that, decided Grimes, by now fairly incinerated by hot lips and quivering curves pressed against him, was a sensible idea. . . .

BY THE TIME SHE FINALLY LEARNED MOST OF THE REASONS FOR GRIMES' SUCCESS IN EAST Texas, Esmerelda was too drowsy to discuss hideouts; which made it all the better for the next move. He extricated himself from her relaxed arms, but as he slowly twisted the doorknob, the latch click was followed by an inward slam of the panel.

It caught Grimes off guard, being whacked in the face by that door; and while red spots still danced before his eyes, Esmerelda's startled yeep was drowned by a wrathful feminine voice: "Stick up yore hands, yuh wretch! Whut yuh mean, busting intuh a innocent gal's room?"

All that came from behind the double-barreled shotgun jammed against Grimes' stomach. Moonlight from the window showed him all that he cared to see of that grim faced battle axe in the flannel nightgown: Mrs. Simms, light-sleeping frontier woman, must have been aroused by some phase of the argument concerning hideouts, and had deliberately set about investigating.

"Maw," protested the horrified Esmerelda as she lit a lamp, "I was too scared to holler. Is he a burglar or something?"

"Burglar!" Mrs. Simms scornfully snapped. *With all that red hair a-sticking tuh his shoulder?* I'll burgle you, yuh shameless hussy! Say yore prayers, yuh skunk, afore I blow yore insides out the window—"

She meant business. Not a chance of grabbing the gun barrel. But Grimes kept his head, and protested, "Listen, m'am! Ef yo' all shoot me, it'll be sorta embarrassing, explainin' how come. But ef we 'uns jest keep this quiet like, I'd sho' be the last one to say a word. 'Specially since I wants to marry her."

That sank home. After all, Maw Simms didn't know, exactly, how many cowhands had fondled that hellion of an Esmerelda; so about all the good shooting Grimes could do would be to start people speculating.

"Maw!" screeched Esmerelda, abruptly and to make the shingles shudder. *"They's another one of 'em—look!"*

The sound, rather than the words, distracted Mrs. Simms. Her start, though brief, was enough for a man whose life had a dozen times been saved by drawing a gun in less than a split second. Grimes thrust the gun barrel aside just as she recovered and jerked a double charge of shot through the mirror.

"Git in there, m'am!" he growled, wrenching the gun from her hands and thrusting her into the clothes closet. "I'm elopin' with yo' daughter, an' I don't aim tuh have no interference!"

"Oh, darling!" gurgled Esmerelda, diving at him, arms outspread.

"Git yo' clothes packed!" he ordered, "awhile I find some hosses. But you tell 'em I run thattaway—" He gestured in a direction exactly opposite to the one he intended taking.

That shotgun blast would precipitate a riot. Saloons would empty; sheriff and deputies would come a-helling, any minute, toward the house. And his gag would keep Esmerelda busy. It might work!

Fuming shotgun in hand, he bounded down the stairs. His destination was the jail. It would be unguarded if those blasts had the usual effect. And no one would expect a fugitive heading in that direction.

But as he reached the hall, he heard pounding footsteps. A familiar voice rasped, "Myra! Whut the gol danged hell's up? Who's shootin'?"

Sheriff Simms, guns drawn, was kicking at the door.

Grimes had but one chance, and he took it. Huddled beside the jamb, he prodded the bolt out of its socket. The door slammed inward, and Simms lurched into the hall.

Whack! The shotgun barrel bent across his head, and both the sheriff's .45s blasted slugs into the floor.

Simms was out cold. He was not even kicking when Grimes went through his pockets, snatched his keys and dashed around to the rear. He cleared the back fence just as the town turned out to see who was smoking up the sheriff's house.

"These here," he panted, buckling on Simms' revolvers as he ran down side alleys and toward the jail, "is going to be jest as good as them they was going to give me tomorrow, fo' bein' a hero!"

LUCK WAS WITH HIM. THE JAIL WAS UNGUARDED. JUDGING FROM THE UPROAR, THE WHOLE town was at Simms' house. Grimes dashed down the corridor. He passed the cell whose bars Leila was gripping. Her eyes widened, seeing the keys in his hand.

"Let me out, honey. Honest, I'll be awful nice to you—"

"I hope yo' rot!" he snarled. "I'd be a hero, ef it warn't fo' yo' dang falsehoods!"

Then, reaching Brent's cell: "Quit that filin', dad. Let's git out of here whilst the gittin' is good!"

Sabina's father leaped down from the sill, bounded toward the door. As the lock grated open, Grimes said, "We kin damn nigh walk out! Ain't no one 'lowing I'd be heah. I'm supposed to be fixin' to elope with the sheriff's daughter."

"Dad gum it!" laughed Brent, "I shore wisht yuh was ee-lopin' with my gal, Sabina!"

So did Grimes; but every second counted. They dashed to the adjoining livery stable, forked a pair of nags the hostler had not yet unsaddled. Easy as pie! And would Sabina be thrilled!

Then, unaccountably, the mob at the sheriff's house came surging into the plaza, and toward the jail. Men were mounting up. Flame laced the darkness, lead whistled.

"Jailbreak!" a hundred throats were yelling above the trample of hoofs.

The sheriff couldn't have recovered from his clouting and missed his keys; it should be hours before he knew his own name. But as Brent quirted his horse, Grimes caught the point: Esmerelda, watching from her window the direction taken by her husband-to-be, had suspected him of trying to liberate Leila, the road agent's accomplice, and had spread the alarm.

Lead raked them, stinging horse and man. Brent sagged, groaned, but carried on, spurring and quirting. Finally, as the sounds of pursuit died in the rear, Grimes pulled up to wind his panting horse and bandage himself—though his wounds were not serious.

Old man Brent, however, was done for. He lurched, almost fell from the saddle, but steadied himself.

"Bub," he coughed, "yore a stemwindin' hero, takin' an old man's part thattaway—"

"Seems mo' like I was a ignorunt hootowl," muttered Grimes, supporting Brent. "I might a knowed that gal would be watchin'!"

"An' tell Sabina—when yuh see her—"

But that message ended in a rattle. Brent was dead; and Grimes, hearing the far-off mutter of hoofs, had neither time nor need for protecting the body from scavengers.

HE RODE ON, SWALLOWING THE LUMP IN HIS THROAT. HE HAD FAILED, AFTER ALL, IN HIS rescue. And with Esmerelda's story of an elopement, made worse by the riot that had started in her room, he'd never be able to face Sabina. He couldn't look her in the eye and convince her that the redhead had been just strategy which had miscarried.

Not a nice gal like Sabina, whom he'd left to toy with that redheaded wench! Though, if old man Brent hadn't died as the result of that disastrous error, it would have been different.

"Hero, hell! Next jasper that calls me that, I'll kill him!" he somberly muttered, spurring his horse to a gallop.

Then he grinned sourly and added, "Leastways, I done got me a pair of bone-handled pistols from the admirin' citizens of Rock Springs!"

• • • • •

Skeleton Creek Feud

The gangling boy whose ewe-necked mustang had just scrambled up the west bank of the Pecos lifted a bullet-riddled slouch hat, brushed back the straw-colored cowlick that persistently reached down into his coffin-shaped face, and stared at the large signboard ahead of him:

SKELETON CREEK: SHUCK YORE GUNS OR KEEP OUT.

"This here is a gal-danged outrage!" Simon Bolivar Grimes spat a jet of tobacco juice at the offensive sign. "If they think I'm a-goin' to appear in public plumb naked, they's crazy!"

But the hell of it was, the boy from Georgia had to stop at Skeleton Creek to find out how to get to Uncle Carter's ranch.

A buckboard was heading down the wagon trail that swung toward town. Grimes, starting at the sound, saw that a girl had the reins. That gave him an idea. He wheeled his sorrel and trotted upstream.

They met in the arroyo that joined the Pecos.

She was a golden brown, delicious armful, with lustrous blue-black hair and large, devil-haunted black eyes. Tiny feet, cocked up on the dashboard, were shod with scarlet slippers, and a blue calico dress generously revealed bare legs and shapely calves.

Though she pulled her flimsy skirt down over her knees, Grimes was not cheated; towering above her on his horse, he got a glimpse of the shadowed valley between the pert brown breasts which quivered delightfully as she heaved back on the reins to halt the team.

"M'am," he said, "maybe yo'all kin help me out of a heap of trouble."

"I bet," she countered, narrowly eyeing him, "you're Simon Bolivar Grimes."

"I ain't, neither!" He was alarmed by the chance that news of his gunslinging had preceded him. "Is they any reward notices out?"

"No. Only, I've heard a lot about you. I'm Susie Wrinkled-Meat—"

"Why—uh—er—ain't nuthin' wrinkled, nowhere!" he stuttered, heart thumping as he surveyed the thin calico that revealed every line of her shapely young body.

"My father," she explained, "was John Wrinkled-Meat, War Chief of the Comanches. He was seventy-eight when he got drunk and tried to kill a bear with a Bowie knife, and the bear won."

"Hell, ma'am, yo' don't look like a Injun," Grimes protested, dismounting and clambering to the buckboard.

"Well, maw is Spanish," she allowed.

"Anyway, Mis' Susie, mebbe yo' all kin hide one of these smoke poles in yo' wagon, wheah I kin git it after I'm in town. They won't be searchin' a lady fo' weepons."

He drew his left pistol, fumbled with the horse blanket that padded the seat.

"Ain't no use hiding your gun. You wait here till I get the buckboard loaded with supplies and then go to the ranch with me."

"What ranch?"

"Why, your uncle's. You're the spittin' image of him, so I reckonized you right away. Maw's cookin' out there."

"Home, sweet home," sighed Grimes, getting a fresh glimpse of legs plus as he stepped from the wagon. "But how come Uncle Ca'tah didn't send a cow puncher fo' groceries?"

"When he went to the express office in Skunk Valley and got the *five hundred dollars* you shipped him from El Aguila, he was dry-gulched and robbed, only they didn't quite kill him. He was going to take that money to the Skeleton Creek Bank to pay the back interest on the mortgage. Now they're going to foreclose, sure.

"And there's not a cowpuncher left at the ranch. Rustlers smoked them out and run off most of the cattle. But didn't you notice the Box-G branded on this team?"

"Not with the way yo' laigs was cocked up on the dashboard," countered Grimes. "I'll wait here, an' cool down a bit."

He no longer had any reason for going to town; not until he had seen his uncle and learned more of the feud that promised to ruin the ranch. For a law-abiding place that prohibited belt guns, Skeleton Creek seemed unusually lively!

AN HOUR LATER, SUSIE RETURNED. GRIMES HADN'T COOLED DOWN ENOUGH TO HELP, BUT her smile promised pleasant ways of whiling away lonely evenings on the Box-G.

Late that afternoon, the trail led into an arroyo. Grimes, who had been riding since sunrise, dismounted to tighten a latigo strap. The buckboard creaked on, rolling and pitching over the boulder-strewn bottom.

After several attempts to work out a wrinkle in the blanket, he removed the saddle, then replaced it, so as not to reopen a scarcely healed gall on the shoulder of his hastily acquired horse. And when he mounted up, the wagon had rounded a bend.

He wondered why the creaking of the buckboard ceased, a moment later. Perhaps the trail forked, and Susie was waiting. He spurred ahead; and as he cleared the turn, he saw that he had ridden into a trap.

Three masked men had halted the wagon. One covered Susie with a drawn pistol; a second was scattering flour and coffee and beans over the rocks; and the third, warned by the sound of Grimes' approach, had a carbine leveled.

"Git offen that hoss, an' yuh won't git hurt," commanded the man behind the rifle.

"Sam, yuh better take his guns," counseled the one whose Colt had kept Susie from warning her companion.

"Mebbe so, Fin. But he looks too dang dumb tuh come in outen the rain," was the answer.

Sam, however, was taking no chances: "Unhook that belt, an' don't make no false moves, er I'll plug yuh."

Grimes slowly lowered his hands to the buckle. Fin holstered his pistol; and the man in the buckboard, his work of destruction but half completed, began to figure it was time for relaxation.

"Run along," he chuckled, "while we has a confidential talk with this yere lady."

Before Susie could shake off his paws, he had her half dragged from the seat and into the back of the wagon.

"How about lettin' me in on the fun?" proposed Grimes, whose holstered guns lay on the ground. "She won't mind."

Susie, panting and screeching, tried to break from her assailant; but all she accomplished was the ripping of her flimsy dress from the neck yoke to the waist. Fin, licking his lips as he saw the play of her lithe brown body, guffawed and allowed Grimes might as well stay around with the grown-ups.

"Yuh wouldn't understand, nohow!" snapped Sam.

"Et'd sho' be fun learnin', suh," protested Grimes.

Susie, bare torso and legs dazzling the spectators as she clawed and screamed, was too much for watchfulness. The muzzles of Sam's carbine shifted; and then Grimes flung his slouch hat.

It sailed straight into Sam's face. The carbine roared, but the slug went wild. Grimes lunged for his guns before Sam could lever home another cartridge or go for his Colt. And then the trio learned that the boy they had regarded with such contempt was a gunfighter from the Salt Fork of Hard Water Creek!

Fin fired as his Colt cleared the holster; but Grimes' .45s were already dancing. Fin died with red flame blotting out that last glimpse of Susie's skyward-pointing legs. The team bolted, deflecting the pistol blasts cut loose by the girl's assailant as he kicked clear of her. And Sam, throwing lead too hastily to cut down the long, lanky boy who wove and sidestepped like a whirlwind, dropped with three slugs in his chest and a half-emptied gun in his fist.

"Those gents," grunted Grimes, dodging the last shot fired from the tail of the buckboard as it careened around a curve, "ain't no gentleman—didn't even give the gal a chance to say if she liked 'em."

He was in the saddle now, galloping down the arroyo after the panic-stricken team. The gunner in the wagon was still trying, but his fire was wild. Then Susie, fighting the fuzztails, yanked them to a halt; and Grimes won the exchange by a hair. Three down!

Nothing to do but decide how much more calico could be taken away before Susie would be really undressed. The answer might have been fascinating, but this was no place to linger; so Grimes said, "You git yo'self pinned together, an' then we'll have a look at these heah jiggers."

He jerked the masks from the dry-gulchers.

"Ain't never seen 'em," the girl declared. "But their hosses are both H-Bar-H. Looks like Happy Hardwick's behind all this dirt. He's got the spread next to your uncle. Wouldn't be surprised if he was figuring on bidding in the Box-G when the bank forecloses."

That made it clear enough why three men would raid a wagonload of groceries: part of the campaign to get Uncle Carter out of the Box-G.

Since there was going to be war in Crockett County, Grimes rounded up the weapons of the three lead-slingers, including the .30-30 carbine and their cartridge belts.

IT WAS LATE THAT EVENING WHEN GRIMES STRODE INTO THE RANCH HOUSE, WHERE Susie's mother was preparing supper. She was comely, full-breasted and not more than twice her daughter's age; and as Grimes caught her smouldering, speculative glance and generous smile, he had a hunch that John Wrinkled-Meat's widow hadn't been languishing for kisses.

While Susie explained how she had been almost peeled to her bare skin in defense of her virtue, Grimes went to his uncle's room. There he found him, lean, grim-faced, his iron-gray head and left leg masked with bandages.

"Next time they better send enough to make a job of it, bub," chuckled Uncle Carter. "In anuther day or two, I'll be forkin' a hoss again."

"They's short of men," countered Grimes. "That's how I got this carbine."

"That's mine!" exclaimed Uncle Carter. "They grabbed it along with my money, leavin' me fo' dead."

And before they had spent long comparing notes, it was certain that Happy Hardwick was behind the conspiracy.

"Ef I could jest get that five hundred dollars back," grumbled Grimes' uncle, "an' pay the back interest, they'd be a chanct of you and me stagin' a cleanup an' smokin' out that thievin' sculpin. Now you better git some grub and sleep."

The old man resumed his work with a harness maker's awl, stitching a heavy bullhide trace.

That night, Grimes' rest was interupted by the creaking of a hinge and a soft rustling in the darkness. The arm that slipped around his neck was plump and substantial as the well-rounded curves that pressed warmly against him. His visitor was not Susie, but Catalina, the Comanche chief's widow. Grimes didn't know just what to say, until he finally managed to stutter, "M'am, yo' sho' sta'tled me plumb silly. But ain't yo' all makin' a mistake?"

"I 'ave breeng you wan dreenk." Catalina's throaty whisper was as warm as the bottle of tequila she thrust into his hand. "You must 'ave had the beeg fight thees afternoon.

"Sooch a brave boy," she murmured in his ear; and as he finally set aside the bottle at which he had been pulling to gain a moment more for thought, Catalina planted a juicy, whole-hearted kiss squarely on his mouth.

Before he knew it, Grimes had an armful of billowing curves whose generous sweep made him tingle to his ankles. Half off balance, he instinctively caught at Catalina to steady himself. That bit of unintentional encouragement made her embrace tighten about him. He could feel her heart trying to hammer through her thin gown. One more squeeze and he'd be overwhelmed by that affectionate armful—

But Grimes, always a gentleman, checked himself in time.

"M'am," he gasped, "my uncle'd jest lambaste me til I couldn't set in my saddle fo' a month! He don't believe in sech goings on."

Somehow, he managed to extricate himself from her arms and edge her toward the door without being unduly rough. By way of clinching it, he compromised, "Mebbe some other time. . . ."

Catalina knew when she was beaten. He watched her figure fade in the gloom of the hallway. He told himself that Uncle Carter's enforced neglect probably had made Catalina forget herself.

Finally, after a restless half hour, he decided it was late enough for a word with Susie. Anyway, with a parcel of Latin exuberance like Catalina around the house, Uncle Carter had probably become a lot more broad-minded than the Georgia branch of the Grimes family.

So, barefooted and stealthy, he picked his way down the hall to Susie's room. The well-oiled hinge did not creak. Before she was fairly awake, his kiss muffled her gasp of astonishment; then, aroused and clinging to him, she whispered in his ear, "Simon, you oughtn't come in here. Maw's just a bit down the hall, and if we wake her—"

Grimes, however, had a ready answer. Susie was on her feet in an instant, tip-toeing after him. And as she crossed the threshold of his room, Uncle Carter's snoring reassured them.

"I'd been thinking of you all evening," she murmured, "and I'd have come over, but I was sort of scared you might holler right out, waking suddenly."

No doubt that she'd had something on her mind! Grimes came to that conclusion when simmering lips and pert young curves simultaneously flattened against him. And as her arms twined about his neck, the boy from Georgia knew that, for once, a good deed was its own reward. . . .

The reward, however, was dismaying; and he collected it when the door slammed open, admitting Uncle Carter. Behind him was Catalina, holding a lamp and screeching, "I tol' you, that young devil is after my daughter! *Por Dios—*"

"Yo' gol-danged young skunk, fust it's rustlers stealing my cattle," roared Uncle Carter, wounded leg dragging as his good arm flailed the harness tug, "an' then it's you, stealin'—"

Whack! Slap! The lambasting rivaled anything Grimes' pappy had ever dished out; and though he was a shooting fool among strangers, he no more thought of fighting back now than he would have at home. And when Grimes did succeed in dodging the blistering smacks of the leather, Susie's ripest curves got a share of the whaling.

Uncle Carter's arm gave out before the harness tug. Leaning against the door jamb, he panted, "An' ef they's any more of this shameless conduct, I'll run yo' off the ranch."

"Yo' don't need to run me off!" flared Grimes. "I'm goin' to Skeleton Crick and git myself a job riding."

He jerked on his boots and buckled on his gunbelt as Uncle Carter stamped out of the room; and a few minutes later, Grimes was saddling up his horse.

But as he rode into the darkness, he remembered the malicious gleam in Catalina's eyes, and his uncle's wrathful outburst, "Fust rustlers stealing my cattle, then it's you, stealin'—"

That hadn't registered during the bombardment of leather; but now he got it. Unwittingly, he'd poached on his uncle's reservation! No wonder Catalina had been griped when nephew and uncle both rejected her kisses!

Grimes, however, was too stubborn to go back and make his peace with Uncle Carter. On the other hand, tradition demanded that he stick with a kinsman involved in a disastrous feud.

That was his decision, early that morning, a few miles from Skeleton Creek. He dismounted, cut a pair of coat straps from his saddle and drew his left-hand gun. One end of the spliced straps he tied to his suspenders; the other end he attached to the triggerguard of his .45 and slid the weapon down his pants' leg. And after a bit of experiment, he had the gun out of sight, but handy for a quick draw.

THIS TIME HE PASSED THE OFFENSIVE SIGN THAT TOLD THE WORLD THAT SKELETON CREEK was a law-abiding town. Ahead of him was the main street, a deeply rutted expanse of prairie lined by two general stores, seven saloons, a bank and a jail. And just before he was abreast of the last-named, a crusty, hatchet-faced man with a large star and a tobacco-stained mustache emerged.

"Listen, I ain't done nuthin'." Grimes feigned confusion and alarm.

"I ain't sayin' yuh has!" rumbled the marshal. "Didn't yuh read that there sign at the city limits?"

"Mistah, I ain't nevah had any book-learnin'—whut—"

"It says yuh kain't tote belt guns in town!" The marshal explained as he took Grimes' holstered Colt. "Yuh kin git this smoke pole back when yuh leaves."

Grimes rode on. Halfway down the main street, he sized up the saloons, then dismounted at the Corkscrew Inn, whose hitching rack was most crowded with the horses of early drinkers.

"Whisky, ef yo' please, suh," he boomed, stalking to the bar. Then, voice treacherously rising to a piping treble: "Yo'all know if they is anyone round heah that needs a fust class cowhand?"

"They is," admitted the bartender. "But it's fer men, not boys."

"Who's lookin' fer a job?" demanded a rasping voice that dominated the rumble of conversation in the far corner, where several men were gathered about a table.

Grimes turned, downed his whiskey, and saw a tall, redheaded man hitching about in his chair. He had hard eyes, a freckled face and a square jaw.

"I am, suh. Simon Boggs from Nashville, suh," he improvised.

The bricktop shook his head, spat his disapproval; then, catching the wrathful gleam of Grimes' eyes, he laughed good humoredly and countered, "Kin yuh sling a gun?"

"Tolable, suh," admitted Grimes.

"I'm payin' sixty a month, as long as yuh live."

"What's so dangerous, suh? An' who'll I be riding fo'?"

"Whut's so dangerous?" The redhead's laugh was bitter. "Three of my men got bushwhacked last night. I got two new ones, an' I need another. I'm Happy Hardwick. Meet me here at noon."

"Thank you, suh," acknowledged Grimes.

And then two of the cowpunchers at the table lurched to their feet. The short, squint-eyed fellow said to Hardwick, "We're gittin' ourselves some grub at the Chink's."

"Good idea," approved Hardwick. "With all yore likker, yuh need suthin' on yore stomicks. An' keep outa trouble, er I'll kick yuh slabsided."

Squint Eye laughed and grunted to the other puncher, "C'mon, Lanky."

Grimes was hungry enough to eat a pack saddle. Moreover, he wanted a few words with his fellow employees, mainly to find out what the town thought of finding the three riddled gunners in the arroyo. Thus, after buying another drink, he stepped to the street.

In the middle of the block was Ling Fu's restaurant. Grimes entered. Squint Eye and Lanky were at a table near the door. Before he could address them, the Chinaman came slip-slopping from the rear and hailed him, "Wantee glub?"

"Gimme a dollah's wuth of ham an' aigs," demanded Grimes, "an' about two dozen flapjacks, an' plenty of molasses, an' a gallon of coffee."

"Yuh better eat hearty!" jibed Squint Eye. "Might be yore last chanct."

Amiability was decidedly at a discount; so, instead of joining the two cowpunchers, Grimes seated himself at the counter and watched the Chink pour out the first installment of the coffee, then deftly spot the ham and hotcakes on the griddle.

Food, however, was forgotten when he saw the girl who entered Ling Fu's place. She wore fancy stitched boots and a trim riding skirt that flattered the sleekest hips west of the Pecos; but Grimes skipped those swaying curves. What caught his eye was somewhat further up.

She wore a vee-necked silk blouse, whose thin fabric rippled from the quiver of her breasts. She was more substantial than Susie, and the blue-veined fascinations that protested against their frail confinement were bewitchingly outlined.

The twinkle of her eyes seconded the sweet malice of a smile that was just long enough to let her loveliness sink in, and let Grimes know that she had noted his intent scrutiny; then, turning to the Chink, she said, "Ling Fu, can you spare a dozen eggs? A skunk or weasel must have cleaned out our chicken house."

"No hab got, Missee Patton," deplored the Chinaman. "Evelly body wantee ham an' egg."

"You' kin have the half dozen I ordered," Grimes cut in. "He ain't busted 'em yet."

"You're awfully kind," the blonde girl acknowledged.

Then, picking up the newspaper-wrapped parcel Ling Fu handed her, she flashed a dazzling smile over her shoulder and headed for the door.

"Wait a minute, sister!" hailed Squint Eye, on his feet and blocking the door. "How come I missed yuh last night?"

"What's Big May mean, holding out the best gal in town!" grumbled Lanky.

Squint Eye, a bit unsteady on his feet, reached out to catch her arm. He missed his aim, but brushed a ripe curve that fairly sizzled against his hand. The blonde girl, jerking clear, dropped the parcel of eggs. Lanky laughed at her wrathful outcry, and snatched the vee of her blouse.

Instinctively recoiling, she slipped on the egg-splashed floor, landing with a thump, toes waving at the ceiling, skirt high above her knees. Most of her sheer blouse remained in Lanky's grasp. The boys howled; this beat anything the town girls could offer.

But as the blonde screamed and tried to cover the generous upper exposure, Grimes' fist caught Lanky a wallop that knocked him into a corner. Squint Eye, cursing wrathfully, made a dive for his bootleg.

Grimes spun on his heel and snatched the heavy coffee cup from the counter just as Squint Eye's hand came up with a snub-nosed .38. The blistering java, however, had the edge by a split second. Scalded and half stunned, the gunslinger jerked a wild slug as he slumped face down.

Lanky, still groggy, was tugging at his hip pocket. He didn't realize that sitting on a gun slows up the draw; and Grimes didn't have time to tell him. A jerk of the leather thong brought his own weapon from concealment. The thunder of the .45 for a second drowned Ling Fu's frantic yells. Lanky, drilled three times, flattened to the planks.

Grimes, unable to throw anything but lead at the man he had knocked behind the table, had shot himself out of a chance to ride for Happy Hardwick. If he had realized how consistently the anti-weapon law was violated in Skeleton Creek, he might have subdued his gentlemanly impulses, but it was too late now.

One leap took him over the threshold—and face to face with a sawed-off shotgun which the marshal was leveling. Another lawman, followed by the hangers-on of the saloon across the street, was coming on the run.

"Hist 'em, er I'll cut yuh off, hip-high!" growled the marshal. "Yuh ain't got a chanct."

"That's gospel," Grimes wryly admitted, dropping his gun. "But this heah's self defense."

"Yuh was packing a hideout," was the grim retort, "in vi-erlation of a city or-dinuns. An' I'm arresting yuh fer dry-gulchin' Sam Moss and Fin Wallace and Pecos Farley, out the arroyo. When yuh knocked the shells outen yore guns after yuh bushwhacked them hombres, yuh pulled a dumb play leaving 'em there. The empties matches them that's in the smoke pole yuh left with me."

"Hell," protested Grimes, "Findin' .45s don't prove I fired them."

"Usually they don't," admitted the marshal, prodding Grimes down the street, "but yuh fergot that they ain't no one around Skeleton Creek that uses the brand of cartridges in yore guns."

He'd entirely forgotten that the manufacturer who supplied the shells for towns several hundred miles east might not be represented in Skeleton Creek!

The marshal booted Grimes and Squinty into adjoining cells.

"Listen, Terrill," protested Happy Hardwick, who had led the crowd of spectators to the jail, "Lanky started it, an' Squint Eye didn't hurt no one, anyway."

"They all had hideout guns, an' that's agin the law," snapped the marshal.

"Yuh old coot!" grumbled Hardwick, "fust my men gits shot, an' when I get some new ones, yuh throws them in jail. This hoss-faced kid is a purty good lead-slinger, an' I need him—"

"This yere tow-headed brat kilt yore three cowpokes yestiddy," countered Terrill, "an' I kin prove it."

"Ef' you kin, I'm all fer hanging him! Let's git a drink."

Grimes' entire plan was blown up. While he could prove self-defense, they'd nail him for smuggling a gun into town; and in the course of his trial, his identity would be exposed. He'd be useless to Uncle Carter.

LATE THAT AFTERNOON, GRIMES' SOMBER THOUGHTS WERE DISTRACTED BY FOOTFALLS IN the corridor. Terrill's muttering was countered by a woman's familiar voice. The blonde girl he had defended in the Chink's restaurant accompanied the marshal toward the cell.

"Git out, Boggs," Terrill grumbled. "But I'll fix yuh at the trial."

"I'm Melinda Patton," explained the blonde. "I persuaded dad to sign a bail bond. And since we're responsible for you, you're going to be my prisoner, out at the house."

Grimes blinked, stuttered his thanks, then contrived to ask, "Do yo'all live outta town, m'am?"

She did; so he turned to the marshal and demanded his guns.

"You win, yuh onery skunk," grumbled Terrill, surrendering the weapons. "But even if her old man is a banker, tain't goin' tuh help yuh at the trial."

Banker! With Melinda's gratitude backing him, it'd be a cinch to get in a word in favor of Uncle Carter.

Side by side, they headed west. In half an hour, Melinda pulled up at a well-kept, spacious ranch house. He dismounted, tossed the reins to a Mexican and followed Melinda into the living room.

"Oh, I know you must have thought it was terrible," she began, "the way I ran out on you, this morning. But I was so humiliated—"

Grimes nodded and cut in, "Considerin' how much of yo' dress was missin', an' how small yo' hands are, it jest wouldn'ta been right fo' you to stay. But wheah's yo' pappy?"

"He'll be late," explained Melinda. "I rode to Skunk Valley and had him sign the bond."

A Mexican maid served supper. And later, once more in the living room, Melinda was getting thrills out of a blow-by-blow account of the riot. Nor was that one sided: Grimes was recollecting fleeting glimpses of dazzling flesh betrayed by her ruined blouse. He slipped a tentative arm about her. For a moment, she yielded, then protested and tried to draw away.

"Please don't," she half-heartedly objected. "Mr. Boggs—Simon—you mustn't—"

But Grimes persisted. He sensed that, despite her reticence, she wouldn't scream if he kissed her; so he drew her closer, and when she cheated him by turning aside her face, he kissed her shoulder and the hollow of her throat.

She shuddered, then tried to thrust him away; but that effort left her off guard. Before she realized what had happened, he had found her lips. Then, unable to pry him loose, she made the most of it.

"I ought to hate you," she whispered, snuggling into his arms. "But you've kissed me so much that—"

So he made a job of it. When they finally broke for breath, Grimes didn't know whose heart was pounding the hardest. They were so close together, he couldn't tell one from the other.

And then, as he got a bigger and better hold, Melinda's protests began anew: "Don't—Oh, Simon! You *mustn't*—I didn't know—"

The rest of it was a bit inarticulate. Her breath was coming in gasps too quick for speech, and anyway, she wasn't certain she wanted him to stop. . . .

But finally, looking up at him with misty eyes, she murmured, "Darling, I had the maid fix you a room right next to mine . . . and maybe dad won't be home tonight. . . . "

But while he planted his boots in the guest room, he was too wary to leave his guns with them when he followed Melinda.

"Simon," she sighed, very much later, "I hope dad won't kick when you tell him you want to marry me."

"Honey, yo' leave it to me to persuade him. I'm jest honin' to learn the bankin' business. A man finally gits tired of hootin' around with a gun in each hand."

Grimes meant every word of it. True, if he married the banker's daughter, he could readily snake Uncle Carter out of a ruinous fix; but that thought was only a side issue. Marry Melinda? Even if he had to kick her pappy slabsided; even if she was a hash-slinger, not a banker's daughter.

So they kissed and planned; and the footsteps in the hallway did not arouse them until it was too late for Grimes to slip to his own room.

"Dad always comes in to kiss me good night," she whispered. "Ever since Maw died. So you hide under the bed. He doesn't know I invited you to stay. But

I'll have to tell him—no, you mustn't slip out—the servants saw you—I'll tell him you're in your room, and he won't want to see you because it's so late."

That was a sound move; and Grimes took cover just as Patton tapped at Melinda's door. But the knock and hinge creak were muffled by the hoofbeats of an approaching horse. Heavy feet pounded on the veranda, and a rasping voice hailed, "Hey Patton! I want tuh see yuh fer a minute."

The banker turned from the door. Grimes heard him say, "What's the idea, Hardwick? Anything wrong? Hello, Potts! Come in."

"Yeah," answered Hardwick, "plenty's wrong. What the tarnation hell do yuh mean goin' bond fer that young skunk of a Simon Boggs?"

Patton began to explain, but Hardwick cut in, "Yeah, I know he pertected your daughter. But those boys was strangers and didn't know who she was. They didn't mean no harm. Just drunk an' playful-like."

"Wait till yuh hear what they done!" snapped Patton. "Melinda! Git dressed and come out."

"Me and Potts are here tuh apologize, but what I want tuh know is, how come yuh go bond fer Carter Grimes' lead-slinger?" rasped Hardwick.

"What? Yo're crazy!"

"I ain't crazy. Potts, here, coming from Skunk Valley yestiddy seen a jasper riding along with that half-breed gal of Carter Grimes. That was this yere Simon Boggs what killed the men I sent to scatter all her wagonload of vittles. Are you fixing tuh go back on me? Or are we playing this hand tuh a finish?"

"Shut up, you damn' fool!" snarled Patton. "I didn't know Simon Boggs shot up yore men. Yuh think I'd back down, when we got dang nigh every cow critter from Grimes' spread, and that mortgage is ready to foreclose?"

Grimes heard Melinda's slow exhalation of breath. He knew that she understood as well as he did that her father, secretly acting as banking agent for a crew of rustlers, was behind the scheme to ruin the Bar-G. She knew everything, now, except that Grimes was the nephew of the victim of the conspiracy.

"Simon," she gasped as he emerged from cover. She caught his hand, nails sinking in. "Darling—I don't care—if you are working for Carter Grimes—I love you anyway—I won't tell them you're here. Dad doesn't know yet you're in the house. You can trust me."

Grimes turned. The moonlight now invading the room revealed every sweet curve of her, silver white through her frail gown. For the first time, he fully saw the sweep of her long, shapely legs, the sensuous curve of her hips, the proud, youthful breasts he pressed to him as they exchanged kisses and promises.

Her eyes widened, seeing the grimness of his face. She recoiled, half frightened; then, as he bent over, Melinda realized that he was going to kiss her, and wondered again at the fierceness of his caress.

Grimes had made his decision. He was in an enemy's house; there was a feud, and generations of Georgia tradition left him no choice. Melinda, however, did not understand until he flashed panther-like down the hall.

"Simon!" she screamed. "Oh, Simon—don't—"

He knew that it was fear for him, not a warning against him. That made it worse, but only for an instant.

They came a-running, reading Melinda's voice, not her words. And then the hall was laced by spurts of flame, shaken by thundering guns. Hardwick, caught amidships, spun and collapsed. Patton, ducking to the cover of the doorjamb, hosed the passageway; but Grimes, gun dancing, chewed the wood away with a rain of slugs. He was himself raked and seared, stunned by the devilish concussion, and his right leg had suddenly gone numb.

Potts, panic-stricken at Patton's death, turned toward a window; but he tripped across an overturned chair. That saved his life. His gun had slid beyond his reach.

"I quit!" he yelled. "Fer God's sake—"

Grimes, .45 smoking, bounded forward. He was too shocked in mind and body to hear Melinda's scream as she flung herself across her father's body. Grimes was moving automatically. Though this was a feud, he had to use Potts instead of killing him. He snarled, "Git on yo' laigs, an' mebbe I'll not blast yo' gizzard out!"

Once out of the house, he made Potts mount up; then, piling into a saddle, Grimes herded his prisoner toward the Box-G. He was dizzy and faint from loss of blood, but wrath gave him strength; wrath, and the memory of what it had cost him to be loyal to his clan.

Sunrise ended the nightmare. Catalina, seeing the haggard wrecks that slid from their saddles, ran screeching into the house. Uncle Carter, gun drawn, came limping out. Susie was at his heels.

"I told this skunk," gasped Grimes, "if he'd be yo' witness in co't, to prove that Patton an' Hardwick was con-spirin' to rob yo', I'd not blow his haid off. This gives yo' a fresh start, an' I hopes it chokes yo'!"

He caught the door jamb, tried to stagger toward his horse, but his legs failed. Uncle Carter, pistol covering the prisoner, gestured to Susie. As she approached Grimes, the old man said, "Simon, I guess it jest warn't right fo' me to make any claims on Susie. Me an' Catalina has . . . uh . . . er . . . so't of arranged things, an' ef yo' still care fo' the gal—"

"Uncle Ca'tah," said the boy, "when I git the lead picked outen my carcass, I'm ridin' west. I jest shot old man Patton, a hour after his daughter said she'd marry me." Then he sat up, and his smile was wry and bitter. "But mebbe it's jest as well. Ain't never heard of a Grimes having a banker fo' a father-in-law, an', anyhow, a feud's a feud, even if it's in Skeleton Crick."

• • • • •

Feud's End

"SIMON! YOU, SIMON! WHUT THE TARNATION HELL YO' THINK THIS IS, A GOL DANGED hotel?" Uncle Carter, bawling like a four-year-old bull, shattered the early morning silence.

Simon Bolivar Grimes had heard the first raucous bellow some minutes earlier, but untangling himself from the ranch cook's lovely daughter took time and determination. The girl had developed the art of clinging to the utmost possible degree.

Susie Wrinkled-Meat, slim, shapely, and brown, had inherited an inappropriate name and piquantly prominent cheekbones from her late father, a Comanche chief; and her Spanish mother's contribution was a pair of devil-haunted black eyes and an insatiable urge for just one more kiss.

She wore a gown heavily paneled with hand-made Mexican lace. It concealed this and revealed that—particularly *that,* of which Susie had plenty: such as sweetly rounded hips, and firm little breasts, coyly hinted at by the transparent yoke of her gown. She was sultry enough to need ventilated garments. . . .

"Simon, darling," she sighed. "I hate to think of you're going with the pool herd to Abilene. I'll miss you awfully."

She kissed the gangling, tow-headed boy from Georgia until he tingled all the way to his cowhide boots. He had been telling Susie goodbye since eight o'clock the night before.

"Honey, I jest got to be rep of the Box-G," he panted. "But—"

"Simon, you blasted, girl-crazy horn toad, wheah are you?" howled Uncle Carter from outside the cook's 'dobe shack.

Grimes pried the armful of torrid lace from his shirt front and stumbled toward the ranch house. His coffin-shaped face was longer than usual. Maybe if he stalled long enough, he could devise some way of taking Susie with him.

"Uncle Ca'tah," he began, planting himself at the kitchen table, "I got a whale of a headache. Anyway, they ain't going to be through putting the trail brand on all them critters till tonight."

Grimes' uncle, however, was almost psychic: "Bub, they ain't no use thinking of takin' Susie along. Them cowpokes would be so danged busy murderin' each other fo' one of her kisses, they'd plumb fo'get ridin' herd."

"I warn't thinkin' of that!" flared Grimes. "I jest been tryin' to figger out why Melinda Patton ain't putting any of her H-P critters in the pool. They's suthin' funny theah."

"You might ask Melinda," was the malicious retort.

Grimes, white with wrath, leaped to his feet. He and Melinda had been very much in love until he shot her father, the crooked banker, who, as front for a cattle rustling syndicate, had nearly put Uncle Carter out of business.

The impending civil war was blocked when a sweet voice purred from the threshold, "Señor Grimes, I 'ave jest notice there ees no flour, and the bacon, she ees damn' near finish."

It was Susie's mother, Catalina. Her comely face had a well-kissed look; and every quiver of her firm, generous breasts made Grimes wonder if his uncle wasn't mighty lucky in his arrangements to take care of John Wrinkled-Meat's daughter and widow.

"Simon," grunted Uncle Carter, "mebbe you an' Susie bettah take the buckboard and load it up with vittles. She kin drive it back."

It was so arranged; and, presently, they were on their way.

WHILE NOT QUITE HALFWAY TO SKELETON CREEK, GRIMES NOTED A LARGE HERD NEAR THE bank of the creek that gave the town its name. The critters were branded "BB." He had never heard of such an outfit. Frowning, he handed Susie the reins.

"You wait heah. I'm goin' ovah to the camp," he said, mounting the saddled palomino tethered to the tail gate of the wagon.

Grimes was moved by more than mere curiosity; it was part of his business to keep posted on who was who.

He skirted Skeleton Creek; but he had scarcely ridden fifty yards when he pulled up. The woman at the edge of a dawn-kissed pool, just visible through a thicket, was built to make Venus at the fountain look like a Piute squaw. Her hair, gilded by the early light and streaming to her hips, was a passable substitute for the last flimsy garment that was settling about her ankles.

He got just a flash of a bosom that quivered like delicate pink-tinted jelly. Then, before he could get a look at her face, she turned to the creek, tentatively tested its temperature with an outthrust foot. Though that move cheated Grimes of a fuller view, it gave him a chance to remember that no gentleman would spy on a lady's morning bath. He headed for the camp.

Two men squatted at the fire. Half a dozen others, likewise black dots against the horizontal rays that made Grimes blink and squint, were hustling about with their work.

As he approached, the two at the fire started to their feet, hands darting to their belts. The move, however, was checked when Grimes hailed the camp, but while that gesture had been natural enough, they did seem just a shade jumpy. One, short and squat, ducked out of sight; the other, tall and rangy, rose and approached Grimes.

As the gap closed, Grimes for the first time was able to see that the boss of that outfit had a black beard, a hatchet face and bushy brows; a salty, hard bitten hombre if there ever was one.

"Light and set, stranger," he invited. Then, gesturing at the pot on the fire, "they's still time fer some cawfee."

"Thank you, suh. I done et. I'm Simon Bolivar Grimes, suh, an' seein' yo' critters, I thought at fust you was some local outfit headin' fo' the pool herd."

"Yo're jest half right, bub," grinned the bearded man. "I'm Bart Bailey from Del Rio, which ain't exactly local. But, last night, I heard about a pool startin' from here, and with so many cattle thieves on the prowl, I reckoned it'd be sensible tuh join up."

They chatted for a moment, then Grimes wheeled his horse and rode back to the buckboard. Susie was at the creek ford, waiting. The blonde woman was no longer in sight. But Grimes was not thinking of the beauties of nature.

"Mistah Bart Bailey," he pondered, "sho' drove his herd slow-like, fo' a gent what's afeerd of owl-hooters. Them critters is too fat fo' a fast run from Del Rio."

HALF AN HOUR LATER, AS THEY APPROACHED THE MOUTH OF AN ARROYO, HE HEARD THE whinny of a horse. It came from the right; and the greeting to his beasts was cut off before it was fairly out. Someone had blundered. The abrupt choking of the sound was a dead give-away. There was an ambush ahead.

Grimes, pig stubborn, refused to retreat. In the arroyo, the light was still tricky for long range fire. As they were for a moment sheltered by a thicket, he said to Susie, "Grab my hoss and git out while I attend to that gent."

"I'm not scared," she countered; but she wisely dropped to the bed of the buckboard.

Grimes' drawn pistol, a single action .45 the length of a siege gun, lay on his knee. He was ready—

Whack! But the rifle blast came from the side of the arroyo opposite from the one where the concealed horse had whinnied.

A slug gouged a ragged welt along Grimes' ribs, thudding into the seat beside him. He yelled, pitched to the floorboards. The fuzztails bolted. The clattering drowned everything but the triumphant hoot from the left, and the answering shout from the right.

A man popped up from cover, high above the bottom of the arroyo. He was certain that he had plugged his victim; but a correction was on the way. The galloping mustangs had closed the gap; and then the long barreled .45 bellowed like artillery firing in battery. The lurker pitched headlong down the slope.

The mustangs wheeled sharply, wedging the wagon wheels on a boulder. The impact spilled Grimes from the seat and piled Susie on top of him. The resulting pinwheel of bare legs, cowhide boots and red calico settled to the rocky bottom just in time to miss the hail of pistol slugs that poured from the opposite bank. The choked whinny from the right had been guile, not stupidity; but for poor marksmanship, Grimes would have been plugged from the left before he caught the trick.

Sheltered by the half-upset wagon, he hosed the slope with lead. His second gun, however, had dropped far beyond his reach; and as he frantically jacked the empties from his smoking weapon, a howl and a clatter of departing hoofs mocked him.

No chance to pursue. The saddle mount had broken from the tailgate and bolted. Susie was screeching to the high heavens, "Simon, they killed me!"

For a mortally wounded person, she was tolerably noisy. Helping her to her feet, he saw that a slug had creased her hip. So while Susie nonchalantly tore a strip from her skirt, Grimes pacified the mustangs, who were industriously kicking the dashboard to pieces, maneuvered them to extricate the wedged wagon wheel, and then caught his saddle mount. That done, he approached the pie-faced man who lay gaping stupidly at the sunrise.

He was a stranger, and the contents of his pockets were not enlightening. His accomplice, escaping with both horses, had removed the most serviceable clue; but Grimes, after bundling the stiff into the buckboard, circled around the scene of the ambush.

One of the hidden mounts had a broken shoe, he learned from the hoofprints; and he found a lead-riddled hat near the spot where the lurker had watched the horses. It was a Stetson with a silver ornamental band. On the brim was an old bloodstain, almost obliterated. Though the law would not accept such a flimsy identification, it was good enough for Grimes.

That hat belonged to Lem Potts, the shyster lawyer who had been the sole survivor of the gunfight in which Grimes had blotted out Melinda Patton's father. There was no mistaking that bloodstain.

The implications, however, reached much further. The signs indicated that it had been an impromptu ambush. There were no cigarette butts, no blurr of footprints to indicate a long vigil. Potts and the rifleman must have hastened from Bart Bailey's camp to intercept him.

Then he caught the play: Bailey and his companion had not realized that Grimes, dazzled by the horizontal rays, had not been able to recognize the man ducking from the camp fire. Thus the ambush was to keep Grimes from drawing any conclusions as to why Potts, survivor of the rustler syndicate, had had important business with Bailey.

Grimes, though unable to prove his suspicions, drove on toward town with his convictions.

THE LAW AGAINST CARRYING BELT WEAPONS IN SKELETON CREEK HAD JUST BEEN repealed, mainly because everyone homocidally inclined concealed guns in bootlegs, hip pockets and shoulder holsters instead of wearing them openly. This repeal, mainly due to Grimes' blasting the gizzards out of a pair of ruffians who had underestimated him, got him a sour glare from old Hob Terrill, the town marshal, who sat near the jail.

"Mawnin', Hob," beamed Grimes, jerking his thumb toward the corpse in the wagon. "I got some new business fo' you, an' the sheriff."

"I guess yuh got another alibi?" He helped Grimes unload the dead.

"Suttinly, I has. Ef I'd fired fust, this gent wouldn't never lived to pour a .45-70 along my ribs an' through the wagon seat. An' I got a witness."

The gritting sound Grimes heard as he clucked to the nags was the marshal's teeth. He turned back and added, "An' fo' six bits extry, you kin look an' see wheah that wild shot scraped Susie."

"Six bits, nothing!" mocked Susie, patting her hip. "It'll cost you both your eyes, Señor Terrill!"

The marshal, regarding the shapely bare legs Susie had cocked up on the dashboard, looked as though that would be cheap enough. Then he said, "I'll git yuh yet, yuh gol blamed trantler."

Grimes pulled up at Link Simpson's general store. Then, leaving Susie to stock up the wagon, Grimes headed toward the Corkscrew Inn, which was headquarters for the cattlemen who were pooling their herds for the long drive to Kansas.

HALFWAY TO HIS DESTINATION, HE HALTED, CONFUSED AND EMBARRASSED. A GIRL WEARING stitched boots and a trim riding skirt that flattered the most fascinating hips on that side of the Pecos was approaching him. Her sweet, serious face was framed by pale golden hair. The upper fullness of a vee-necked silk blouse rippled deliciously with each stride. She had everything!

This was Melinda Patton. Dreading this first meeting since he'd shot her father, he turned to duck into the Last Chance Saloon; but the swinging door slammed outward, blocking him.

Grimes, lips dry and heart hammering, caught the glance of her blue eyes. She recoiled; a gleam of tears contrasted strangely with the sudden hardening of her face.

"Melinda—honey—" he blurted.

She swept past him. He suddenly was glad he was riding with the trail herd. That meeting had undone every effort to forget the way she had once smiled at him in the moonlight stealing through her window. She had to hate him now, just as it had been his duty to avenge the unexpectedly revealed duplicity of her father.

Worst of all, the blowoff had come just as they'd decided, after an evening's conference, that they'd be married the following day.

He stumbled back and into the Corkscrew Inn, where he gargled two shots of whiskey. Then he glanced about and saw the reps of the other outfits that were to pool their cattle. Sitting in their midst was Bart Bailey. White-haired Gil Stewart of the Lazy M was saying, "Shore. I'm trail boss. But we kain't let in any outsiders onless the reps from each ranch agrees, unanimously."

"Hell," said Bailey, "you gents has jest as good as admitted they ain't no objections tuh me."

"Makes no difference," contended Stewart. "We ain't heard from the Box-G outfit yet, and until—" Then, seeing Grimes, he hailed him: "Hi, thar, Simon! Come here an' meet Bart Bailey—"

"I done had that pleasure, Gil," the boy cut in. He grinned guilelessly at Bailey.

The bearded man, if he really were surprised to see Grimes, betrayed no amazement. He nodded, then said, "I'll jest leave whilst yuh do this votin', Stewart. An' as soon as yo're done, I'll get started trail-brandin' my critters."

Stewart led the local cattlemen to the proprietor's private room.

"That was jest a formality, fellers," he said. "Ain't no objections, is they, lettin' Bart Bailey team up with us."

"I'm objectin', suh," Grimes interposed. "Fo' the Box-G, what's got mo' critters in this herd 'an any other outfit."

For a moment, there was a clamor of amazement at his vote. Bailey, apparently, had won the good graces of the four reps during the time he had gained by riding instead of deliberately driving to Skeleton Creek.

"What fur, Simon—? What's wrong with him—? What yuh got agin him—?"

"That's none of yo' dang business!" he retorted to the babbling trio. "Yo' asked, is I got objections an' I done said I has."

"Listen, young whelp!" Jeb Terry, broad as a chuckwagon and belligerent as an old bull, advanced a pace, "I asked—"

Pop! Grimes' fist snapped him back on his heels; but the blow just enraged Terry. With a wrathful bellow, he recovered, tugging leather.

That was a mistake. Before his gun half cleared the holster, a blast shook the room. Jeb yelled. Blood spurted from the hammer thumb that had been cut by fragments of the bullet that knocked the gun from his hand.

"I'll knock the two of yuh loose from yore eye teeth," growled salty old Gil Stewart, interposing. "Simon, what yuh got agin' Bailey?"

Grimes scratched his tow head and frowned. "Gil, I jest don't exactly know. Yo' might call it a permonition. Kain't prove it, so I ain't sayin'."

To explain would only warn Lem Potts, if he actually were in cahoots with Bailey in some devious piece of skullduggery. Grimes had a deep-seated grudge against that slick customer; but for Potts' twisted legal advice, Melinda's pappy might have stayed straight, and young love would not have gone up in gunsmoke.

"Yo're right, not sayin' what yuh kain't prove," Stewart grudgingly conceded. "But yo're a damn ornery brat, an' ef I was yore uncle, I'd lambaste yuh till yore hind end looked like a Scotch plaid."

"My uncle has been doin' that fo' months, an' ain't another man living what'd have guts to try it," Grimes frigidly retorted, stalking from the room, and the others followed.

Before Stewart could break the news, Bailey chuckled sourly, shrugged and said, "I done heard most of it. Grimes, I dunno whut yuh got agin' me, but supposin' you come up tuh my room at the White Hoss Hotel? It's only fair tuh tell me in private."

Grimes had to concede the justice of his contentions.

"I'll sho' admire to give yo'all satisfaction, Mistah Bailey," said Grimes. "In two hours, ef it's agreeable to you. I got to see how many of my critters is branded."

"It's Room Four," added Bailey, as Grimes turned toward the street.

The drover's affability in the face of that direct affront convinced Grimes that Bailey was too diplomatic for an honest man; but that was all the more reason to accept his proposition. Bailey could hardly have guessed that Grimes had connected him with Lem Potts; and, in his efforts to placate the stubborn boy, he might unconsciously drop a revealing hint.

Grimes headed for the branding pen at the further side of town; but he at once looped back and down a side street, to find Potts before Bailey met him.

LEM POTTS, HE PRESENTLY LEARNED, WAS NOT IN HIS HOTEL OR OFFICE. NEITHER WAS HE at the bank, the jail, nor in any of the other saloons. It took Grimes only a few minutes to make the rounds. Then he played his last hunch.

Melinda Patton's sorrel mare was no longer at the hitching rack. She must have left town during the conference at the Corkscrew Inn. Grimes reasoned that Potts, who could not be proved guilty of the attempted dry-gulching, would scarcely shake his hocks; instead, he'd merely hide out until the trail herd left Skeleton Creek. And Melinda's ranch house was the one place where he'd expect to stay clear of Grimes, a gunslinger no one in Skeleton Creek cared to face.

Half an hour later, he was approaching the ranch house of the late Hank Patton. Though neat, it already showed signs of dwindling fortunes. The cracking of the rustlers' syndicate had cut heavily into the fortune Melinda's father took in and spent each year. Then he noted hoofprints: rider and a led horse had not long ago galloped toward the house.

One of the beasts had been bleeding. *And the led horse had one cracked shoe;* the sign Grimes had noted at the ambush. Melinda had sent Potts to bushwhack him.

A feud was a feud, and he couldn't blame the gal. But if Potts were carrying on her vengeance—

"Gawd a-mighty!" he groaned, catching all the implications. "She wouldn't *hire* anyone to plug me! She ain't that low. But ef someone was making love to her, she'd have a right to *ask* him to settle me."

He dismounted, stealthily approached the house. He knew all too well in what wing the living room was. As he came nearer, he heard a murmur of voices. The garden afforded him adequate cover from observation by any employees who might be about the bunkhouse or stables.

He was tall enough to get a peep between the curtains that screened the barred windows; and what Grimes saw was more than enough.

The woman must be Melinda. A man was bending over her, drawing her toward him. Her face was thus not visible, but there was no mistaking that riding skirt, well over her knees, nor the dazzling curve of her white legs.

"Oh . . . Lem . . . you mustn't . . . not now . . . . I do appreciate what you've done—what you're doing for me—but I can't—please—"

Grimes drew his .45; but those slim arms, and her incoherent gasps unnerved him. His entire body trembled, and a red haze blurred his eyes. He turned from the window.

Killing Potts in Melinda's house would damn Grimes, who had no right there. If he were jailed, he'd be foiling Uncle Carter, whose old wounds kept him from going with the herd.

". . . Lem, darling—please don't—but tomorrow night—come back at eight—"

Grimes stumbled back to his horse, spurred his beast to a gallop. He'd made a fool of himself, suspecting Bailey. The only thing to do was to apologize for a piece of Georgia orneriness and square himself with Gil Stewart and Uncle Carter's other neighbors.

HIS TWO HOURS WERE ALMOST UP WHEN HE CAME LARRUPING INTO SKELETON CREEK. AS he dismounted in front of the Corkscrew Inn, he saw Gil Stewart, and said, "Jest fergit what I said about Bailey. I done made a hell of a mistake."

"All right, bub," answered the trail boss. "I'll tell him—"

"I'd ruther tell him myself, Gil. But ef you want to tell Jeb Terry and the others, I'd sho' thank you. I feel so't of foolish about this mess."

He stalked toward the White Horse Hotel. Bailey was not at the bar; Grimes therefore ascended the rickety stairs to the second floor. He tapped at the door of Number Four. A woman bade him enter.

He halted a pace across the threshold, and devoted the next moment to gaping and stuttering. Her blue robe trailed half open, and what little she wore beneath it accentuated the high spots between waist and collarbone. There were the sleek legs he'd viewed by sunrise; and now he caught more fully the dazzling beauty which distance had that morning withheld. Her smile was a crimson challenge.

"Uh—ur—beg yo' pahdon, m'am—I'm lookin' fo' Mistah Bailey's room—I'm Simon Bolivar Grimes, m'am—"

"Oh . . . Mr. Grimes? If you don't mind—" She paused, basking in his hungry glance, yet seeming to grope for a tactful way of reminding him that she could dress just as well without an audience.

The comb slipped from her fingers. Grimes sank to his knees to retrieve it, and did his best to keep his eyes on the floor and his fingers steady. When he straightened, she was so close that he felt her warmth and roundness against him.

But that was nothing to the next shock! Hungry lips pressed a moist, clinging kiss on his mouth, choking his gasp of amazement. Her arms twined about him and she arched herself closer, breathing an inarticulate sigh of contentment.

"Lawd, m'am!" He was thrilled and horrified. "You kain't do that—not heah—with that door—"

His mouth went dry and ice raced through his veins when heavy footsteps came clumping down the hall. Then the robe slipped from her shoulders. Sheer horror paralyzed him.

In desperation, he reached for her wrists. She cried out, and while one hand broke away, her feet laced treacherously with his boots, tripping him. He was hopelessly tangled with a writhing armful when the door burst open.

Bailey was at the threshold. At his heel was the marshal, Hob Terrill.

"I'll kill the skunk!" roared Bailey, gun drawn before Grimes could kick clear and protest that it was a frame-up.

"Drop it!" snarled. Terrill, knocking the weapon aside just as Grimes got to his own gun. "Yuh fool, yuh'll jest embarrass yore wife ef yuh kill him and have tuh explain why. She ain't been hurt none, not exactly—"

He cocked a critical eye at the hysterical Mrs. Bailey, who was laughing, sobbing and pouring out an incoherent account of how Grimes had gone wild seeing her state of array when she turned from the dresser. Terrill didn't blame Grimes for having notions; he was getting a few himself; but he sternly went on, "Yo're under arrest fer assault and battery, improper and unfittin' conduck, an' attempted—"

He choked, groping for just the word to use before a lady. But Bailey cut in, "Hell, marshal, ef yuh arrests him, *yuh'll* be advertising my wife's humiliation. Supposin' him and me go outside the city limits and settle this."

"Kain't do it." Terrill was adamant. "I kain't countenance dueling. If a couple gents gets riled an' on the spur of the moment shoots each other, that's jest a act of God. But planning it, with malice aforethought, it's down right iniquitious an' it don't go. Not in Skeleton Crick."

Bailey's wrath subsided. "Maria, I done tol' yuh that that dang open-front nightgown—"

"Bart, it's a negligee—"

"That open-front nightgown was downright indecent," he persisted. "So mebbe I shouldn't git too hostile, specially as he ain't done no—no—uh—damage."

Grimes was sweating, embarrassed, and wrathful. Bailey was a skunk; but having told Gil Stewart that he'd withdrawn his objections, Grimes couldn't back down. And then Bailey said, "Since this here ain't got beyond the four of us, I'll fergit it, ef yuh let me in on the Skeleton Crick pool."

"You damn' ornery polecat!" fumed Grimes.

"Yuh agrees," Terrill cut in, "er by God, I take yuh to the hoosgow."

"I ain't agreein' because Terrill's caught me with my galluses hangin' halfway to my ankles," raged Grimes. "I jest done told Stewart I was mistaken about you, and that I wouldn't vote agin you. So I kain't back down.

"But once this trail herd gits to Kansas, I'm scatterin' yo' guts all ovah a quarter section! Now, ef yo' wants to join, yo' ah plumb welcome, suh."

Bailey chuckled. Grimes stamped into the hall. And to forget the morning's humiliation, he spent the remainder of the day at the branding pen.

THE FOLLOWING MORNING, THE TRAIL HERD SURGED NORTHWARD, CHUCK WAGON AND remuda at the rear.

Grimes, watching Bailey's critters joining the pool, saw something he had not noticed the previous morning. It became plain enough, once a trick of the early light made him for a second time scrutinize the "BB" on the flank of one of the beasts that supposedly had come all the way from Del Rio.

It was slick and skillful branding; but his resentment and his initial suspicions had sharpened his eyes. The "BB" had not long ago been "HP"—Melinda Patton's brand! Instead of having come from Del Rio, Bailey had, by a circuitous route, taken Melinda's disguised cattle from her spread and then back again to Skeleton Creek.

Neither could it be wholesale theft; particularly not when Potts, Melinda's lover, had been conferring with Bailey the morning previous. It was becoming intricate beyond reckoning; each possible answer was contradicted by some other fact.

Gil Stewart, though he had heard nothing of the clash between Bailey and Grimes, kept them far apart, just on the chance that the boy's initial opposition might, in the tension of the long march, cause an outbreak of hostilities. The most even tempers would crack after the first week of long marches, nights broken by guard duty, by alarms real and false, by rumors of rustlers, by threats of stampedes.

FOR THE FIRST NIGHT'S CAMP, GRIMES WAS ASSIGNED TO THE THIRD WATCH. INSTEAD OF spreading his tarpaulin near his fellows, he made his bed somewhat apart, and near the river. All day long, whenever a "BB" could be picked out of the herd, he received fresh confirmation: positively no doubt that they had all been "HP." He was still simmering with wrath and humiliation and jealousy; he had to get to the heart of the riddle.

Something crooked was in the wind. He now had two on his list of men to blot out, once Uncle Carter's cattle had been delivered and the money banked: Bart Bailey, and Potts, Melinda's new lover.

Yet, despite his brain-wracking, he finally must have dozed. Something was creeping toward him; a silent shape whose advance he had felt rather than heard.

The hair on the back of his neck bristled from the shock of realizing that an enemy had almost crept up on him. Then, silent as the stalker, Grimes drew his pistol, thumb ready to flick the hammer back when the enemy was too close to retreat.

"Simon, I thought it'd never be dark," whispered a soft voice. "Last night, I sneaked to the chuck wagon—"

"What? You hid in it?"

"In that bull's hide stretched under the wagon bed. I shoved out some of the brushwood they put in fer fuel."

She was in his arms, eyes agleam in the dim light, hungry lips seeking his mouth, stopping his protest, "Yo' kain't follow us. Uncle Ca'tah was right. Though I did so't of reckon it'd be nice ef yo' could—"

"Just tonight and tomorrow night, honey," she explained, wriggling closer, a supple length of quivering loveliness. "Then I'll take a hoss and go back. Won't be nothing—I can make it in a day, riding. I hid some grub—"

But by that time, Grimes wasn't interested in details concerning the bull's hide "hammock" in which Susie had stowed away. He drew her closer, thrilled as her breath sighed in quick gasps in his ear. . . .

The trail day is long, and the night woefully short, yet there were a number of hours before Grimes was due to stand watch. And though kisses made him drowsy, he watched the slow circling of the dipper overhead.

An owl hooted . . . then another . . . just a night sound; and, but for the girl in his arms, Grimes would have ignored it as did the herd guards and the nighthawk of the remuda. But it would be a mess, having the second watch slip up on him and catch Susie.

He relaxed. Then, peering toward the men stretched out near the chuck wagon, he saw a dark shape emerging from a blacker patch. The moon's upper edge was just peeping from the horizon, though trees still shadowed most of the camp.

The figure moved silently, infinitely cautiously. There was a gleam of steel.

Murder! Grimes, thrusting Susie aside, snapped his .45 into line. The blast shook the silence; but even as the gun jumped in his hand, he knew that he had been an instant too late. The blade sank home. The slayer leaped, whirling toward the report.

Grimes bounded forward. Tongues of flame laced the gloom. Susie cried out, stumbled; but that shot stretched into a prolonged drumming. The gunner, bolting toward the remuda, pitched headlong.

"Cut down, hip high!" yelled Grimes. "Susie—fer Gawd's sake—"

She was on her feet, but the hand that caught his wrist was wet with blood. And then the camp became a howling madness.

"I got him!" Grimes roared. "Quit yo' shooting—see who he knifed— You, Jeb!"

Matches flared. Gil Stewart plucked at the knife haft in his chest, coughed, and slumped back, dead. The assassin Grimes had shot down was Bart Bailey.

The reason for his treachery became apparent an instant later. Rifle fire crackled from the flank of the bedded herd. Horsemen charged out of the darkness. That explained the owl hoots!

Grimes made a dive for the wagon, passing out rifles. The cowpunchers aroused in time to beat the ambush, raked the raiders with a withering fire. Saddles emptied, horses pitched end for end. Instead of a camp gutted by a stealthy assassin, they charged into a hornet's nest.

They broke; and as the drovers piled into their saddles, Grimes got the answer: Melinda, Potts and Bailey had conspired to plunder, then peddle the stolen cattle to traders in wet beef.

But as the enemy fled, a new peril threatened the camp. The cattle were stampeding. A long, rumbling line thundered along the flank. The raiders, defeated, had precipitated a panic to block pursuit. The drovers again were on the defensive; and against a deadlier peril.

Grimes jerked Susie from her feet and into the saddle in front of him. No time to get a second horse. Not a chance to fan out the roaring herd. They had gotten too good a start. Moonrise revealed a surging sea of long, deadly horns; and the main body, blindly following, was adding to the irresistible flood of beasts.

"The river—Simon—the river—" gasped Susie.

"Not a chanct, honey! They's cut us off, both sides—"

She tried to worm from his arms, but he checked her.

"Simon—you're silly—I can't last long—I'm just tiring your hoss—a wild shot—plugged me—"

Good God! Then he remembered how she'd let out scarcely a yeep. The morning before, she'd yelled bloody murder, just at a scratch. She must be badly injured.

"Shut up, you little fool," he snapped, turning in the saddle. "We'll make it."

His .45 crackled. A longhorn pitched in a heap, another, and a third. The mountain of beef was too high for those behind to hurdle. Horns locked, they could not swerve. Bones crushed as tons of frenzied beasts piled up, held like a timber jam by one key log.

"We're gainin', honey—hang on—"

He swung to the left, trying to outrace the further tip of the crescent. He emptied his other gun, gained a few more precious yards.

Then the overloaded mustang's stride broke. He had lamed himself in a gopher hole. Terror drove him on, but he couldn't last long. Escape every instant became more hopeless.

"Simon—you fool—"

Susie's frenzy caught Grimes off guard. She slipped free, thudded to the earth. One bit of devotion in a solid front of treachery. He wheeled, reloaded his guns, bounded to her side. It was insane; perhaps Grimes knew he hadn't a chance, even though he did ride on.

"That buffler wallow—scrunch into it! I'll shoot the hoss!" he yelled. "And pile up some cows tother side of it—"

And then, far ahead, he saw a rider skylined in the moonlight; a rider suddenly blossoming white, and wildly waving something white. A pistol blazed. The point of the onrushing crescent swung, fanned out. Hundreds of frenzied beasts with a single, insane mass mind responded to the new terror. Those further to the rear wheeled, snorting, bawling, hoofs rumbling, horns clashing. Grimes whirled, picked up his limp burden, swung to the saddle.

He flogged his lamed mustang with his pistol barrel, booted and spurred the beast till it forgot its tortured leg.

And when the horse finally pitched in a heap, the stampede had been turned. Other riders, who had outraced the right wing of the herd, came scrambling up the bank to press the advantage. The critters were milling now. Hundreds dead, but the most were saved.

Grimes, struggling to his knees, saw the white rider reel in the saddle. It was Melinda Patton, peeled down to her boots and a few scraps that only an expert in ladies' wear could have described. She slid to her feet, swaying as she clutched the saddle horn.

"Simon," she panted, "I came to warn you—they were going to murder—you and Stewart and as many others—as they could—then loot—"

Grimes, kneeling beside Susie, looked up and snarled, "Yo' came to save yo' own critters!"

"No! It was you. Do you suppose, if they planned to stampede the herd, they'd try murder by hand, when the herd would do that?"

That clinched it. Grimes felt Susie snuggle closer. She smiled and murmured something, then slumped against his arm.

"I wonder," he finally muttered, voice dry and strained, "if you really are in a class with this gal?"

Melinda knelt beside him. "Let's forget our feud. Dad was in the wrong. I finally saw your position. Then I suspected Potts—"

"Potts?"

"Yes. After dad was exposed, and all the cattlemen got damage judgments against his estate, the bank began wobbling. The only way I could save myself was to disguise my HP cattle as BB, and get Bailey to drive them north. The money I'd raise would go into the bank in a blind account and tide me over, instead of having everything cleaned out by judgments against dad's estate. Just judgments, but ruinous.

"I was wrong, but desperate. Potts had been courting me for some time, and, finally, I pretended to encourage him. But when he came in yesterday, with a wounded horse and a confused story, I suspected dirt.

"Then the marshal told me how Bailey and his wife tricked you. That nasty play set me thinking more. And when Potts, early this evening, left me on a flimsy pretext—instead of trying to force himself on me, I became more suspicious, and followed him."

"Mebbe," said Grimes, very slowly, "yo'll are in a class with Susie after all. When I git back from Kansas, I got a shooting party with Potts—"

"No, Simon." She leaned closer, till he felt her warmth against him. "There's been too much hate and killing. This is feud's end. I'm grieved—but dad was wrong—you couldn't help it—"

"Honey," he groped, "ef yo' mean that, I'll even kiss Potts when I git back."

● ● ● ● ●

Hoodoo Town

THE BLUE ROAN GELDING PRICKED UP HIS EARS AND GAINED FRESH LIFE AS HIS TALL, gangling rider reached the outskirts of Skeleton Creek. The horse smelled water and stables, and knew that the heart-breaking ride from Kansas was over; knew that the saddle bags, heavy with nine thousand dollars gold, would soon leave his sweat-caked flanks. But Simon Bolivar Grimes anticipated more than food and rest.

He was thinking of Melinda Patton. His coffin-shaped face relaxed in a boyish grin, and he seemed strangely young to be wearing a bone-handled .45 with enough notches to give a buzzsaw a start in life. And then he saw the red-haired girl in the doorway of the Corkscrew Inn, the biggest and best of the town's eleven saloons.

Her spangled bodice was low-cut and nicely filled, and to enhance her fascinations, she was leaning against the jamb in a way that flared out the generous curve of her hip. The evening breeze, stealing down the dusty street, played tricks with her short skirt, which coquettishly revealed glimpses of whiteness as it whipped over her knees. She started; then the dance hall smile changed to something warmer when she recognized the dusty rider.

"Simon—so you got back?" She heard the tinkling gold in the saddlebags as he reined in. "But where's the cowpokes? Ain't heard any shooting, or yelling, like when trail drovers get back to town."

"I done left them at Cross Plains."

Her eyes widened. "You idiot! Wonder you wasn't held up."

"I was, twict," admitted Grimes, wheeling his horse.

"Oh." Sally allowed that another couple of gents had made the error of thinking he was awkward with a gun, just because he always seemed on the verge of stumbling over his own feet. Then she invited, "Light and have a drink, honey."

He shook his head. "Kain't—not now, Sally."

The redhead made a moué, then taunted, "Hopin' to see Melinda so bad you can't even stop fo' one little drink?"

He spurred the roan, and a moment later, he was dismounting at the office of the express company at the further end of the street. There, he drew two heavy buckskin pokes from his saddlebags, and routed out the crusty old night clerk, Lafe Simmons.

Lafe gave him a receipt for the money, flung it into the ponderous safe and locked it up. Then he demanded, "Simon, whut y'all got in that passel on yore back?"

Grimes reddened, and blurted out, "A guitar, ef its any of yo' dang business."

He left his horse at the livery stable, got a fresh mount and then went to the Drover's Tavern, next door to the saloon. Sally was no longer at the entrance. Half an hour later, he was back on the street, his long face scrubbed clean and the fuzz hacked from his chin. The guitar still hung from his shoulder.

Once out of the city limits, he took the instrument from its case and twanged a few chords from *La Paloma.* Wouldn't Melinda get a thrill, being romantically serenaded!

"Mighty dang good," he conceded, "considerin' I learned it all in a week."

Maybe it would have been sweeter if Lupe Romero hadn't had satanic eyes, legs that got lovelier the further the eye reached above her hose tops, and a hip wriggle that gave meaning to everything. She was the darling of Abilene, and Grimes' music lessons had thrice been interrupted by indignant lovers who wanted her kisses reserved for the town.

They had been buried with military honors, but Grimes prudently lit a shuck from Abilene. After all, he was going to marry Melinda Patton; and three killings a week, he reflected, counts up in a year.

A light was burning in Melinda's window. Dismounting, he twanged away at his guitar, and he sang in Spanish. It was like a yearling bull competing with odd, tinkling noises; but Melinda would lean out, any minute now—

Wham! A shotgun poured flame and whistling pellets into the yard. It was a wild blast; most of it peppered Grimes' tethered mustang, for darkness made the shooting erratic. He took a dive for the shelter of the grindstone, guns blossoming in each hand as he howled, "Come out shootin', yo' gol-danged bushwhackin'—"

Then a woman screamed, "Simon—my God—I didn't know—"

It was Melinda, her streaming hair gilded by soft lamplight. She still clutched the fuming shotgun, and her gasp of dismay lifted her lovely breasts against the lace work of a honeymoon gown that revealed every curve from her white shoulders to her shapely, substantial hips.

And then, clearing the sill, Grimes saw that Melinda's blue eyes were tear-reddened. "Honey, whut's been the matter?" he demanded. She choked a sob, and for a moment her eager lips clung to his mouth as though she'd never take time for a breath. Every contour, flattening to his embrace, seemed of its own accord to seek him. For a moment, he thrilled to the soft crush of thinly-covered breasts, the warm clinging of her curving, undulant body. Then—

"Oh, Simon—I wish you'd stayed away," she gasped, breaking away. "I've been dreading your return—but I'm so glad to see you—"

"Uh—um—whut—the hell—" He stuttered. Women still puzzled him.

But being a man of action, he didn't try to figure it out. Instead, he took one stride toward the lamp and blew it out. Then he eased her to the spacious lounge and he kissed her until she quivered and gasped. He'd learned more than music from Lupe.

Melinda made inarticulate little sounds, and by the time his kisses left her parted and gasping lips to creep down to her throat, they were both breathless.

Suddenly, Melinda slipped from his arms and thrust him away from her when he tried to regain his hold. "Simon, darling, I didn't know it was you singin' out there, so I fired. I was just all broken up. I can't marry you."

"Whut—us kain't get married—why—"

"No, Simon. The town's against me. I can't marry you, after your shooting Dad—"

"But—honey girl—listen—" His voice broke. "Yo' pappy was tryin' to git me. I couldn't—"

"I know you couldn't help it," choked Melinda. "Dad was stealing your uncle's critters—he was dead wrong—and you had to fire to keep him from killing you—but, don't you see, it just wouldn't look right, us marrying."

"I thought we done settled that."

"We did, Simon. But while you were taking your uncle's herd to Abilene, I've been hearing things—"

"Who—?" He was on his feet, gun drawn.

"Women's whispers. Enough of that will get under the hides of all the men, your friends included. They'd back you if you committed murder, but friendship can't last long with their women folks back-biting you and me, morning, noon, bedtime, all the time."

"I don't give a tarnation-damn—"

She caught his hand. "Simon, you listen. Your friends'll be thinking I'm a no-good wench, marrying you after you killed Dad, even if 'twas his fault. You'll hear something, some time, accidental-like. There'll be more killings—"

"I like killings, every so often," he growled.

That stopped her, just for a minute. Then she sighed, hopelessly and went on, "The truth is—I love you—and hate myself for it. So I'm going—to my aunt's spread in New Mexico—"

He stared, and for once his eyes did not brighten as they picked the sweet, white curves that glowed through that frail, revealing silk. "You mean it?" His voice was dry and monotonous.

Her eyes dropped. "Yes."

He turned and without a word hurdled the window. Then he picked up his guitar, smashed it on the pump handle and kicked the pieces against the rain barrel. Then he recaptured his mustang and galloped like a madman toward Skeleton Creek.

Get pig drunk with Sally. She liked him, she was awful nice, only he'd never done any more than maybe give her a pinch or a pat, and then buy her a drink when she pretended she didn't like it.

THEY WERE WHOOPING IT UP IN THE CORKSCREW INN. ALL THE HORSES FOR MILES AROUND were tethered at the hitching rack. Music blared, feet scraped; Grimes heard the riot from a distance. It jarred, and grated. He reined in his mustang and sat slouched in the saddle, suddenly cold to prospects he had considered. But he entered town at a walk, stubbornly determined to carry on.

Then he heard new sounds: a yell, the squeal of panic-stricken horses, stampeding from the hitching rack. A dull boom came from the express office, almost at hand. Gusts of nitrous smoke poured into the street and men came tumbling out. They ducked into the side alley.

As Grimes spurred forward, they emerged on horse. It was a hold-up, and Skeleton Creek's mounts a-helling down the main street, in the opposite direction.

Grimes, lying along his horse's neck, hosed the raiders with lead as he charged to meet them. A man running from the emptied hitching rack cut loose with a sawed-off shotgun. Grimes' .45 beat him by a hair. He pitched headlong, his weapon pouring buckshot into the harness-maker's window.

It was a short, deadly melee, with the lanky towhead's murderous gun spraying lead into the surprised bandits. Another, fighting his frenzied horse, sagged from the saddle; men came dashing from the Corkscrew Inn, guns blazing.

When the smoke cleared away, the raiders were hightailing it westward, and Grimes' horse, wounded, piled him in a heap before he could pursue.

Two bandits and a citizen lay sprawled in the gory street. Lafe Simmons, blood trickling from his ears, was done for; a tap across the skull had cracked it as effectively as dynamite had ravaged the iron safe. But for Grimes' unexpected return to town, the getaway would have been perfect.

HALF AN HOUR LATER, GRIMES WAS IN THE SALOON. SKELETON CREEK WAS ON THE warpath, and the Sheriff and City Marshal were catching hell.

"That's the fo'th time Wells Fargo's been held up," stormed Amos Diggs, shaking the kinks out of his streaming white hair. "And, by gravy, hit's got tuh stop!"

"It's a-goin' tuh kill business," raged hatchet-faced Mel Hawkins. "The express company warned us, one mo' hold up an' they jerks their office outen this town."

"Yo're damn' double right," chimed in the manager of the company, who had been routed out of bed by the riot.

Old man Diggs had the answer. "We'uns is organizing a Vigilante Committee, an' hang every owlhooter so high yuh kain't see the buzzards peckin' his eyes out. Belly up, gents and gargle!"

"It's on the house, gentlemen," yelled Lyman Byrnes, the red-faced proprietor of the saloon.

They all did so—except the disgruntled marshal, who had ridden hell-bent to get the sheriff from Skunk Valley. But that interested no one; vigilantes would be the answer! No one could identify the fallen looters, but everyone was guessing.

"Me, I'm going to be a vig-gilanty myself," declared Grimes, downing another whiskey. "They got my uncle's nine thousand bucks afore I could git it into the bank in the mawnin."

The organization meeting was a roaring success, until someone took a notion to play rough with Sally, the red-haired dance hall girl. When she left her room, she'd given them a fair start on account of the brevity of her costume; so the three amorous gents who wondered what made the sequins of her bodice sort of glitter and wobble every time she took a step didn't have heavy work, as far as garment went.

Sally screamed. It was getting to be more than frontier humor. Her hair was down over her white shoulders, and with both hands trying to hide her swaying, almost bare breasts and thrust away her playmates, she had no chance to protect her skirt. It came away with a short tearing sound.

Grimes, attracted from the bar by the ruckus, allowed that she did have nice legs, especially above her hose tops, where sleek thighs melted into the dainty concealment of her brief undergarment. Nearly all of Sally was nice, quivery and soft. So he grabbed her two tormentors by the shoulders and jerked them loose. They sprawled, each clutching a piece of the redhead's gown—which they dropped as they made a dive for their guns. Sally stumbled back, palms partially covering her shaking breasts.

There was a general scrambling for cover; but it stopped when Grimes' boot kicked the Colt from one gunner's hand and sidestepped the other's wild shot.

There was no second. The boy's .45 smacked down across the fellow's head.

"Quit it!" he snapped. "Any gent that paws a lady thataway in public ain't no gent. An' ef'n I wasn't a law-abiding vig-gilanty, I'd of blasted yo' danged teeth out."

So saying, he stalked to the bar, downed some more whiskey, and then gravely tottered to his room at the Drover's Tavern. But he had scarcely kicked off his boots when there was a tapping at the door. Sally, wrapped up in a robe, slipped into the room, and didn't move away from him as he closed the door. All her make-up had been removed; she seemed younger and softer, except for the hard little lines about her mouth.

"Simon, I'm so glad you came back to see me," she cooed, snuggling closer.

Whatever she wore beneath that sleazy robe couldn't have been made into more than two small handkerchiefs. Sally lifted generous lips and eager eyes; a warm feminine scent exhaled from between the blue-veined breasts that were crushed tantalizingly against him.

He was suddenly dizzy, and she helped him to a chair. "Gol dang this joining committees," he muttered thickly. Then, long, somber face propped in his hands, he stared at the dusty floor. Sally sensed that his thoughts were elsewhere.

"Simon," she whispered. "why'd you come riding back to town so sudden-like?"

"Shut up!" he barked. "Or I'll handle yo' wuss'n those jaspers down t' the saloon."

But Sally murmured sympathetically, and tried to brush the cow-lick out of his eyes. Then she said, "It's dangerous, Simon, you this drunk and a oil lamp right where you'd knock it down."

So, to keep him from knocking over the lamp, she lifted his face with her hands, smiled, and sank onto his lap. Grimes laughed bitterly; he'd made a similar gesture only an hour or so ago. This time, he did not repulse Sally. She was whispering endearments, clinging to him as he held to her for support. Her mouth was humid and persuasively tender, brushing over his lips and face and throat. And the tingles incited by those kisses sent his arms about her more determinedly. She was warm and yielding; her flesh was not as firm as Melinda's, but it was luxuriously silky and scented.

He was mortally weary, rather than just a bit too drunk. He was tired of everything . . . he thought it'd be nice to cushion his head on Sally's shoulder, but the touch of rounded breasts that were so thinly covered by Sally's robe was a stimulant. She insisted on kissing him. So he humored her . . . especially as he couldn't keep his eyes from the gleaming skin of plump thighs, where her skirt had fallen back into her lap as she crossed her knees. And before he knew it, he was as thrilled and ardent as the girl who had so long wanted to exchange kisses with him.

He didn't mind how the room seemed to spin. He scarcely caught the significance of what Sally whispered in his ear as she nestled snugly in his arms: "Simon, those jaspers that took your money out of the safe are from Clovis—New Mexico.

"I heard two strangers—just afore the hosses stampeded—talkin' about Clovis. They were gone when the riot ended. But I didn't tell no one. Didn't have a chance, till later, an' then I allowed I'd let you know, private, so's you can get the credit yo'self. Now I got to go . . . and . . . don't be too worried about Melinda. . . ."

But when she wriggled out of his arms, he wasn't worried about anything. Battle and whiskey and Sally's kisses had combined to give him a sense of peaceful unconcern. To hell with everything. . . .

And down the street, drinks on the house kept the newly organized vigilantes too busy to take up the trail. They were shooting out the lights. Someone sang *La Paloma.* Grimes heard, cursed, but lay there. Finally, his snores blended with those of the committee. . . .

THE NEXT DAY, THE RED-EYED CITIZENS WERE ON THE WARPATH IN EARNEST. NO MORE drinks on the house. And just as the posse was about to take the trail, Uncle Carter, gray and sour-faced, came galloping into town with the cowhand who had brought him the news of the robbery.

"Seems like to me," he growled, pulling up beside his nephew, "some skunk knowed you got here ahead of time. Warn't nuthin' else in the safe till you turned over that *dinero.* "

Grimes remembered that Sally had seen him, and must have heard the tinkling gold. No one else could have. And certainly no one could have anticipated his early return from Abilene. Then how account for the strangers and their carefully planned raid?

They rode all day, following blood splashes and hoofprints. Later, buzzards circling drew the posse to a horse that had dropped from wounds and exhaustion; and a peculiarly high-heeled bootprint clinched the lead: the raiders had passed this way. Sally's story was already verified—partially, at least—by the northerly direction of the fugitives.

Close to the New Mexico line, they found the smoldering remains of a stage-coach. The driver, bullet-riddled but doggedly hanging to what life remained, crawled out of the mesquite and muttered a few words: "We passed through Skeleton Creek, three-four hours after the hold-up—had thuty thousand in gold—so we changed our route—but didn't do no good—gimme a drink—fer God's sake—"

He swallowed the tepid water, but he died before he could give any details. Yet his few words cast light on the past night's doings. The bandits apparently had been waiting for the stage, intending to trail it to ambush; and during their lurking, they had seen a chance to get Grimes' money, in addition to achieving their original objective.

Inside information, no doubt. Otherwise, they'd have expected the contents of the express safe to be loaded on the stage, and would surely not have made their daring raid in town.

Lyman Byrnes, mayor of Skeleton Creek and owner of the Corkscrew Inn, then and there offered five hundred in gold for the capture of whoever had committed this new outrage. And the posse rode on, spurred by vengeance and the urge to appease the wrathful express company, whose station was what kept the town on the map.

THREE DAYS PASSED. THREE BLISTERING, DUSTY, THIRST-HAUNTED DAYS. DESPITE ALL arguments, Grimes persisted in his contention that the bandits had not ridden toward the Mexican Border.

"I got a hunch!" he asserted, stubbornly refusing to reveal his reasons. And Uncle Carter, though inwardly dubious, chipped in with his gunslinging nephew, which convinced the posse.

Late the next afternoon, his hunch was justified. After hours of scrambling over volcanic wastes—they were in the badlands now—they found that familiar, high-heeled bootprint in one of the few patches of sterile soil. And that was the turning point.

Presently, a horse scented water; one of the freaks in this savage desert. Men could be hiding out. And they had scarcely pressed on a mile when rifle fire blazed from a butte that towered up like a castle turret in that land of ancient fires.

A man dropped. The others took cover as bullets droned like bumblebees overhead. Grimes, protected by crevasses in the lava bed, ran hell-bent, his uncle after him.

They emerged just as the bandits came trooping down on the far side, the sortie disguised by the frontal fire that held the main party. Uncle Carter's .60-caliber buffalo gun poured one-ounce slugs into the flank of the bandits. Grimes, recklessly breaking cover, ducked in and out, a dancing jack in the box with each hand blazing. Lead raked him, but surprise made the enemy fire wild. He emptied a saddle and charged on, yelling.

Uncle Carter and Old Man Diggs were on his heels. Then the fire from the further face of the butte slackened, and leaden fury came pouring out to meet them. They were driven back, and soon they saw that it was a stalemate.

The bandits could not come out; neither could the posse close in and scale that steep cliff. But they had the enemy's horses, and the water hole as well.

That night, however, the odds were leveled. Rain pelted in drops as big as baseballs. The depressions and pockets in the butte must have collected enough water to float a boat. And by noon the next day, the bandits had gained a temporary advantage. Under cover of darkness, some of them had worked into sniping posts that commanded the spring; and that made it bad for the besiegers.

"Hell," growled Uncle Carter, "kain't rush 'em. We're in owlhoot country, and fust thing we know, we're going tuh git ourselves bushwhacked by other sculpins. Simon, y'all ride to Clovis and tell the sheriff—"

"Like hell, I will," protested the boy. "If the sheriff wanted to, he'da come out here afore now to smoke out these skunks. But I got a better one. 'Member that mine, way back yonder? Git some dynamite. An' some timbers—we kin fix up a cattypult and heave a passel of bombs up into the blow holes in that butte."

That was a good gamble; but Grimes refused to do anything as dangerous as hauling dynamite. Instead, he took a .45-70 and settled down to a sniping duel. He soon learned, however, that it was not like picking off squirrel, back home in Georgia. The hell glare of the desert kicked up heat devils and spoiled his aim.

Under cover of darkness, they devised the crude catapult that would hurl dynamite into the bandit's nest. They could hardly hope to blot them out with a single bomb; but the terrific concussion, the gusts of nitrous smoke, the very shock and surprise of such a blast at the first gray of dawn, when man's vitality is the very lowest, would give the vigilantes a chance to close in without suicidal odds.

THAT NIGHT, TONGUES OF FLAME STABBED THE GLOOM. THE VIGILANTES, MAKING A BLUFF at eagerness to smoke out the bandits, were firing at every sound or sign of motion on the crest of the butte or its cavernous face. The trick was to keep the besieged on edge, expecting a rush that did not materialize. Then, when the shooting at last ceased, the bandits would relax and their vigilance would slacken, giving the bombing device a chance to get close.

Grimes, whose post was well forward, heard a suspicious stirring. He slovenly shifted, getting his .45 into line. The moon had not yet risen, and the wind distorted sounds, so that he had to hold his fire. From the pit at his left, a rifle blazed, and a slug spattered to bits some yards before him. A woman screamed. Grimes yelled, "Hold it—don't shoot!"

The vigilantes broke cover. And then Grimes saw the huddle of white in the gloom ahead. It was a girl; the ivory blur of her face, the fullness of her breast and the roundness of her thighs were plainly perceptible. He caught her in his arms and carried her to the cook's fire, far to the rear and behind a sheltering rock.

It was Sally, wearing what was left of a street dress. Her hands and arms were lacerated and the jagged rocks had raked the tender flesh of her arms and legs. Thorns and mesquite had left her open-work blouse a sorry handful of shreds and the scratch-reddened contours of full breasts were partially visible, even in the near darkness. She gasped, "They sent me—I was leaving town—I left on the stage, that night—"

"Yuh was caught in the stage holdup?" demanded Old Man Diggs.

"Nice way you walked out o' my dance hall!" grumbled Byrnes. "Sarves you right. What'd you leave fer?"

"Hell!" growled Grimes, suspicion suddenly knitting his brow. "I bet she knew I had the money—"

Sally flashed Grimes a single imploring glance and cut in, "I didn't! I was a prisoner! They sent me down here to bargain. They got another prisoner—Melinda Patton—"

Grimes' fists clenched. While he had been lying dead drunk in the Drover's Tavern, Melinda had been boarding the stage for Las Cruces. He turned on Sally and demanded, "Prove it!"

The redhead fumbled in the wreckage of her blouse, ignoring the eyes that caressed her half-bared breasts. Then she found what she sought: a robin's-egg nightgown, wrapped about her waist. It had a lace inserted yoke, and right over the spot that would have centered on a well-shaped woman's heart were embroidered initials. But Grimes already recognized the garment.

"Let those bandits go," Sally said, "and they won't hurt her. But if you don't, they'll—oh, Lord, you know what they'll do—"

Grimes was on his feet, and saying, "They so't of got us. I guess we'll have to—"

"Like hell, we will!" rasped Uncle Carter. "Ain't no cattle rustler's daughter going to make me lay off."

"Ner me, neither!" chorused others of old man Patton's enemies. Melinda's father, unmasked, had been buried, but the indignation of the town still lived.

"Yo're a pack of skunks—yuh ain't men, jest skunks!" stormed Byrnes, unexpectedly taking Grimes' part, "Leavin' a pore gal in the hands of them renegades."

But the vigilantes, wrathful and weary, many of them wounded, swamped the saloon keeper's generous impulse. Grimes, however, shouted them down: "Yo gol-danged buzzards, y' ain't goin' to heave no dynamite into that butte—" He whirled, jerking his gun; but before he could drive a slug into the cache of explosive, some yards away, Uncle Carter knocked his .45 out of line and the shot went wild.

A rifle barrel smacked down across Grimes' knuckles and the weapon dropped from his hands. Raging, he turned on his allies, but they overwhelmed him. Disarmed and kicked lop-sided, he was booted out of camp. "An' stay out!" howled

Uncle Carter, "until you learns that a cattle thief's daughter don't count when justice and the welfare of Skeleton Creek is in the jackpot!"

"An' run that redhead out!" howled others. "She musta knowed that jug-headed kid had money in his saddlebags! She done tol' the owlhooters!"

GRIMES PICKED THE CACTUS SPINES OUT OF HIS HANDS AND KNEES, AND STALKED, CURSING, into the gloom. For two cents, he'd take the outlaw trail himself. He'd had hard luck ever since his arrival at his uncle's ranch. But he was unarmed, except for a Bowie knife. His mustang was with the remuda. Maybe they'd let him take it, if he asked; but wrath and humiliation made him pause.

Why not creep back, bushwhack the horse wrangler, get himself a mount and guns? To hell with Skeleton Creek, and Melinda as well; her dang fool notions about what people would say was to blame for this sorry mess.

Maybe she could escape in the panic caused by the bomb. Then, thinking of her in the hands of those renegades, his aching head whirled. He was useless, futile, burned out by his own vain rage and helplessness.

He started, drawing his knife as he heard a sound from the side. A woman said, "Simon, it's me. I followed you."

It was Sally, and as she crept up beside him, she went on, "I didn't tell them! Honest, I didn't! I just left town, figuring I'd better, account I told you about those two fellows talking about Clovis. I was afraid if any escaped, they'd suspect and come back and kill me. Looks now as if you and me ain't got a friend left. But maybe we can go somewhere."

"If I kin steal us a hoss," muttered Grimes.

They waited at the far side of a boulder some hundred yards or more from vengeful men whose voices rumbled in the gloom. Sally, shivering in the desert chill, snuggled against him for warmth. He slipped his leather vest about her, pillowed her head on his shoulder. She murmured, "Simon, there wasn't anyone in town that was ever nice to me. Somehow, I'm not worried, being with you."

Then, sensing even in the gloom that he was staring somberly at the ground before him, too dejected and beaten for thought of action, she ran her fingers through his hair, hungrily clung to his lips, murmuring desperate words into his mouth. "She don't love you, Simon—I was talking to her on the stage . . . she was all broken up, but if she really cared, she'da stuck with you."

"That's gospel, honey," muttered Grimes, warming to her friendliness. He drew her closer, felt the soft suppleness of her body, the luxurious yielding of her flesh as his embrace closed about her. She shivered as he kissed her, and breathed, "I've always loved you, Simon . . . couldn't you care for me, just a little?"

"Heaps, Sally," he answered, pulse hammering from the warm exhalation breathed into his ear. Loneliness had brought them close, but the redhead's throbbing breast and possessing arms were inflaming him so that he forgot all but their own little corner of that black waste. "But maybe we kain't get to any town—maybe—"

"Nothing makes any difference," she sighed. "They can't take this minute away from us. . . ."

BUT WHEN THEY FINALLY SLIPPED FROM EACH OTHER'S ARMS, SALLY KNEW THAT HER kisses had given Grimes more confidence than she had reckoned. That was when he said, very purposefully, "We been a pair of damn' fools, honey. They kain't prove you sold out the stagecoach, or told anyone about my money. They was jest madder'n hell, an' you hadn't oughta blame 'em. And if you came down out of that butte, *I could sneak up it.*"

"Simon—" Her nails sank into his arm, and for a moment he felt her eyes stab him in the darkness. "You fool—you'll git killed—which is more'n is going to happen to that high-nosed gal—she'll live through—"

"Shut up!" snapped Grimes, jerking her to her feet. "I'm going to risk it. Them hard-hearted jaspers ain't dynamiting that butte till I get Melinda out."

Sally exhaled a long, tremulous sigh. "Darling—I might have figured you'd be a damn' fool—I hate it like snakes, but I sort of am glad you are thataway— ain't never had a honest-to-God man love me before—"

"Compliments ain't helping me none," he reproved. Then, pulling her to him, he kissed her, very gently. "Bye, Sally—"

"I'm going," she said. "To show you the way, so's you won't be kilt. She'll have me to thank for having you."

So that was it. Grimes never could figure what women would do next, and he was weary from trying. So he stealthily picked a course between the sniping posts that girdled the butte.

Once inside the circle whose intermittent sniping was keeping the bandits on edge, Sally took the lead. Slowly, perilously, she worked her way to the very foot of the towering lava formation, which uncounted centuries of rain and wind blown sand had so fantastically chiseled.

Then came the ascent of the seemingly impassable face. Without Sally's guidance, he could never have found that treacherous trail. Halfway up, she reached back, fingers closing on his shoulder.

"Can't tell what's coming next," she breathed. "Wait a spell, then trail along and use your head."

No time for questions. She was beyond whispering distance and the snipers were no longer harassing the besieged. Nothing now but the eerie tricks of the wind to mask his advance.

Someone snarled a low challenge. Sally said, "They run me out of camp. I ain't got nowhere else to go. Where's the boss, Walt?"

"Fixing fer to smoke his way out, hosses or no hosses," Walt answered. "C'mere, Sally . . . whut yuh want to see the boss fer?"

Grimes, stealthily ascending, did not get the girl's answer. It was muffled, and she was gasping. And as he rounded an angle of the rock, he could just distinguish her bare legs gleaming through her shredded skirt, the whiteness of her arms, the sway and ripple of her hips as she pressed closely to the bandit who had pulled her toward him. He hoarsely panted, "Yuh damn' fool, stick with me . . . ef yuh snuck up here through the posse, yuh an' me kin sneak back an' out. Tain't no sense goin' out smoking. . . ."

"Walt," she gasped. "Not yet . . . wait. . . ."

And wait he did. There was no cry, just a gurgle that Sally's lips stifled before they recoiled in horror. Grimes' knife, sinking hilt-deep below Walt's shoulder-blade, released a red flood that drooled from the bandit's lips, spattering the girl as he slumped, thrashing. Lung and heart lanced by the Bowie knife, he was dead before he dropped.

"Wheah's Melinda?" whispered Grimes, buckling on Walt's pistol belt.

Sally had picked up the red blade and was wiping it on Walt's shirtfront. As they crouched in the shadow of an upthrusting tongue of rock, she brushed aside the remains of her skirt, stretched a garter to the limit and snapped it back over the heavy blade, securing it high on her plumply rounded thigh, where there was the least chance of its being observed.

"I'll show you," answered Sally.

"Stay here," ordered Grimes. "Jest tell me. . . ."

A woman screamed. The sound was eerily distorted, and so was the harsh laugh of the man who answered. It came from one of the blowholes that honey-combed the butte, Grimes, lunging recklessly into the darkness, heard the mutter-ing voices of desperate men awaiting their leader's order to make a sortie. The hour for the bombing was relentlessly drawing nearer.

"Hi, Walt," hailed a guarded voice from Grimes' right. "What'd the redhead say? How come she's back?"

Sweat cropped out on the boy's tense body as he realized how narrowly the lurking outlaw had missed sensing his comrade's fate. But the treacherous acous-tics of the butte had helped: a dying gurgle had sounded like some trick of the wind. Melinda was gasping, somewhere, then she screamed. A man laughed tri-umphantly, and her cry was cut off.

Grimes turned to his right and snarled in Walt's manner, "Plenty . . . whar's the boss?"

Trigger finger twitching, he crouched, and just caught the blurr of a man's upturned face. If he only had that knife! And then the outlaw countered, "Y'ain't deef, are yuh? Whar yuh think the boss is? Hey. . . ."

But Grimes, diving into the blowhole, had him by the throat. The man was built like a yearling bull, but the boy from Georgia was long and wiry and the sounds that taunted him from somewhere in that tricky darkness whipped him to a slaying fury. Teeth sank into his arm. A knee jabbed him in the pit of his stomach. Then, lurching forward, himself half paralyzed, his weight drove his throttled op-ponent against the rocks. A dull pop and the fellow slumped, Grimes across him.

"Quit yore scratchin', yuh hellcat!" raged a voice that drowned Melinda's renewed screams. "Afore we goes out smokin', I'm a-gittin' suthin' fer my trouble . . . ooow. . . ."

Grimes, gritting his teeth, contrived to stir. Then, as that ever-lastingly de-layed breath gasped into his lungs, he recovered his gun, smacked it across his unconscious enemy's head and bounded back to the surface. The next outcry and curse came from directly in front of him.

He did not hear the guttural voices to the rear, the surly, suspicion-laden exchange from where he had left Sally; he was too wrathful and desperate to consider that his luck could not continue, that despite the intentness of the outlaws in their watch for some move on the part of the besiegers, he could not hope to carry on undetected. He'd found Melinda, and beyond any doubt, he was too late.

But he had a gun in his hand, and slaying blazed in his heart. He bounced around a rocky knob. A dull red glow marked the opening of a tunnel that reached far into its heart.

By the light of the embers, Grimes saw a tangle of flailing arms and bare legs. Melinda, peeled down to a few scraps of flimsy lingerie, was overwhelmed by a broad-shouldered hulk she was clawing in her vain endeavor to keep his bearded lips from her upturned face. He was crushing her to him, subduing her renewed struggles. Grimes' captured six-gun was useless; from where he stood, he could not drive a shot between the ruffian's shoulders. The heavy slug would go through, riddle the girl's writhing body.

"Come up shootin', yo' gol-danged skunk!" yelled Grimes, bounding down the tunnel.

One more leap and he'd have his pistol against the bandit's ear; but Melinda, hair streaming and shaking breasts thrusting through the remains of her dress as she wriggled clear, rolled against his shins, breaking his stride. He stumbled, and though his recovery was cat-quick, it gave the girl's assailant his chance. Instead of reaching for the gunbelt that lay on the ledge beside him, he lashed out with a heavy hand, snatching Grimes' wrist. The cocked .45 poured lead against the rocks; and, jerked off balance, the Skeleton Creek vigilante nosed headlong against his enemy.

Grimes had his hands full. He and Melinda and the outlaw were tangled like a bucket of angleworms; bare, throbbing flesh, streaming hair, clawing paws, desperately kicking boots, all in one hopelessly confused mill. He smashed home once, but the gun barrel glanced, clipping Melinda. A heavy fist hammered his jaw, knocking him groggy.

And then the rumble of voices outside came booming into the cavern. A man shouted, "Jud, you damn' fool . . . the both of you . . . quit fightin' about that gal . . . the posse's fixing to heave dynamite at you. . . ."

"Git on yore laigs!" howled another, dashing in after him.

Grimes, recovering from the blow, wrenched his pistol into line. As he moved, he recognized the first speaker . . . Byrnes, mayor of Skeleton Creek, and proprietor of the Corkscrew Inn. And in that deadly instant, he understood why he had an ally in his attempt to stop the bombing, knew that his own try at destroying the dynamite had led the vigilantes to keep an eye on Byrnes, lest his openly expressed sympathy lead him to a like endeavor. He now knew why Byrnes had declared open house to celebrate the organization of the vigilantes, getting them drunk enough to give the safe wreckers a head start.

It all flashed through the boy's mind as he thumbed the hammer. Jud, boss of the bandits, heard the warning . . . but he never heard the blast of the pistol that coughed flame and lead into his gaping mouth.

Byrnes had had no chance to recognize Grimes. Neither did the men who followed. All they had seen was hand-to-hand grappling, and a girl whose battered flesh was covered by scarcely more than wisps of lingerie. Her outstretched legs, rounded and luxurious, her full breasts lifted by her indrawn breath, were reason enough for battle. But the blast that spattered blood and brains on Melinda's quivering body got the two into action.

Grimes' weapon shifted, picking the quicker of the two. That was the bandit who had followed Byrnes. The guns thundered; the fellow pitched on his face. But the treacherous mayor of Skeleton Creek, knowing now with whom he dealt, had made good use of that instant. Instead of shooting, he leaped, gaining the shelter of a jutting rock just as Grimes' smoke pole roared a second time, its sluggish action making him a split second too late.

And then, as Grimes rolled for cover, a white streak flashed from the tunnel mouth. There was a gleam of steel. Sally, plucking the Bowie knife from her garter, nailed Byrnes as he snapped a shot at Grimes. The bullet flattened against the wall. The redhead's skirt had scarcely settled to her knees when the traitor's forward lurch drew her with him; screaming with excitement, she was still desperately tugging at the hilt to withdraw the blade for a second stab.

"He's done!" yelled Grimes, jerking Melinda to her feet. "Now duck . . . here they come . . . a-shootin'!"

The darkness outside was shaken by pounding feet, confused yells. Grimes, thrusting Melinda into shelter with the redhead, snatched Byrnes' fuming pistol and bounded to the tunnel mouth. But he had half-light behind him, and the bandits were in the gloom. They could not yet quite understand; that was his only chance. This was other than a toe-to-toe shooting, where skill could win.

His gun blazed, sweeping the shadows, its blasts rippling like a rattler's tail. . . .

Then a terrific concussion threw him against the opposite wall. For an instant, a hell glare of flame broke the darkness. He felt a mighty rush of air, beating him as with caulking maul; his chest seemed to cave in, his eardrums were at the snapping point. Acrid fumes choked him as he sagged, half conscious, dropping from the wall against which he had been kicked.

Dynamite from the catapult! The vigilantes had sneaked up close enough to use it. Far below, men were yelling. And, just outside, men were groaning, dazed and torn and battered; dizzied by the echoes that still mocked them from the blowholes. Grimes, bleeding and numb, scarcely followed what happened. When he tried to crawl to the tunnel mouth, his pistol to add to the roar of .45s and the booming of buffalo guns, the whiplash smack of Winchesters, Sally caught his shoulder.

"It's all over, Simon . . . they's cleaned out. . . ."

"Don't shoot!" screamed Melinda, tottering out of the cavern.

They didn't fire; not with her almost bare body silhouetted by the glow of embers behind her. And then the vigilantes of Skeleton Creek holstered their smoking guns and listened to Grimes' account of his singlehanded raid.

"I didn't know for sure," Sally cut in, "that Byrnes was teamed up with those jaspers that blew the express safe, an' he was too important a citizen for me to accuse. But that's why I left town on the first stage, after telling Simon I allowed they was heading for Clovis. I was afraid he might talk out of turn, and if Byrnes didn't murder me, someone might of remembered that me and Lafe Simmons was the only ones that knew Simon had all that money."

Uncle Carter regarded Melinda from head to foot. There was plenty to see, despite her efforts to arrange what remained of her under garments. "I figgered you was crazy, cuttin' up that way about this gal," he said. "But mebbe yuh warn't wrong after all."

Then the posse turned from the tunnel, Melinda eyed Sally, saw the redhead's possessive arm about Grimes' neck, and the glance she flashed at Jud, the bandit chief. A flush raced all the way to her breast; then she said, "Simon . . . after seeing what happened . . . you won't want . . . oh, it's my fault . . . I don't blame you. . . ."

"Hush up, honey," said Grimes, very gently. "You couldn't help anythin' that happened. An' ef you was scairt of people's talkin' afore this, mebbe yo' better go on with yo' plans, cause they's goin' to talk plenty from now on." He drew the redhead closer and added, "Me an' Sally's both lighting a shuck from a hoodooed town. We'uns all needs a fresh start, somewheah else."

• • • • •

Salt Crazy

Simon Bolivar Grimes, dismounting to rest his horse, took a pair of field glasses from his saddlebag, and brushed from his eyes the tow-colored cowlick that persistently invaded his coffin-shaped face; but before he had fairly scanned the back trail, he chuckled and said, "Shucks! Won't be no one followin' me. Ain't shot anyone for dang nigh three weeks. A gent sho' does git absent-minded!"

But, having his glasses unlimbered, the gangling boy from Georgia allowed he might as well survey the pleasant valley that stretched out below him to his right and left. If it looked like good cow country, there was no use heading to El Paso to look for a job.

On the green slopes, he saw plump, white-faced cattle. Far off to his left, there was one whose brand he could easily read: Rafter-FL. And then Grimes saw the girl.

In spite of a ripening grudge against women—they had kept him in trouble ever since he came to Texas—this one stopped him in his tracks. Her hair gleamed golden in the sunlight; her face and throat were ivory white. She was riding hellbent after a recently branded calf. The breeze made her blue silk blouse cling close, outlining a slim waist and pert breasts that quivered deliciously. The first cast of her loop was good, and in a flash, she was out of the saddle.

The powerful glasses seemed to bring her within arm's reach. When she knelt to hog-tie the critter, the space between the embroidered tops of her boots and the bottom of a short skirt, disarrayed by her posture, was a fascinating revelation. She had legs as lovely as her face.

He watched her deft little hands set to work with a small bottle and a wooden paddle. There had evidently been a rain right after branding, and she was now applying medicine to counteract the screw worms that usually attack calves at such a time.

For a moment, as she leaned forward, the glasses reached well into the vee of her silk blouse. Grimes' pulse stepped up and he swallowed his heart. That gal was shapely all over! Then he licked his lips, resolutely wheeled his horse, and rode in the opposite direction.

"No, suh! I ain't asking the Rafter-FL fo' a job! Wheah they's got wimmen folks, they's a heap of trouble."

As he approached the head of the valley, instinctive caution made him rein in. Two riders emerged from the cottonwoods along the creek. Each had a gunny sack across the pommel of his saddle. As they rode, they poured a gleaming white substance from the bags. Grimes frowned. They must be teched in the head, scattering sugar on the ground. But, after all, it was their sugar.

One of the riders, sensing Grimes' presence, started as though a hornet had stung him. Then, without hail or warning, the other drew his .45. The range was too long for effective shooting, and the puff of smoke and the menacing gesture warned Grimes. He ducked and went for his own six-gun, just as the first rider jerked a Winchester from its scabbard.

Grimes might have wheeled and escaped, but his back was broad enough to make a good rifle target; so he leaned forward and charged. The blast of his Colt was a split second ahead of the sharp crack of the Winchester carbine. His shot emptied a saddle; and, for a moment, the cottonwoods echoed with the roar and thunder of handguns.

Grimes felt the cold breath of lead whisking past him. He whirled his mustang, then pulled down on the surviving gunner. And now the boy from Georgia, warmed up to his work, not only plugged his surviving enemy, but drove two more shots through him before he hit the ground.

Both horses bolted. Grimes, certain that neither gunner was playing possum, dismounted and jacked the empties out of his weapon.

One of the pair stared skyward. The other lay face down near his Winchester.

"Most danged onsociable jaspers I ever seen," grumbled Grimes. "Jest blazing away 'thout as much as saying who be you, or nothing. They mighta knowed that a stranger wouldn't of got this fur south onless he could shoot tolably well hisself."

He stroked the straw-colored fuzz on his chin, pondered on the tee-total dumbness of some gents, then knelt and cautiously tasted the white stuff they'd been scattering along the range. It was not sugar, but table salt. Grimes was more puzzled than ever. That was downright extravagance. Uncle Carter always spread out rock salt for his cattle, and generally buried it in a trench.

He had never realized how powerful his uncle's field glasses were. It took him some time before he reached the spot where the blonde girl had thrown the calf. In the meanwhile, she had moved on.

It was getting hotter'n sand! And Grimes, thirsty, headed for the creek to get a drink.

Presently, he passed more Rafter-FL cattle. He noticed a palomino grazing along the creek bank. The blonde girl, it seemed, had gotten herself out of the sun. And then, skirting the stream, Grimes saw a pair of tiny boots, a blue blouse and sundry other feminine doo-dads neatly laid on a rock. He heard a splash, and from the contour of the land, he knew that just ahead was a pool—and one probably fitted out with a mermaid.

No gent would sneak up on a lady who was cooling her toes. Grimes wheeled his horse, intending to swing wide of the pool. He had scarcely changed his direction when he heard an agonized bellow, and saw two steers charging like mad, kicking their heels sky-high.

His first thought was that, like everything else in Skunk Valley, the cattle were decidedly loco. Then, after losing a precious instant, Grimes understood.

Heel-flies had nailed the two steers, driving them mad with pain. That accounted for their kicking; and true to form, they were heading right for the nearest water. They were hog wild, and could not be headed off. Nor was there any use in trying to use his *riata*. He couldn't rope both brutes.

He spurred his horse to the edge of the pool and shouted, "M'am, git outa there, quick! Two critters is headin' yore way, crazy from heel-flies!"

While the blonde girl had not peeled down to the absolute, she might as well have. Her frail garment outlined the loveliest curves in all Texas, which is an eleven-hundred-mile stretch, any way you cross it!

She flashed a startled and indignant glance at Grimes. Then she made sense of his words, heard the insane bellowing of the cattle. Escape was cut off. They were ploughing toward her, frantically kicking as they headed for the deep water. She snatched at the *riata* Grimes tossed her, but she slipped from the rocky ledge over which a small waterfall tumbled.

In another brace of seconds, she'd be cut up by their hoofs or gored by long horns. Grimes' .45 drowned her scream. The leading steer crumpled, a slug between the eyes. *Wham!* The second one, hurdling the carcass that blocked his rush, dropped thrashing in the center of the little pool.

Her momentary pallor became a flush that reached to the upper edge of her clinging garment. She laughed tremulously and said, "I'm shaking all over, stranger. And being as how it's a mite late for you to pretend you're blind, you can give me a hand so I won't slip on those two critters."

Grimes plunged in to help her. He lost his footing, and with his delightful armful tightly clasped, splashed with her into the troubled water. By the time he got her to the bank, he was sorry it wasn't a mile away. And when she planted a warm, wet kiss on his mouth, his good resolutions abruptly snapped.

As she dried herself in the sun, she told him that she was Florabelle Lawson, and that her father owned the Rafter-FL spread. She concluded, "Only, dad's been dead drunk the past two-three days, and two of our hands got shot up kind of bad in a poker game the other night, so I had to go out and tend to screw worms."

Grimes frowned, left off eyeing her long, sleek legs, and said, "But they's the dangdest craziest people out this way. Scattering table salt over the range."

Florabelle sat bolt upright. "Table salt? Who did that?" Her eyes blazed. "With the rains we've had, and the natural sweet water in this creek, all our critters'll be salt hungry, and a lot of green grass makes them worse."

She went on to explain how cattle, if they gorge themselves on fine salt, will quickly die. She concluded, "Who were they? How much did they scatter?"

"M'am, they shot at me afore I could ask 'em. They jest had two sacks. I guess they 'lowed using a wagon'd make it too easy to trail 'em. And their hosses got away afore I could notice the brands."

"Two of them, and you shot it out?"

Grimes shrugged. "Didn't have no chanct to run," he apologized.

104

Flora regarded him intently. "Simon, I want you to ride for the Rafter-FL."

"No, m'am," he declined. "Wimmin has been gittin' me into a pack of trouble ever since I come to Texas."

His feet seemed as though he must perpetually stumble over them, and his hands were built to match. But Flora had seen enough of him to realize that appearances are deceptive. So she looked up through her long lashes and pleaded, "Please, Simon. Someone's been stealing our critters, and now they're fixing to kill those they can't steal."

She was leaning against him, and to keep from being overbalanced as he sat on the flat rock, Grimes had to get a good hold of Flora. His arms betrayed him. They seemed to remember the curves and softness they had held while lifting her out of the pool. And Flora made the clinch closer, instead of edging away.

"Simon," she begged. "I need a reliable man."

The flexion of her slim young body, its warmth and closeness, kept Grimes from getting her precise meaning. "You got one," he said, kissing her upturned mouth.

"Oh—" She gasped, tried to turn her face; then she decided she liked it. She shivered and clung closer, whispering when she got her breath, "Simon, you young devil! Do you always act this way?"

"Only when they asks fo' it!" he answered, and kissed her until she was gasping and breathless. "An' I ain't scairt of trouble!"

"You ought to be—*ooooh!*"

LATER, AS HE ACCOMPANIED FLORA TOWARD THE DISTANT RANCH HOUSE, SHE WENT ON, "Dad's an awfully good cattleman when he's sober. But a drop of liquor, and he's hog-drunk, like that! He realizes it, so he fixed it for me to handle all his money, and I swore I'd shoot any cowhand that brings him a bottle from town. Only, every once in a while, he somehow gets hold of some."

Grimes pondered on that for a moment, then said, "I been thinking you'd better not tell anyone—not even yo' pappy—about my run-in with those two salt experts. Sheriffs is funny about sech things, an' them two jaspers might have ornery friends, an' I'm plumb sick of shooting people onless it's necessary."

The owner of the Rafter-FL was tall and wiry, with amiable blue eyes that twinkled from a leathery face as hard as a meat axe; but he was still a bit shaky from his last jag. He nodded appreciatively as he heard of Flora's narrow escape. But later, he drew Grimes to one side and bluntly warned him, "Bub, yo're all right, but keep away from that gal. I been watching the way she eyed yuh all evenin', an' I been figgering as how it took you two a right smart time tuh git back from that pool."

"Listen, gol dang it!" blurted Grimes. "You ain't got—"

"Mebbe yuh saved her life and mebbe yuh didn't," Lawson interrupted. "But she's goin' tuh marry Cal Marston. He's my foreman. Yuh ain't seen him yet, account of he's gone tuh Skunk Valley an' ain't come back. So don't yuh go foolin' around, er they's trouble."

But Lawson had missed a trick. Grimes already had an engagement with Flora. And that night, he slipped from the bunkhouse to the hay loft. Presently, the ladder creaked and a slender white shape came toward him. It was Flora, wearing her boots under a frail nightgown.

"Honey," she whispered, sinking into the hay beside him, "I heard what dad told you after supper. But I ain't marrying Marston."

She was all white and gold in the moonlight that reached in through the loft gate, and almost touched her beaded boots. Her lovely face and firm young breasts had a new glamour, and as he kissed her, the glow of her eyes made her the most marvelous critter he'd ever seen.

And in a moment, they were close in each other's arms, lips and breath blending. "Simon," she sighed, "don't ever stop loving me. . . ."

THEN, LATER, AS SHE SNUGGLED AGAINST HIM FOR SHELTER FROM THE CHILLY BREEZE, she went on, "If you can find out who's raising all the ructions with our cows, Dad will probably forget what he told you. Marston ain't done nothing but make excuses for not getting to the bottom of things."

She shivered, then slipped from his arms, adding, "Now I got to get back. I don't know what we'll do after tonight, account of Dad's room is right next to mine. And it's risky, meeting you out here."

He remained in the hayloft, watching her dart from shadow to shadow until the ranch house swallowed her. Later, he climbed down; but clattering hoofs warned him. It must be Cal Marston, returning from town. And when the rider dismounted, unsaddled and turned his horse into the corral, that settled the question. This was no time for Grimes to be conspicuous, so he ducked into the granary.

Instead of heading for the bunkhouse with his horse gear, Marston was coming toward the barn. There was no mistaking the direction of his footsteps. Could he have been lurking and seen Flora's approach or departure?

That jasper must be a mind reader, was Grimes' next uneasy thought. *He's heading right fo' the granary!*

A vagrant gust of wind stirred up a bit of fine chaff and dust. It tickled Grimes' nostrils. And during the ages that he fought a sneeze, Marston reached the threshold. He struck a match. Grimes, still racked by his silent efforts, tried to shrink to the cover of the open door. He made it, but knocked down an oat measure. The tinny clatter in that silence was like the ring of cathedral bells.

"Whut the tarnation hell yuh doin' in here?" growled Marston. "Gol dang yuh, Barry. I done tol' yuh—"

So he thought it was Barry, one of the cowpokes, did he? Grimes wanted that error to stick; otherwise, when Lawson heard of the encounter, he'd begin wondering. He heaved himself against the door, slamming it against Marston. The match blinked out. The foreman cursed wrathfully as he recoiled, toppling back over a knee high stack of oat sacks.

"I'll tear yore gizzard out, yuh ____ ____!" he howled.

Grimes lost a split second opening the door he had slammed in Marston's face. Since the foreman thought he knew the identity of the prowler, he would not shoot. Grimes therefore risked a dash, but he had not counted on Marston's quick recovery.

Long arms wrapped about his knees. As he was thrown off balance, he snaked an arm around Marston's neck. The sudden application of weight dragged the foreman sprawling along. They tangled on the barn floor, grappling and slugging. In a moment, this human pinwheel burst out into the moonlight.

Grimes booted his opponent a glancing one to the chin, breaking the clinch, but the outdoor light exposed the boy from Georgia. Marston saw the strange face and went for his gun.

In the struggle, Grimes' belt had shifted. That saved Marston's life. Still groping for his Colt, Grimes hurled himself to the corner of the water trough. Marston, pummeled groggy, fired wildly, hosing the trough and the ranch house.

"Quit it, both of yuh!" roared a voice from the right, "Er I'll splatter yuh with buckshot till yore stummicks looks like a lace curtain!"

Lawson, wearing a short nightshirt, was not an especially stately figure by moonlight, but the long, double-barreled goose gun in his knotty hands gave him more dignity than the goddess of liberty.

"I caught this yere sculpin prowling in the—" Marston checked himself abruptly; he gulped, got a fresh start. "Who the hell is he, anyhow?"

"New cowhand I hired today," said Lawson. "Now stop yore gol dang fightin'! Grimes, whut the hell was yuh doin'?"

"Um—uh—lookin' fo' a jackknife I done lost. In the granary."

The disturbance had aroused Flora. A lamp now glowed in the kitchen, casting a patch of radiance through the unshaded window. She came out, wide-eyed and frightened by the shooting, and glanced at the three men. Grimes knew that she had deliberately lit a lamp in order to gain time to compose herself.

For a moment, she stood there like some lovely ivory statue clad in a nightgown too sheer to resist the lamplight that came through the open door. The breeze played with the filmy fabric, outlining her lovely legs, the flare of her hips, the breathless tension of her breasts. Then she relaxed, exhaled a quavering sigh, and gasped, "Oh—Dad—what happened—anyone hurt?"

Her father eyed her, then said to the foreman, "Marston, I guess that's all fer you. I'll tend tuh this jigger."

Once the foreman was out of earshot, Lawson said to Grimes, "So yuh lost a jackknife in the granary, huh? I guess she was a-helpin' yuh hunt it!" His hand darted out, catching a strand of Flora's streaming hair. "Jedgin' from the fox tails she ain't had time tuh comb out, they's been a hay mow party."

"Uh—listen—I tell yuh—" began Grimes.

"Git out!" growled Lawson, shifting the goose gun. "Right now."

"Dad," protested Flora. "Please be reasonable! I—"

"Shut up! Git in the house afore I clout yuh! An' you, Grimes, ef I ketch yuh on my range, I'm a-shootin' hell outen yuh! Now git!"

Grimes, when he rode from the ranch, had a plan for overcoming old man

Lawson's wrath. It was just a matter of going to Skunk Valley and learning who was raiding the Rafter-FL. That might be accomplished by scouting around until he found out who was buying unusual numbers of hundred-pound bags of table salt.

EXCEPT FOR THE SEVEN UP SALOON, SKUNK VALLEY WAS ASLEEP WHEN HE ARRIVED, BUT he routed out the livery stable keeper, and, after a good deal of pounding, awoke the night man at the Silver Dollar Hotel. While he was convincing the clerk that he wanted a room, and not the contents of the cash drawer, the stable boy came dashing over.

"Stranger," he informed Grimes, "yore hoss has got a shoe with a hunk busted out. On the off fore foot. My Uncle Ab's a blacksmith—"

"I allowed suthin' was making him stumble," said Grimes. "Thank you very kindly, and have yo' uncle fix it up whilst I pound my ear."

It had been a long day, and the boy from Georgia was already half asleep on his feet. But his last waking thought was that it would be an easy job to cover the general stores of Skunk Valley.

AROUND NOON, GRIMES SET OUT TO GET HIMSELF A DRINK AND SIZE UP THE TOWN.

The Seven Up furnished not only a shot of tonsil-scorching liquor, but like-wise a buzz of excitement. Grimes had scarcely downed his whiskey when the town marshal stalked in. He wore a star as big as a sunflower and on his heels came a hatchet-faced man whose shiny, greenish frock coat betokened important doings. The citizens who trooped after him confirmed that impression.

"I'd sho' admire to know whut the excitement's about in the back room," Grimes observed.

"That gent in the long-tail coat," answered the bartender, "is the coroner, and he's a-holding an ink-west on two of Emmet Eastley's cowpokes. Someone shot the wadding out of both of 'em."

"Heh? Who done it?" Eastley was a total stranger to Grimes, but the death of two cowhands was vitally interesting.

"Ef we knowed who done it," snorted the bartender, "we wouldn't be having no ink-west. All we know is that jest one hombre drilled them some time yes-tiddy. Both was shot with a .45, and all the empties was jacked out in one place. The same kind of shells."

Grimes headed for the back room. He was tall enough to look over the heads of the group gathered about the two men laid out on pine planks supported by saw horses. The faces of the deceased were familiar.

The coroner was listening to a square-faced cowpuncher testify, "We done found pore Hardpan and Lanky all shot up in Bear Gulch."

Grimes knew that that was perjury. Bear Gulch was four or five miles from where he had shot it out with the two gunners. There was no longer any need of tracing the sale of salt. Since Emmet Eastley was killing a neighbor's cattle, he would also steal them; and Grimes' problem now was to get the deadwood on him.

The citizens were fidgeting; they'd been discussing the testimony an hour before the inquest. So the coroner rapped for order and rendered his verdict: "Seein' as how both of the deceased, to wit, Hardpan Lewis and Lanky Mills, was gunslicks from way back an', moreover, both fired their weapons, we find that the aforesaid deceased come to their death from slapping leather with a damn good man, the same being a person or persons unknown. All right, gents, funeral this afternoon."

Shortly after the inquest was adjourned, Grimes learned that Emmet Eastley's brand was the Diamond Double E, and that neither the owner nor his foreman had left the ranch to attend the funeral. Then he went to the livery stable to get his horse.

The beast's four feet had been shod. As he paid his bill, Grimes asked the way to Eastley's spread. The liveryman told him, then eyed him from head to foot and said, "Son, a lot of folks don't like Eastley, and someone musta hit back. Don't look like it's healthy, ridin' for Diamond Double E."

"Ef a man don't look fo' trouble, he usually don't find it," was Grimes' sage rejoinder; and so saying, he mounted up.

IT WAS WELL PAST MID-AFTERNOON WHEN GRIMES APPROACHED THE DIAMOND DOUBLE E ranch buildings. A middle-aged Mexican was in the shade of the house, spinning horsehair rope. Grimes hailed him. The old chap returned the salutation, motioned toward the corral, and said, "No spik Englees." His gesture, however, was plain: it meant, "Light and set."

Grimes still had a handful of horse-gear when a woman's scream came from the spring in a clump of poplars at the far side of the house. A man's voice blasted in high pitched Spanish: "I will kill him—and you too!"

Startled, Grimes leaped back from his horse as the rope spinner left his wheel. Somebody's domestic bliss had gone loco. From where he stood, he could see that the girl was plump and olive-skinned. Her bare legs were kicking frantically as she screamed, "Ignacio! *Sanctisivm madre,* I didn't—I do not love heem— Father! Help!"

The young Mexican's hands clawed at her throat. She wrenched herself free, ripping her *camisa* to the waist. Grimes caught a glimpse of shapely breasts and streaming black hair; then a gleam of steel as Ignacio bounded after her to carve the comely flesh he had exposed.

Grimes dropped his saddle and went for his gun, but the trees now blocked the view. Before he could shift, the old rope spinner, who had the advantage of some yards, leaped to the rescue. When Grimes reached the shaded spring, Ignacio, knocked silly by the old man's boots, was staggering toward his gaily caparisoned horse. He had not even paused to retrieve his knife, and he did not have breath enough to curse. It was not until he was in the saddle that he turned back to shake his fist and growl, *"Puta!* I will kill you and him too!"

The rope spinner was half blinded by a wild slash across the forehead. The girl, who had stumbled over an outcropping root, did not know whether to pull her skirt down from around her hips or to regain her feet. Grimes gave her a hand; and as she flung back her hair, then rearranged the tatters of her *camisa,* he noticed the golden chain and locket that gleamed from the grass. He picked it up, saying, "Is this yourn?"

And that, Lola explained, taking the trinket, was the cause of the trouble. "Of course, Señor Eastley did give heem to me. That Ignacio, he ees so jalous.

"But even if my father 'ave not save me, you come running weeth that beeg gun, *verdad?"*

Old Bernal Higuera, after having his daughter tie a bandanna about his forehead, went back to his rope spinning. Lola's jealous lovers apparently were just part of the day's work. Nor was that surprising, Grimes allowed, as he warmed up to the glance Lola flashed him when she caught his hand and said, "Ees much cooler by the spring, no?"

If she referred to the weather, there was no argument. But Lola's tattered *camisa* and short skirt revealed an enticing assortment of extremely torrid curves. She had lovely legs, and her devilish black eyes were as inviting as her generous lips. Lola was built for ardent kissing.

"Don't pay no attention to Ignacio. I do not love heem. And not Señor Eastley. But my father, he is cook—"

She shrugged, which somehow explained that a chef on the Diamond Double E had to have an amiable daughter, or else become an ex-cook.

"How's Mistah Eastley to git along with?" wondered Grimes, retrieving Ignacio's knife and thrusting it down his boot leg. "I'm lookin' for a job."

"Ees always nice to me. Only, I don' like heem." But Lola moved close enough to prove that she did like present company, "An' you must not get the job. You weel be kill. Ees two men dead yesterday."

"I kin take care of myself," persisted Grimes.

"Please, go," pleaded Lola, catching him by both shoulders. "Right after supper. You are a nice boy. Too young for thees business."

This was interesting; so Grimes went stubborn. But instead of explaining, Lola served an armful of tropical logic, which she punctuated with a kiss that made his head spin. They were both gasping when he suddenly thrust her aside and said, "Ef yo' pappy hears us—"

"He ees deaf. He joost hears the loud scream." Her dark eyes were now aglow with more than pity for a boy rash enough to work for Emmet Eastley, and her lips were turned up for another kiss. "Maybe," she sighed, cuddling close, "you will believe when I tell you more, no?"

Every generous curve cried for a closer hold. And as her arms slipped about Grimes to draw him nearer, he hoped she was right about her father being deaf. . . .

LATER, LOLA RESUMED, "YOU ARE TOO NICE FOR THEES JOB. SEÑOR EASTLEY STEALS THE cattle and keeps them in the box canyon until the changed brand ees all heal up. You *sabe?"*

But before she could tell him the location of the secret corral, the clatter of hoofs interrupted. As Lola followed him from the spring, she told him that the tall, hook-nosed man riding toward the ranch house was Emmet Eastley, and that the one beside him was Red Harris, the foreman. Behind them trailed half a dozen dusty, sweating cowpunchers.

Eastley's hazel eyes appraised Grimes from head to foot as he announced that he was looking for a job. Harris spat a jet of tobacco and cut in, "Yuh might wait till Squarehead Smith comes back from the funeral. Mebbe he's done brung a couple riders with him."

Eastley nodded, then said, "Wait, an' tie intuh some grub."

Lola helped her father hustle out the biscuits and beans and steaks, but despite the good food, the men were oddly restrained. Though they still reeked of wood smoke and burnt hair, there was no reference to branding, nor any of the usual chatter about the day's work.

Grimes was not enjoying his meal. To avoid suspicion, he had to stay until morning. He knew already that he would get no job. What Eastley needed was running-iron experts who could change Rafter-FL to Diamond Double E. Very simple, but it took just the right touch.

Sitting at the foot of the table, Grimes had a perfect view of the kitchen. But this meant nothing until the back door opened and a man slipped in, knife drawn. It was Ignacio, vengeance crazed. Lola screamed. Bernal Higuera dropped a platter and leaped to intervene.

This time, Ignacio moved with cat ferocity and speed. Before the men at the table could realize what was happening, the trio in the kitchen were in a deadly tangle, with steel dancing like heat lightning.

Grimes fired just as Eastley whirled. Ignacio dropped, plugged through the head. In his fall, he carried Bernal Higuera with him, leaving Lola with red welts visible through her slashed dress. The boss of the Diamond Double E caught her as she reeled and collapsed, more frightened than hurt.

The cowpunchers eyed the lanky boy who had shot down the length of the spacious dining room, and by the dim light of kerosene lamps, to pick Ignacio from the two who struggled with him. While Grimes had had the advantage of position, it was nonetheless a shot to talk about.

SOME MINUTES LATER, EASTLEY GRINNED AND SAID, "I SMELT THAT BULLET! IT TOOK A shot through the head tuh stop a feller that's hopped up with marihuana. Any place else, an' he'da cut the hell outta Lola and her dad."

"Shucks," grinned the boy from Georgia, "that wa'n't nuthin' a-tall. Yuh oughta see my pappy, back home."

Eastley stroked his chin and said, "Sort of runs in the family, eh?"

Grimes had a thoroughly interested audience. No doubt now that he'd get a job with the Diamond Double E! Thus he was caught off-center when a pistol prodded him in the back.

"Hoist 'em!" growled the man behind the gun.

"Whut—whut the tarnation hell—"

Eastley explained, "Ain't never heard of more'n two men in Texas could make that shot, and neither of them's in these parts now. So they couldn't of kilt Hardpan and Lanky yestiddy. Yo're it, bub."

He turned to the foreman, who was returning to the dining room. He demanded, "Red, how about it?"

"His hoss has brand new shoes, fore an' hind," said Red Harris.

Eastley said, "Then send a man tuh Skunk Valley tuh git the old shoes from the blacksmith. Ef they looks like they made the tracks whar pore Hardpan and Lanky was smoked out, this jasper is yore meat. Take his smoke poles an' lock him up in the 'dobe."

They marched Grimes to a thick-walled building that had been the ranch house before Eastley evicted the Mexican owner. It was old, but the windows were barred, the door was solid, and the great squared rafters were solidly covered with withes, which were in turn thickly plastered with earth.

Lola's pitying glance gave him no hope. He heard Eastley call for the key to the padlock. And with such an important capture on his mind, the boss would have no time for any love-making that might give Lola a chance to steal the key.

The clatter of hoofs outside told Grimes that a man was riding hell-bent toward Skunk Valley. That he had not been killed then and there, he reasoned, was that Eastley first wanted to find out who had put Grimes on the job. It certainly was not that he had any scruples about executing the wrong man.

Then Grimes realized that, while his display of shooting had gotten him into a deadly predicament, it had also gained him one advantage. Gunners of his caliber seldom bother with knives, so his captors had not looked in his bootlegs. Ignacio's weapon, which Grimes had abstractedly picked up and stowed away just to clear the ground about the spring, was still in place.

He stealthily hoisted himself to the broad sill and began to whittle away at the withes on which the mud roof had been laid. His work, however, was far from complete when he heard a rider approach. His own sweat suddenly froze. The messenger could not already have returned from Skunk Valley—but the horseshoer might have become talkative during the drunk that followed the funeral. If Squarehead Smith was returning with gossip, the jig was up!

Grimes tried to wedge himself through the small opening in the roof, but failed. He turned to leap to the door. He had no time to enlarge the hole enough for quick escape, but he might spring a surprise with his knife. Then he recognized Cal Marston by the light of the lantern Eastley carried when he went out to meet his visitor.

Grimes remained on the sill, and heard the Rafter-FL foreman come to the point, "Emmet, I got Lawson hawg drunk agin. We kin drive off half his dang herd. Couple of his boys is disgusted about not gittin' their pay, an' they quit. It's easy."

"I dunno," objected Eastley. "That's so damn sudden like. And the box canyon's chock full of critters now, waitin fer their hides tuh heal up. Anyway, they's some dirt bein' stirred up—"

He described Grimes and his dazzling gunplay. Marston cut in, "Yuh don't need tuh wait fer them hoss shoes! That's the sculpin that musta kilt them boys afore he come home with Flora. Yuh better bury him deep, right now! Whar is he?"

"In the 'dobe. But do yuh reckon Lawson put him tuh work, quiet?"

They were fumbling with the lock. Grimes, instead of risking a surprise party with a knife, succeeded in forcing himself through the roof. But before he could make use of the moment during which his captors would be puzzled by his disappearance, there was a scream from near the barn, and a man's hoarse outcry.

Eastley and Marston had turned from the door and toward the disturbance. Grimes, however, did not make a dive for the treacherous foreman's horse. It was not Lola, nor was the Mexican girl among the men who crowded the yard; the woman was Flora Lawson, struggling with a cowpuncher.

The lantern light picked the gleam of white curves that peeped from her torn blouse and skirt. Her captor grunted, "Hell, I didn't know it was a gal until I got me an armful. I saw someone snoopin' around a few minutes after Marston got here."

Eastley cursed luridly as his lovely captive glared at him defiantly. Most of her remarks were directed toward Marston. "You dirty skunk!" she raged. "I suspected you ever since you hollered about that boy in the granary. I looked and found the liquor you been giving my dad. So I followed you tonight to find out who you were doing this dirty work with."

Grimes groaned as he watched from the top of the 'dobe. Flora, blazing with wrath at her capture, did not realize her peril; but Grimes did, even before he saw Marston's expression change.

"You're fired, you sidewinder! And let me go—"

"Emmet," cut in Marston, "I didn't know she was follering. Yuh better let her go afore they's trouble."

"You blockhead!" growled Eastley. "We can't let her go. Her seeing you here's a dead giveaway. She'll talk. Like Grimes. Lucky we got him."

"But yuh cain't kill her!" stormed Marston. "We're pardners, yuh an' me. Gimme anything yuh want fer my share of the Diamond Double E, an' I'll take the gal to Mexico."

"I'd rather be shot!" defied Flora, regarding the circle of muttering ruffians who were avidly eyeing her half-bare figure.

"Yuh led her here an' got us intuh a nice mess," snarled Eastley. "She's ourn."

So that was the way out. Force Marston to defend Flora, then blot him out. And no one would ever learn what had happened.

Marston was sick with more than fear. Grimes tugged frantically and tore a large 'dobe brick from the coping. He could not hope for more than winning a break for Flora. Death hovered, ready to swoop.

"If you've got Simon Grimes here," said Flora, with scarcely a catch in her voice, "let me see him. For a little while. Then I don't care what you do."

"I reckon yore entitled tuh a few last words together," admitted Eastley.

Grimes, clutching his brick, waited for Marston to go for his gun. But the traitor's courage was failing. He would not turn a hand to save a girl who preferred Grimes!

And then a distant rumbling startled the tense group. The bellowing of a thousand steers and the pounding of their hoofs shook the ground. A fence crashed. Terror seized the dismounted cowpunchers, but Eastley roared, "Stand fast, yuh _____ jugheads! They's just salt crazy!"

He checked the panic for a moment. The cattle were tearing down a small wooden building, crashing into the ranch house, demolishing everything that blocked their search for salt. And in the terrific confusion, Grimes hurled his 'dobe brick.

Eastley dropped. Before Flora's captor could let go of her and reach for his gun, Marston had drawn and shot him. But Grimes, taking a nosedive from the roof, interrupted his belated rescue. He landed, driving Marston to the hard ground. The pistol blast made the cowpunchers turn from the horses they were hastening to saddle, so that they could drive the salt-hungry cattle away before the buildings were utterly ruined.

But Grimes now had Eastley's guns, and their fire hosed the surprised clump of men. "Ketch Marston's hoss!" he yelled, flinging Flora aside and ducking to the shelter of a grindstone. "I'll hold 'em!"

Lead spattered against the heavy stone. The boy from Georgia sniped the flashes, and the surviving gunners broke in panic. They would not face the gunslick who had popped Ignacio on the fly! They already knew that it could not be Marston.

Flora was in the saddle. "Get up behind me!"

"Take thees horse," interrupted a woman, slipping from the back of a winded beast. "I turn those cow looz so I get the chance to turn you looz. But you are too smart, no?"

It was Lola. She vanished in the shadows before Grimes straightened up in the saddle. He turned back, waved once at something that seemed to move in the gloom. But with Eastley and Marston dead, there would be no one to suspect or harm Lola—except, perhaps, another jealous lover.

"Simon," said Flora as they galloped clear of the milling cattle, "don't ever bother to tell me why that girl had wits enough to remember that salt-hungry critters will go on a rampage to the nearest house, looking for the stuff. The joke's on Eastley, forgetting to tend to stock that was getting so much sweet water and green feed."

"My uncle," was Grimes' sage observation as he leaned over in the saddle to take an armful of Flora, "allus 'lowed it was bad luck to spill salt. Now ef yo' pappy don't shoot the gizzard outta me—"

"Darling," gasped Flora, when the kiss had to end for fresh breath, "Dad's hawg drunk . . . won't it be wonderful, now—"

"An' the rest of the time, too," added Grimes. "Mebbe ef we keep him drunk, we'uns kin run the Rafter-FL."

• • • • •

Too Many Cooks

"OH—SIMON! YOU SCARED ME HALF SILLY!" FLORA LAWSON SAT BOLT UPRIGHT, HER FIRM young bosom rounding out the low yoke of a frivolous, half transparent nightgown. Moonlight stealing in through the ranch house window warmed their ivory firmness, brought gold from her blonde hair. "You mustn't—dad's not drunk tonight—"

Belatedly, Flora drew the edge of the sheet up to her collarbone, but her white shoulders and face were too lovely to profit much by the sudden veiling of competition. The long-faced boy from Georgia blinked incredulously, brushed the persistent cowlick from his eyes.

"Why—listen, I put a quart of red likker right wheah he'd git it!" Simon Bolivar Grimes began to develop suspicions. "Ef that skunk of a Barry—"

"I took it myself. Darling, we can't be seeing each other this way. Barry has been eyeing me— Simon, you stay and listen!"

She caught his wrist and he slowly seated himself beside her, letting his half-drawn .45 settle back into its holster.

"Now that you're foreman of the Rafter-FL," Flora went on, "you've got to keep the respect of the men. And so do I."

"Hell!" grumbled Grimes, hungry glance straying to the luscious curves again exposed by Flora's sudden gesture.

Women were funny critters. She hadn't been so dang fussy before. "Ef yo' all are tryin' to git rid of me, yo' kin say it right out."

"Don't be so hot-headed!" Flora pleaded. She leaned toward him, and a slim, bare arm slipped about his neck. For a moment, she yielded, lay in his arms, throbbing as she clung to him, lip to lip. Then she thrust him away and softly moaned. "Simon—I want you to stay—all the time—"

Grimes licked his lips and blinked. "All the time—yo'all mean—"

"Always, Simon. We'll get married. Won't that be wonderful?"

"So dang wonderful I jest kain't imagine it."

He meant that, and he looked it. For a moment, Flora accepted that silent tribute. Then she smiled and fished a parcel from under her pillow. "I got you these when I was in Skunk Valley, only I wasn't going to give them to you till breakfast."

"Suthin' fo' me?" He blinked, fumbling with the wrappings.

"Of course. You were so wonderful, saving us from that gang of cattle rustlers while dad was too drunk to stir. I'm so grateful, and I wanted to prove it."

A musical tinkling broke into the crackle of paper, and Grimes saw that she had given him a pair of silver spurs, exquisitely chased and embossed. The two-inch rowels each had a pair of tiny bells. The chains were fine, four-fold links. The straps were maroon leather.

"Dawg gone my hide! Ef they ain't scrumptious!"

"Like them, Simon?"

He took an armful of Flora and kissed her until she gasped. She finally looked up with misty eyes and whispered, "Simon—don't go yet—"

"I guess," he panted, "appearances kain't git all shot to hell any wuss fo' me staying a minute mo'. . . ."

BUT WHEN GRIMES TIPTOED FROM FLORA'S ROOM, HE WAS WORRIED. HE SOMBERLY TOLD himself, "This yeah matrimony proposition allus gits me into heaps of grief. Lookit the time I dang nigh married that hoss thief's daughter."

Grimes buckled on the silver spurs. Nobody but Hipolito Pasalaguas, the best saddler in Skunk Valley, would have made them. Only, those dang little bells ought to be taken off. In case of a feud, a gent was liable to be recognized in the dark.

He mounted his gray gelding and rode out across the range to join his men at the camp. From afar, he heard the restless stirring of the mustangs in the remuda, then the clatter of pots and pans and the raucous voice of Jasper, the cook.

The cowpunchers, routed out of their blankets, squatted shivering about the fire as Grimes stalked toward them, just in time for breakfast.

Ford Barry, the top hand who would have been foreman but for Grimes, sourly eyed the boy from Georgia and spat a jet of tobacco juice into the fire.

"An' she shall have music wharever she goes!" he chanted mockingly.

"Ef yo' don't like these yeah spurs," flared Grimes, "yo' kin—"

The cowpokes forgot their morning grouch and howled with laughter. Grimes swallowed and joined the mirth, despite the malicious grin on Barry's broad red face. He shoveled home his flapjacks and bacon, washed the grub down with the corrosive stuff Jasper called coffee. This outfit needed a new cook. Something ought to be done about it.

Barry tasted the steaming liquid, flung his mug to the ground and howled; "Jasper, yuh gol-danged skunk, ef yuh don't quit givin' us trantler juice, I'm a-rawhiding yuh!"

Jasper jerked back on his hocks. "Why, yuh ornery saddle tramp—yuh was cutting steaks offen cattle died of blackleg afore yuh got a job here," he choked. "Yuh contemptuous horn toad, this yere's dang good coffee. Simon, whut's wrong with it?"

"It's larrupin!" declared Grimes, emptying his cup. "Gimme more!"

"Larrupin, is it?" howled Barry. "Why—"

He drew his gun. The big .45 was blazing before it fairly cleared leather. The coffee pot, riddled by a slug, spurted the poisonous fluid into the fire. Steam rose, gray clouds of ash drifted from the glare. Then Grimes cut loose.

The first shot knocked Barry's Colt from his hand. Grimes followed through. One fist holstered his weapon. The other lifted Barry from his feet. He landed asprawl, face down and frozen to his boots.

"I'm quittin' this ___ ____ outfit!" piped Jasper, rage cracking his voice. "Yuh kin cook yore own ___ damn' grub! Ef yuh was tending tuh business instead of gallivantin' around with silver spurs, that sculpin wouldn't dast shoot holes in my cawfee pot!"

He kicked a pan of bacon into the fire and stalked, cursing, into the thinning gloom. Grimes turned to Barry, who now sat up, blinking and wondering what had hit him.

"Next time yo' pulls a hawleg jest fo' fun," he warned, "I'm a-shootin' yo' gizzard plumb through yo' spine. Now git yo'selves in yo' saddles or I fires the passel of you!"

That was good as far as it went. But all day long, as the men fanned out over the range, driving the cattle toward the assembling place, Grimes was worried. The Rafter-FL outfit was already out of hand.

Grimes himself took charge of the chuck wagon, and at noon the men began to realize that old Jasper had been a truly splendid cook! Their wrath centered on Ford Barry.

"Yuh ___ ____ damn' skunk!" threatened one of the victims, "it's all yore fault, an' ef we don't git a good cook, yore a-going tuh be lynched!"

"Jest keep on yo' shirts," chuckled Grimes as he swung to the saddle. "The old man's right smart rasslin vittles when he ain't drunk."

DISCIPLINE, GRIMES REALIZED, HAD ITS LIMITS; SO HE LEFT THE OUTFIT AND HEADED FOR the ranch house to get old man Lawson to act as cook until a new one could be found in Skunk Valley.

Grimes, pretending to smuggle liquor to the ranch without Flora's knowledge, had regulated the jags of the Rafter-FL owner so that they never reached outrageous lengths. A pint would bribe the old chap.

Lawson met him at the corral. His frosty blue eyes gleamed; he seized the boy's arm and boomed, "Simon, whar the tarnation hell's that likker?"

"Shut up!" warned Grimes. "Ef Flora hears—"

"She done rode to her Cousin Sally's place fer a couple days. An' onless she busted the bottle, they's some likker hid somewhar."

Grimes decided that Flora's sudden departure was to avoid any more meetings with him. He resented her stand. Gratitude, hell! A gent can get along splendidly without silver spurs.

"Mebbe yo'all kin find some in the old 'dobe."

He seated himself on the steps and spat tobacco juice at the boot scraper. The clicking hoofs of a burro loaded with household goods roused him from his sour pondering. A white-mustachioed Mexican was driving the beast. Beside him walked a barefooted girl whose scarlet skirt was windwhipped against her thighs.

Pert breasts rounded out her *camisa,* each elastic stride producing a delicious quiver. Her devil-haunted black eyes lighted with pleasure as she recognized Grimes. This was Bernal Higuera and his daughter, Lola.

"Don Simón!" she exclaimed. "My father heard that you need wan good cook on thees *rancho."*

"Buenas tardes, Don Simón!" The wiry old Mexican ceremoniously lifted his high-crowned sombrero. He flashed a reproving glance at his daughter's tactless approach, and went on, "Out of gratitude for your valor, I have come to pay my respects."

Old man Lawson reeled out of the 'dobe with a half-emptied pint of whiskey. He eyed Lola's slim waist and exquisitely curved hips. "Simon," he stuttered, "yuh might as well give him the job. Bein' as how yuh saved his life, he might give the boys some better grub."

"I am the faithful servant who kisses the hands of your excellencies," answered Higuera.

"He means," translated Grimes, "he's chief cook, startin' now."

Lola said nothing; but her sparkling eyes seconded the slow, intoxicating smile that brightened her olive-tinted face.

THAT NIGHT, JUST AFTER HE HAD BLOWN OUT THE LAMP AND WAS READY TO TURN IN, Grimes' bitterness at Flora's notions on propriety was abruptly thinned. Lawson's drunken snoring masked the hingecreak of Grimes' door.

Lola was on the prowl. A long brown *serape,* doubtless her father's, trailed from her shoulders. Beneath its heavy woolen folds, she wore nothing but a frail nightgown. In the moonlight, Grimes could see the shadow of lace cast against her warm skin; panels of drawnwork reached from knee to hip, and from the dip of her waist to the swell of her bosom.

She gestured for silence and tiptoed to his side.

"Querido," she whispered, snuggling against him, "you are surprise, no? But I weel show you."

"Ain't much left to show," gulped Grimes, "onless I git a lamp."

"You do not onnerstan'," explained Lola, pressing close against his buckskin shirt front. "You save my father from that marihuana-crazy Ignacio. The gratitude, no?"

"Wait a second," protested Grimes, fairly overwhelmed by the soft, warm, creature that was making him tingle all the way down to his cowhide boots. "Lookee here, Lola—that warn't nuthing. Yo' bettah run along—ef someone seen you—dawggone it—"

She laughed softly, stroked his unruly hair. Her eyes were wide and gleaming, and the lithe motion with which she shrugged aside the coarse *serape* fanned Grimes to blazing ardor. She whispered, "I onnerstan', my brave hero. The *señorita* weel be jealous, no? But me, I am clever. I see her riding away to the cousin's *rancho* today. I know you weel be lonesome. I have the gratitude. I weel not look at you w'en she ees at home—"

Lola kissed him. Her lips were full and warm and hungry. Mexican fire scorched his mouth, and when his embrace closed about her, the frail gown betrayed every ripple of her supple body.

"Yo' bettah not come here again," he whispered hoarsely, drawing her closer.

"Ey onnerstand," she sighed, hot breath exhaling into his ear. "Bot you are so brave, *angelito mio.* . . . I love you. . . ."

The gangling Georgia mountaineer was far too excited to see anything funny about being called a little angel. Lola's throaty murmurings made anything seem probable. Gratitude had its points. . . .

The clatter of hoofs in the yard brought her from his arms in a breath. Grimes, peeping out the window, recognized Flora's silver-maned palomino. He seized the sash, sent it rattling upward.

"Git out!" he gasped. "Quick—she's back—"

He bundled Lola over the sill and into the backyard. For additional distraction, he stamped out to the front, where he met Flora at the steps.

"Honey," she sobbed, draping herself over his shirt front, "I was so lonesome, I couldn't stand it. So I came back."

He drew her closer. For a moment, they clung to each other, lip to lip. "I'm so glad," she sighed. "Dad's snoring like a buzz saw, too . . . darling. . . ."

She started. A shrill scream lanced the silence. It came from behind the ranch house. *"Valgame dios!* I weel keel you! *Hijo de cabron!"*

It was Lola. A slap *popped* like a pistol shot. A man cursed, then laughed and said, "Dawg gone it, whut yuh running around fer in that nightie?"

"I guess that's the new cook's daughter," stuttered Grimes. "Yo' pappy hired Bernal Higuera on account o' Jasper quit. Yo' remember Higuera?"

"Yes, *and* I remember his daughter!" snapped Flora, looking out the kitchen window at the white figure that scurried toward the cook's shack, and the dark one that stalked toward the bunk house. Ford Barry, beyond any doubt.

Lola's haste gave the moonlight a glowing chance at her shapely legs. Flora added, "The young hussy, running around that way!" Then she caught Grimes' hand. "Darling, how come Jasper quit?"

As she followed him down the hall, Grimes told her about Barry's indignation at the former cook's coffee. He concluded, "An' I'da shot the gizzard outa him, only he's a good cowhand."

"You see, Simon?" They were at his door. "Discipline has been sagging, account of you and me."

He caught her in both arms, kissed the "I told you so" from her lips. For a moment, she yielded, let him ease her across the threshold. Then she wriggled clear and protested, "Don't, Simon—please don't—you mustn't!"

Grimes shrugged, shook his head as she slipped down the hall. "Gol dang it, wimmen is crazy! Whut'd she come back fo', anyway?"

THE NEW COOK SLUNG OUT THE HASH AT DAWN. THE MEN WERE LAUGHING, JESTING, whiffing the savory fumes of honest-to-gawd coffee, and cakes that were cakes!

But when Grimes went to the ranch house to go through the formality of getting the day's orders from old man Lawson, Flora met him with frosty eyes. Her chin was high. One hand held an old brown *serape;* her fingers disdainfully had it by the fringe. She'd found it in his room, where Lola had left it!

"Simon," she demanded icily, "since when do you wear a *serape?"*

"Uh—um—ug," groped Grimes. "I don't never wear one, honey. Only, old Higuera was so gol danged grateful, account I saved his life that night I smoked out the cattle rustlers, he done give me his best one."

Flora's lovely face relaxed as she remembered Grimes' blazing guns and reckless valor.

"Gratitude is mighty nice," she conceded. Then, with gentle irony, "I guess old Higuera's daughter gave you a big tortoise-shell comb?"

Grimes reddened and stuttered. He knew that Flora had put two and two together; that she now understood why a cowpoke had been slapped by the girl running around in a nightgown. "Listen, honey," he groped, ears burning, "I kin explain that. It was this way—"

"You're just like a small boy, Simon! Anyway, I didn't really see anything out of the way. But that grateful old greaser and his grateful hussy of a daughter are leaving right now. I'll fire them, myself."

Which she did, then and there.

LATER, GRIMES SET OUT FOR SKUNK VALLEY TO FIND A COOK. HIS YOUNG FACE WAS DRAWN and weary, and the long miles coated him with alkali dust that accentuated the outward tokens left by the worry of holding a job that would have tested a man twice Grimes' age.

Skunk Valley's single street and dozen cross alleys basked under the flame of a setting sun. Grimes dismounted at the hitching rack in front of the Seven Up Saloon and stretched long legs toward the bar beyond the batwing doors.

He gulped a slug of whiskey and stared sourly at the bottom of the glass. The more he thought of it, the more certain he was that Lola had not been wearing her high, Spanish-style comb, all a-gleam with brilliants. Someone had planted it; and he suspected that skunk of a Barry, whose chances of an occasional smile from Flora had been blocked by Grimes.

Good cowhand or not, Barry was going to learn something from the blazing mouth of a .45. But there was the problem of getting him to shoot it out. Few gunners in Skunk Valley would risk slapping leather with Simon Bolivar Grimes.

Grimes was attracted by the latest innovation in Skunk Valley, a free lunch counter. The savory fumes of chili con carne and tiny tamales invited him; and there was jerked beef, and smoked fish. He stalked over and began to load up.

"Git away from that pickled tongue, bub!" growled a bearded man with a face as unpleasant as his voice. "This yere grub is fer men what buys likker."

Oddly enough, the fellow wore no gunbelt, so Grimes mildly protested. "Ef yo' don't mind, suh, I craves some of that theah tongue, an' I been buyin' a lot of likker."

He plucked the choicest morsel from the platter, and so deftly that the grumbler's stubby fingers for an instant groped at absolute emptiness until he realized what had happened. Then the bearded man cursed and spat a jet of tobacco juice into Grimes' bowl of chili.

The boy from Georgia straight-armed the contaminated dish and cupped the ruffian's chin. The blistering gravy drenched him. A howl of glee rang from the adjoining poker table as Black-Beard smashed against the wall and thumped to the floor.

"Yuh kain't hit my pardner!" roared a redhaired stranger, stamping toward the counter.

He fumbled for his gun. Grimes' weapon was out like a rattler's stroke, but he held his fire. It would be downright murder, shooting a man apparently loggy with liquor. "Drop it—now!" he commanded.

All eyes were on the two; all, that is, except the bartender's. He yelled a warning, Grimes shifted, winning another instant of life. His swift motion pulled him clear of the slug from the .41 derringer that Black-Beard jerked from his bootleg.

Grimes' Colt shifted. Its thunder drowned the cough of the derringer's other barrel. And from the corner of his eye, he saw that the red-headed fellow had fooled him; his guns were darting out, quick as death. Grimes ducked behind the corner of the lunch counter. Lead raked the platters of food, sweeping the space he had blocked but a split second ago.

But even as he moved, his Colt resumed its drumming. It spewed flame and lead. No ear could separate the blasts of that dancing weapon. The second gunner joined his fellow, face down, and a smoking pistol skating from a spreading red pool.

Grimes eyed the devastated lunch counter, and suddenly brightened. "Gol dang my hide! Ef he didn't plumb miss the pickled tongue!"

When the town marshal arrived to investigate, everybody but the two deceased tough customers were bellying up to the bar.

"Have one yorself, marshal!" boomed one of the group. "Them two sidewinders ganged up on Grimes, sorta whipsawin' him, one with a hideout gun and t'other pretending he was too drunk tuh slap leather."

So Grimes, out of gratitude for testimony that cleared him of all legal embarrassments, began to buy the drinks. Then the orchestra arrived; and when the girls entered the dance hall of the Seven Up, Skunk Valley settled down to enjoy an evening that had started out right.

"ARE YOU REALLY LOOKING FOR A COOK?" COOED A SWEET VOICE IN GRIMES' EAR. THE girl whose hip and nicely rounded leg were pressed against him glanced up to flash a dazzling crimson smile. "My old man's pretty good."

She had long, greenish eyes, half veiled by her lashes. The Seven Up was whirling perceptibly and her full bosom, which threatened to burst from her bodice, did plenty to Grimes' whiskey-warmed senses.

"Ef yo' pappy's grub is as scrumptious as yo' eyes, m'am," he gallantly declared, "I'd sho' admire to have him run the Rafter-FL chuck wagon."

"Let's dance, dearie," she proposed, taking his arm. "And we'll have a drink, and then, later. . . ."

Mae's voice trailed to a seductive nothingness that suggested an urge to leave the hallway before closing time. She was a ripe, lithe armful, and her dancing revealed curves that even her gown, low on top and high at the bottom, had not quite advertised.

"Oh, dearie, you're squeezing me as if you really meant it," sighed Mae. Her eyes told him she could stand a lot more. "Get a bottle at the bar and meet me in the alley. Maybe father isn't at home."

All in a pleasant haze, Grimes stalked toward the bar. He had had no time to wonder why two strangers had tried to smoke him out. As he cleared the threshold of the side door, a woman's hand closed on his wrist. When she spoke, he recognized Lola. Her face was a blur in the gloom, but no darkness could conceal the supple curves she pressed against him.

"*Querido,* don' go weeth that woman!" she gasped. "Ees dangerous!"

"Git away from me, yo' dang troublemaker!" growled Grimes, snatching her arms from about his neck. "You an' yo' gratitude!"

Wrath sobered him. After several strides, he paused, wondering. Lola had vanished. Grimes shrugged and went on, but he was frowning. Then he dismissed her approach as jealousy. Mae was at the mouth of the alley.

"Dearie," she sighed, snuggling close and planting an avid kiss, "I hope we can be alone tonight." And, as they walked down the street, "Tell me, where did you get those lovely spurs? They're so attractive."

"I'll tell yuh later, m'am," he answered, keeping a wary eye on the black mouths of the alleys they passed on their way toward Mae's frame house at the outskirts of Skunk Valley.

She left him at the front door, to see whether her father was at home. Grimes, still mulling over Lola's warning, slipped toward the rear. He moved fast enough to overcome the handicap of tinkling spur-bells. Mae suppressed a startled outcry when he pounded at the back door. Her eyes widened perceptibly as he grinned and explained, "Jest in case some gents was waiting to bushwhack me. I'm tolable unpopular-like in Skunk Valley."

Mae understood, laughed softly, and cooed, "You're awfully smart, Simon. Father's not at home. I hope you're not disappointed."

He followed her toward the front. There, he knocked the neck off the bottle. Moonlight made a lamp quite unnecessary, which was more romantic.

"Simon," she protested, "you're hurting me—please don't—let's have another drink—"

But Mae's breath was coming in short, quick gasps and he could feel the quiver of the flesh outlined by her close-fitting gown. They downed another drink . . . and another. Her protests became feeble. Finally she whispered, "Please, dearie! Wait—"

She wriggled out of his arms. From an adjoining room, he heard silken rustlings. He fumbled some tobacco and finally built a warped smoke. He tried to pour himself a drink to dilute his impatience, but he spilled half down his boot-leg. The tinkle of his spurs sounded as though his feet were many miles from his ankles. . . .

WHEN GRIMES AWOKE, HE WAS ALONE IN A ROOM AT LEAST TEN DEGREES HOTTER THAN A locomotive firebox. His tongue was thick and his mouth tasted like an old crupper. Judging from the sun, it must have been mid-afternoon.

"Mae! You, Mae. Wheah are yuh?" he croaked, tottering uncertainly toward the other room.

The echo of his footsteps mocked him. The room was empty, and so was the kitchen. It was not until after he plunged his head into the rainwater barrel that he realized that Mae had played him a dirty trick. His spurs were gone. So was the poke of gold pieces. He hastily probed his bootleg and found the wad of new-fangled paper money that Mae had missed.

He stamped, cursing, through the empty house. Each step kicked up clouds of dust. On the front room table, he found yellowed letters, postmarked months ago, and addressed to one Hob Jarvis, who had skipped to Mexico one jump ahead of the sheriff. Mae had brought him to this vacant house to go through his pockets!

"Good Lawd!" he groaned. "Losing them jingle-spurs Flora gave me! And I don't dast tell no one a woman done robbed me!"

He reeled dizzily through the dusty, blistering street and into the coolness of the Seven Up. There, he downed three slugs of whiskey and felt better. Next, he took his horse to the livery stable, and went to Ling Hung's restaurant and had the Chink cook him six eggs and a dozen cakes and a heap of bacon. Thus refreshed, he began to get the answer to his problem.

He headed for Hipolito Pasalaguas' saddlery. The place was dark and smelled of leather and dust, but from the shadows gleamed the matchless silver work the Mexican artist fashioned for the adornment of saddle and bridle and bit.

A full-breasted woman with sleek black hair hip-swayed from the back room. She had amorous lips and her curves were made for close clinches.

"Como está, señor!" she greeted, her dark eyes lighting up as she saw that the customer was young. "W'at you want? The nize silver bridle? So fine for the handsome *caballero's* horse, no?"

"No," said Grimes. "I want some spurs with bells on 'em. Quick. Where's yo'—?" He paused, wondering whether this was Pasalagua's wife or daughter. She was young, but with generous, mature curves, particularly olive-hued domes that peeped from her *camisa*. "Anyhow," he went on, "I craves a pair of spurs with bells and little eagles on 'em, and a bull's head—"

"Ah—but of course! Like the spur which the Señorita Lawson order from my father, no?"

"Precisely, m'am."

"Come with me, *señor*. I am Camila Pasalaguas." In the back room, she gestured toward a bench. "Please wait ontil my father returns. He weel make you the spur, only three-four days, eef he work quick."

Grimes groaned. She might as well have said as many years! Camila seated herself beside him and sympathetically wondered, *"Que pasa, señor?"*

He explained. Her eyes brightened, and her appraisal became warmly approving. "So you are the *querido* of the lovely lady? Ay, how romantic! Sooch a beautiful girl!"

Camila had nice legs; the thin skirt that clung to their curves left no doubt of that. And she had tiny feet. But she was not wasting any time in trusting to her luscious fascinations to dazzle the young *caballero* who, despite his coffin-shaped face and gangling build, had won the heart of an heiress. Feminine curiosity prompted her to learn the secret of this tow-headed boy's success as a lover. Before he knew it, she was so close to Grimes that he could not move away without being rude.

Then he did not want to move, particularly when Camila's shapely arm slipped about his neck. "I weel persuade my father to hurry weeth the spur," she purred, her free hand stroking his cheek. "But not too fast."

Her smile was a generous expanse of ivory. She kissed him, and the soft contact of her against his shirt front left him only one move. There was enough of Camila to give any man's arms plenty to do. Grimes could not humiliate Flora by letting any Mexican girl think he was awkward.

It was a warm, clinging kiss that left them both gasping. Camila's eyes sparkled with inner fires. Grimes' pulse was pounding. This was going too far, but he did not know how to stop. He tried to speak of silver spurs, and edged toward the end of the bench.

Camila figured that if the young *caballero's* startling success arose from his coyness, no bleached blonde *Americano* could beat her in boldness. So she slipped after him, arms extended and breath coming in quick gasps.

The clinch was a success, but the bench upset. Grimes landed on the dirt floor, all tangled up with Camila. She laughed and let go long enough to get her skirt somewhere below her knees. The back door kicked open. Grimes tried to talk about spurs and at the same time regain his feet, but there was too much of Camila hampering him.

Her father had returned via the back door. *"Caramba!"* he yelled, jerking a knife. "I weel give you spurs! W'at you do weeth my daughter?"

The hurled blade raked Grimes and thudded into the door jamb. Camila kicked loose, bounded to her father and blocked the impending riot. "He is a customer. He wants the silver spurs!"

"I weel sell him nothing!" stormed old Pasalaguas. "Not for wan million pesos! Out of my house, or I weel keel you!"

Grimes could not risk any further publicity about his loss, so he dashed to the front before Pasalaguas could find another weapon. This was the last straw! There was not a saddler within a hundred miles who could replace Flora's gift.

HE SPENT THE REST OF THE DAY AT THE SEVEN UP, SITTING IN A CORNER AND GLARING AT the world. Toward sunset, he admitted he was beaten. Better ride back to the Rafter-FL and face the music.

124

He went to the livery stable to get his horse. Lola was waiting at the door. "Don Simon," she began, "you mus' listen. I 'ave been look for you all over. Even if you hate me, I am grateful, no? I weel tell you—that *cabron,* Barry, he have the girl get you dronk and steal your spur. She ees leave joost now to ride to the *rancho* to return them while you wait for the new one."

"What's that?" Grimes caught her by the arm. "You mean, Mae's pretending she's looking fo' me, an' she stalled all day, so's it'd look like I'd—"

"Si, si!" chattered Lola. "Like you have spend mooch time weeth her."

"I'll blow that dang Barry's guts around his backbone!" Grimes threatened as he swung to the saddle. "Onless I catches that no-good wench and stop her afore she gits to the ranch."

"Wait—Don Simon—I tell you—"

But Grimes was not waiting. The clatter of the gray gelding's hoofs drowned Lola's cries. Whatever she had to say made no difference. She'd told him plenty. As he galloped out of town, Grimes caught the whole trick: Barry, failing to have him killed in the brawl at the lunch counter, had set Mae on his trail to extinguish Flora's affections.

Flora had been broadminded about the comb and *serape* in Grimes' room. But one more accusation, and the game was up!

Wrath drove him on. He made no effort to pick up Mae's trail. She would have to go through a cleft in the hills between Skunk Valley and the Rafter-FL. His only chance was to overtake the lovely traitor in the rocky pass that would force her mount to walk.

The gray gelding, quirted at every jump, struck sparks from the outcropping rocks of the slowly rising trail. Far ahead, Grimes saw a rider, caught the sheen of silk, the glint of ruddy hair. In his eagerness to close the gap, he paid no attention to the rear, and thus did not see the rider who stubbornly followed.

He pressed on, gaining every moment, until the fugitive, sensing pursuit, plied spur and quirt. Grimes, having ridden his horse to the limit, was left behind. His beast was badly blown. He stumbled, lurched, his trembling legs unequal to the ever increasing hazards of the steep ascent.

Grimes finally cleared the first crest, then down into a narrow ravine. Mae was out of sight and hearing. Long shadows obscured the rocky cleft as the descending sun leveled off with the higher peaks. Forced to a walk by the lameness of his horse, Grimes noticed what in haste he would not have seen: furtive, momentary motion in the rocks of the ledge that commanded the trail.

The breeze brought him the faint odor of horses, a whiff of tobacco smoke. A fusillade echoed from the gray walls; but Grimes was already diving from the saddle. He had sensed the ambush with a split second to spare.

A triumphant yell followed the whine of ricochet bullets. Stung by a slug intended for his rider, Grimes' horse reared, slipped, crashed heavily against the tongues of ragged rock. Dismounting on the off side had cost Grimes an instant's delay, and though he landed with drawn pistol, he was numbed by the shock.

The thrashing of the wounded animal savagely jammed him into a crevice.

But the lack of answering fire convinced the drygulchers that they had finished the deadliest gunner in Skunk Valley. They scrambled from cover just as the frenzied gelding extricated himself from the jagged rocks.

Grimes' .45 poured three blasts of flame. The foremost bushwhacker pitched from the shelf, looped once, thudded to the rocks, his skull popping like an overripe melon. But the others had seen that sudden motion; the surviving two flattened, firing as they dropped.

Their wild shots finished Grimes' horse. They now had him bottled up. The beast's carcass, however, afforded him shelter from his enemies. They would have to climb up to a higher position to smoke him out.

That made it a deadlock until darkness veiled the narrow ravine. With poor light, neither besieged nor besieger could risk a break.

The last patch of direct daylight finally was swallowed. Though the range was not extreme for pistol fire, it was now a severe test of skill.

Grimes bobbed up from cover, hands raised. Though he knew that they wanted his hide, not his money, he yelled, "Ef yo' gents wants my poke, yo' kin have it."

One snapped at the bait, and shifted to make the most of the chance. Grimes' body twisted and flashed to his gun. A bullet smacked against the rocks. Grimes fired. The gunner yelled, slumped back to cover. The other, a split second late in taking advantage of a free target, was blinded by chips of granite before he got into action.

Barry, beyond any doubt! No mistaking that voice. Grimes, though untouched in the exchange, cursed wrathfully. "Ain't kilt neither of them! My pappy'd lambaste me fo' sech rotten shooting!"

There was no more thought of escape; no thought of anything but killing Barry. It was now plain that he had been tricked into pursuing Mae so that he would ride headlong into an ambush. And Lola had egged him on!

"The next time they's any talk of gratitude," he gritted, "somebody's getting took to pieces by hand!" Rage gripped him. In that failing light, he could not shoot, except toe to toe. He yelled, "Barry, yo' gol danged sculpin, git on yo' laigs, I'm coming to git you!"

He broke cover, zigzagging across the rocky floor. He was heading for the narrow path that led to the shelf on which the snipers lay. He might make it, but in his blind fury, he didn't much care, as long as audacity gave him Barry's scalp.

Two pistols roared, spraying the ravine with slugs. Grimes, a dancing gray wraith, held his fire as he wove and ducked, darting from rock to rock. Once, he flinched, raked by one of the slugs that rained about him.

Then the fire ceased. The fools had emptied their guns! Grimes leaped to the treacherous path. Get them while they fumbled! Barry was cursing, groaning. Empty shells, frantically jacked from smoking Colts, tinkled down the incline.

"Yo' ___ ____ buzzards!" howled the boy from Georgia, popping two shots into the shadows that concealed his enemies. "I'm a-comin'—"

He had them buffaloed, though his shots were wild. Rocks clattered as he scrambled to make the most of those hard-won seconds. Another dozen yards—

126

Then a yell; freezing fear. "Gawd, look out!"

It was Barry. From overhead came the ring of dislodged rock. A boulder landed on the shelf, tearing half of it away. In that mad instant, it seemed as if a woman had screamed. A man lurched forward, and Grimes' gun roared itself empty. The riddled body caught him off balance. Entangled with his enemy, he bumped and bounced a dozen feet along the path. He snatched at a ledge, but missed. The dead and the battered pitched over the edge, rolled to the ravine floor.

Though Grimes landed on top, the shock paralyzed him. His head was a whirling misery. Somewhere, he heard a low moaning; a woman's voice. A match flared. It was Lola who bent over him. He blinked, licked his lips, groped for words.

"Sanctissima madre!" she cried. "You are not dead! From up there, I think the rock hit you, too! *Ay de mi!* I feared—"

"Huh? Whut's that?" He sat up, and by the light of the match saw that it was indeed Barry's riddled body that had cushioned the fall.

"You would not listen," she sobbed, flinging her arms around him. "I try to tell you, ees something fonny. The trick. But you ride like hell to get the spur! So I take the short cut, only I am too late. I think they have keel you. Then I see you rush, and I roll the rock on those *cabrons.* "

"Mo' gratitude, eh?" he muttered, slowly realizing that, in his fury, he had not noticed bullet grazes and the cut of flying rock chips. "Honey, I reckon I done misjudged you."

He tried to rise, but weakness made him cling to Lola for support.

"Stay here. I weel get the horse. Their horses." She kissed his bruised lips, stroked his blood-caked hair. "First, I get some water."

But Grimes' head was swimming in the gloom. The only reality left in that powder-reeking ravine was Lola's plump, generous body. He slumped, blindly groped for support, and found it. Dimly, he heard her murmuring endearments, felt her pillowing his battered head against her bosom.

Then the clatter of hoofs startled him. Lola screamed, but could not disengage herself from her exhausted burden. Grimes groped for his Colt. Then, in the moonlight that was stealing over the ragged rocks, he recognized Flora. Her hair was all gilded, and her legs gleamed white as she bounded from her panting horse.

At her heels came two Rafter-FL cowpunchers.

"She brought me the spurs," gasped Flora, kneeling beside him. "But she'd heard the shooting, and suspected you'd been dry gulched. So she confessed the trick. But what's Lola doing here?"

The girls eyed each other in the brightening glow. Grimes explained, concluding, "They's been too dang much gratitude and too many cooks. It's all tangled up. But Lola heaved the boulder jest in time. Look at Barry's gun, ovah theah. He'd jest finished loadin' it, an' I reckon the other skunk was ready fo' me as well."

Flora recoiled, eyes wide, breasts suddenly taut against her silken blouse. She exhaled a slow, deep breath, wearily shook her head. She had nothing more to say about Lola, despite the light that smouldered in the Mexican girl's dark eyes as she challenged them all to dispute her right to Grimes.

Flora turned to Barry's battered body, fished from her blouse a pair of silver spurs with little bells. She buckled them to the dead man's heels, then laughed bitterly and said, "That's where they belong, Simon. And that's where you belong. With Lola."

"I think not, *señorita,*" the Mexican girl cut in. "What I did ees for the gratitude. He ees a *caballero,* and not for me to keep. Now I weel get my horse, and you can find yourself the cook somewhere else."

For a moment, she clung passionately to Grimes' lips. Then she choked a sob and dashed into the further shadows. They watched her scale the ravine, where her horse was waiting.

"Simon," whispered Flora, eyes agleam, "maybe we can start all over, in spite of too many cooks."

•••••

Grimes Gets Religion

The afternoon blaze of southern Texas made a simmering hell of the barn, but the tow-headed boy from Georgia didn't notice the heat, nor did the girl whose pale golden hair brushed his face.

Flora's blue eyes were misty. The flush of her cheeks reached all the way down to the ripe young breasts that peeped from the low yoke of her thin calico dress. But, suddenly, she pulled her mouth from his, gasped, "Simon . . . stop. . . . Let me go. I hear someone comin'."

Simon Bolivar Grimes let her slip from his arms. He said, plumb disgusted, "If we was married, we wouldn't have to sneak away like this. Why in tarnation hell ain't we done got married weeks ago?"

Flora shook her lovely blonde head and sighed. "I been worried, darling. First thing I know, I'd be a widow. You're always quarreling."

"Honey," the bewildered boy protested, "I ain't shot no one fo' dang nigh three weeks—"

A raucous voice cut in from the barnyard: "Simon! Gol dang yore hide, wheah are yuh?"

It was Flora's father, drunk as usual. The young foreman of the Rafter-FL made a dive for the door. As he emerged from the barn, he gulped, "I jest come in from—"

Lawson cut him short. "Take this yere money and go tuh Skunk Valley an' put a bet on the fire enjine contest. Shake a hock, Simon, an' whut yuh lookin' so red about?"

"Ah—ug—uh—I reckon it's the sun. Right smart hot," groped Simon Bolivar Grimes as he pocketed the buckskin pouch of money and went to saddle up.

He arrived in town shortly before sundown. It was a sprawl of 'dobe shacks that had won its name, years previously, from the uncommon number of skunks found by the early settlers. Laughter, honky-tonk music, the spatter of broken glass and the occasional roar of a .45 fired through some saloon ceiling gave it animation to accord with the ever-increasing number of cowpunchers who came larruping down the dusty street.

Most of them were from the adjoining ranches, but many came all the way from Poison Well, whose new steam-powered fire engine was to compete with the old hand-operated outfit that was the pride of Skunk Valley. Grimes, going from bar to bar to cage bets, was convinced that Flora's father must be suncrazed!

He came to that conclusion at the edge of the plaza, where the red enamel and polished brass of the Poison Well fire engine gleamed in the glow of kerosene lanterns. Near it was the battered, weather-beaten outfit of the local volunteer company. Not a chance, hand versus steam!

Grimes bit off a chew of tobacco, instinctively hitched his .45s so they sat comfortably for a quick draw, just in case the contest was to decided by blazing guns.

A soft voice purred from one side, "Hello, honey—all alone tonight?"

It was Doris Winfeld. She lived across the railroad tracks with her hatchet -faced mother, Sarah Winfield. Her red hair reflected the lantern glow; a few freckles lent a piquant touch to her heart-shaped face, and she was not over-painted.

Grimes' pulse quickened as his approving, downward glance probed the pale blue silk blouse. Doris was heftier than Flora, but it was all very nicely arranged, which he sensed when she leaned close to him.

"Ma's been hoping you'd drop in some night," murmured Doris. Her soft fingers caressed his hand and a sigh lifted her breast enough to fill out, very alluringly, the filmy blouse.

Grimes' pulse stepped up, but he'd resolved to avoid further complication. Every time he tangled with some gal, he had to shoot a passel of her lovers, and it got monotonous, finally. So he said, "How's yo' maw these days?"

Doris' soft laugh was tinged with bitterness. Wondering about her maw, when he ought to be thinking of a clinch! "Oh, she's all right. Though her pet skunks sort of rile me sometimes."

Sarah Winfield's pets, though perfectly disciplined, had always annoyed Doris. They discouraged visitors. "Ef yuh don't like my pets, yuh kin move out," the old lady had often cackled. "An ef yuh lives as long as I have, yuh'll larn that skunks is better company'n men!"

Doris' chin went up a notch and she wriggle-hipped from the plaza. Grimes called after her, "As soon as this heay contest is over, I'll be seein' yo' all."

Doris flashed a torrid smile over her shoulder. That hip sway never failed. She added, "I sure hope you win, Simon."

Later, the contest was called. The spirit of it got Grimes' mind from Doris' shapely figure, and the way the evening breeze had whipped her skirt against her legs.

The competing fire engines were backed up to pools that remained in the almost dry bottom of Skunk Creek. Whichever pumped its pool dry first was winner.

Skunk Valley made good progress at first. The Poison Well department had not gotten up enough steam. Yells and hoots urged the brass-hatted volunteers to bend on the clanking pump; a mighty jet of alkali water lifted over the crowd, spattered the dusty, baked soil beyond. Then Poison Well got its stride; the hiss of steam, the red glow from the fire box, the triumphant "yippee" of the visiting chief boded ill for Grimes' bet. Their pool was rapidly lowering, despite the wheezing and grunting of the valiant local department.

Suddenly, time out was demanded. "We all ain't got enough fuel fer our biler," contended the Poison Well chief. "Yuh jaspers snitched some tuh git us acrost a barrel."

Oaths rumbled, crackled. But before guns came into play, the judges went into a huddle. They compromised, "Whilst Pisen Well hustles more wood, Skunk Valley can git its breath again."

But Grimes already knew that his prospective father-in-law's bet was as good as gone. And judging from the wrathful muttering, a brawl was impending. One more riot and Flora would turn him down, cold. But he'd be damned if he could see Skunk Valley flim-flammed into a loss. Neither would he turn his back on a possible battle. The Grimeses of Georgia never declined a challenge.

A caressing hand slipped up over his shoulder, and a warm', resilient, feminine curve pressed against him. It was Doris. She whispered, "Don't you worry, honey. I seen a contest like this, up in Topeka. You bust in and tell them they don't need to hustle wood. They can get sides of bacon, straw from the livery stable and some of Ike Wilson's roofing tar. Hustling wood is just a stall so the water can rise up in both pools, and the hand pump men'll all get tuckered out from the race lasting too long."

That was shrewd. Grimes approached the committee, whispered a few tense words. A mighty whoop shook the night. The chairman announced that Skunk Valley's hospitality was beyond reproach; the municipality would contribute fuel of the finest and costliest, and be damned to expense!

So Poison Well's department fired up with sides of bacon and tubs of lard; great clouds black smoke gushed from the smokestack, dark red flames lashed back every time the fire box door clanged open for a fresh charge.

It was working too well! The fierce hissing of exhaust steam, the ominous dropping of the water level of the Poison Well pool brought wrathful glances from the Skunk Valley citizens. Grimes smelled trouble, plenty of it.

Doris was gone. "Gol dang her," he muttered, "she done that on account of I wouldn't come to see her." The perfidy of women was poisoning him. Sweat popped out on his forehead. He'd be lynched!

But the hiss of steam ceased abruptly. Poison Well was cursing, fuming, prodding the fire with a slice bar. There was no draft, and smoky red flame lapped back at the frantic firemen as the door opened. Skunk Valley, not quite understanding, bent lustily on the old fashioned pump, sending a triumphant jet of water far over the city hall.

Bartenders came dashing up, feeding the firemen whiskey as they worked. Pistol fire stabbed the air and men sang in many keys. Then it leaked out: "By gravy, Grimes saved the day! That there bacon and sich-like made so damn' much soot it plugged the flues!"

Before Poison Well could remedy the difficulty and regain the steam pressure that had been lost by the long delay, there was a gurgling and sucking; the Skunk Valley fire hoses became limp. The pool was empty! A mighty hooting shook the night. The bets were won, and local honor vindicated!

But Grimes had no time to collect. There was a ragged roar of pistol fire. A man dropped. Grimes, stung by a passing slug, went wild. Both guns ablaze, he danced into action, a long, lean, gangling terror whose crackling .45s cut down the crowd like a combination binder!

Poison Well fled, leaving its fire engine behind. A score of lead-raked victors scooped Grimes bodily from the ground, carried him to the Silver Dollar Saloon.

Grimes did not see Doris. Long before the night was over, he could see nothing at all. And around sunrise, strong hands piled him on his blue roan mustang; his saddlebags were loaded with gold pieces collected from the stakeholders.

He was far too sick and weary to stay for the barbecue and funeral, and when he reached the Rafter-FL to hand old man Lawton the winnings, he learned that the news of the battle had traveled ahead of him. Flora informed him that she was through forever; a trickster and a gunslinger would never be her husband!

They wrangled well into the day. Old man Lawson, now well drunk, was no handicap. That afternoon, Grimes began applying the higher forms of argument.

"Don't touch me!" Flora ducked his arms. He made a grab at her, but his fingers slid off her shoulder, caught and ripped her neat little calico dress to the waist . . . even tore the flimsy undergarment that only half concealed her breasts and now flashed white as they trembled behind the ripped silk.

She doubled, looped. Grimes caught her. Panting and gasping, she finally ceased struggling and sobbed, "Simon, darling—I do love you—honest, I do— but you're getting to be down right disreputable. Honest, you're worse'n Billy the Kid ever was—"

He stroked her unbound hair, drew her closer, kissed her until her sobs became gasps of ecstasy. But before that went far enough to help, Flora went on. "Simon. I'll marry you—as soon—"

"Soon as which?" he cut in.

"Soon as you reform, for keeps, darling," she solemnly promised, pulling together the tattered edges of her dress. "My maw worried for years about dad gitting killed."

"But he's alive and drunk right now," frowned Grimes.

"I know he is. But maw worried herself to death. And I would, too, about you. Please, Simon—"

"Dad blame it!" he sighed, stamped halfway to the door. "I'll do anything. I'll even git religion."

"Simon—do you mean it?"

"I sho' do, honey."

"Then I'll tell you. Suppose you go to Skunk Valley for a month. You've got lots of enemies there. And if you keep out of quarrels for a whole month, I'll marry you."

And in another moment, he was in the saddle, heading for Skunk Valley.

AS HE RODE, GRIMES' FACE LENGTHENED. HIS PROBLEM WAS COMPLICATED. DESPITE HIS having won a victory for Skunk Valley, he had a heap of enemies there. And he was cursed with a reputation. The gunslicks that passed through that tough little town would not be able to resist the temptation to win fame by slapping leather with Simon Bolivar Grimes.

"Dad blame it!" He sighed gustily, shook his head. "How kin I duck fights? Folks jest seem dead set on quarrelin'!"

Then he was distracted from his pondering. A buckboard was rolling toward him. Despite the dust kicked up by the span of mustangs, he caught a breathtaking glimpse of the girl whose tiny feet were cocked up on the dashboard. She had lovely legs. The tricky breeze whipped her skirt over her knees. She had no eye for Grimes, being too busy with her horses.

The boy from Georgia promptly developed palpitation of the heart. That dark-haired girl had some figure. The jolting of the buckboard made her breasts quiver delightfully.

An' she's powerful purty in the face, too, was his afterthought as she swung to the road fork that led north. *But she ain't got much sense, driving all alone.*

That road passed through a stretch of *malpais* infested with owlhooters who would, out of sheer cussedness, rob a skunk of its smell. Grimes hesitated. "'Tain't any of my broth. Maybe her friends is outlaws. Me, I'm keepin' my nose clean, jest fo' onct."

The buckboard's dusty course led toward the narrow pass that gaped like a black saber slash in the hills. Grimes' resolution wavered. It would be dark before she emerged. He loped after her, keeping a discreet distance. An independent Texan girl would as likely as not tell him to mind his own business; she could take care of herself.

His hunch was better than he realized. The distant rattle of the wagon, now swallowed by the curves of the pass, suddenly ceased. A scream echoed from the rocks. Gruff voices rumbled. Grimes sank the spurs home.

He galloped into the pass, a gun in each hand. Once around the curve, he saw that three men had dragged the girl from the wagon. Her dress was shredded and her hair was streaming. Her screams drowned out the sound of Grimes' approach. Her assailants, eager to close in on the shapely armful of half-bare flesh, were getting in each other's way.

"Git back, Baldy. I seen her fust!" snarled a black-bearded hulk. One paw jerked a comrade aside; the other snagged the girl's bare shoulder.

"Jasper, yuh ______!" raged Baldy. "I'll—"

Grimes holstered his guns. Here and now, he'd make good. No more killing. In a flash, he was out of the saddle. Three long bounds carried him into the tangle of hairy outlaws. He leaped like a cougar, and his yell made the rocky walls echo.

One of the ruffians was catapulted out of the melee. Still tugging at his gun, he looped, landed on neck and shoulder. He crumpled in a still heap. Jasper and Baldy had their hands so full they could not slap leather. The boy from Georgia was slugging and booting them into shreds.

The girl emerged from the skirmish. Grimes tripped, but held his throttling grip. An avalanche of flesh followed him to the rocky bottom. Jasper's eyes were bugging out like saddle pegs. *Chunk!* Grimes bashed the ruffian's head against a rock. "I'll put a dimple in yo' skull, you dad blamed—"

He sprang from a crouch. Jasper, bloody and cursing, had his gun unlimbered. The girl screamed, brought a rock down on Jasper's head. That lesson in geology had its point. Grimes scrambled to his feet, reeled dizzily, tried to look through the blood that was trickling down his forehead.

He leaned weakly against the wagon wheel. The girl's violent exertions made her breasts swell deliciously with each panting breath. Through the remains of her shirtwaist, little patches of white flesh gleamed. "I don't know what I'd have done," she gasped.

Abruptly, she screamed, hurled herself against Grimes. He went down in a flurry of limbs, just as a pistol blazed.

Baldy had recovered from his fall. His first shot had missed. Grimes tried to go for his own gun, but an armful of girl was draped all over him.

That hair-line shaved from an instant seemed ages long.

Oh, Gawd, ef I could git my gun! The prayer flashed through his mind. No lips could have said it fast enough; for the bellow of Baldy's .45 was followed by the squeal of the frightened mustangs. One, his rump creased by the slug, bolted. Grimes desperately rolled clear of the wheel, taking the girl with him.

Too late, he got his gun. Baldy, tottering groggily in his boots, had no time for a second shot. The plunging team bowled him over. He howled, disappeared over the lip of the deep drop that the trail skirted. Baldy hit the rocks for the last time, three hundred feet below.

The girl tried to piece her dress together; then laughed shakily, abandoned her vain efforts and knelt beside Grimes. "Oh—you're hurt—all over—let me help you—I'm Anna May McDavid—"

"Me—I'm Simon Bolivar Grimes, ma'am," he stuttered, heart rising in his throat. She leaned over him as he sat there. She really should have taken time to pin that shirtwaist together. "An' I come closer to prayin' than I have evah since I left Gawgia—"

"Praying?" Anna May moved back, approved the bandage she had fixed.

Grimes told her about why he had gone into action without his guns. "I know it sounds foolish like, ma'am," he concluded apologetically.

Anna May's brown eyes were wide and she shook her head. "No, I think it's awfully noble, trying to reform. Your prayer was heard. Dad will be awful proud to know you. God-fearing young men are so scarce out in this wild country."

"So is gals like you." Grimes was rapidly recovering.

Anna May gasped when the invalid's arms closed about her. But her instinctive recoil lasted no more than an instant. She flushed all over, closed her eyes, turned up her lips for another kiss. "Oh—you mustn't! . . . Mmm . . . please," she breathed. "But—just once more—Ohhhh . . . . Watch out—that one—the one I didn't hit—he's coming to!"

Grimes settled that with a well-aimed kick. But when he turned from the booted chin of the first down, Anna May sighed regretfully.

"No, Simon. We mustn't." She meant it; moreover, this really was no place for kissing. He helped her to the buckboard, and as he joined her, she went on, "Dad will be so grateful. And I know he'll want you to testify."

"Testify!" Grimes sat bolt upright. "Honey, is he a jedge?"

"No. An evangelist. When he preaches tonight—he'll convert a heap of sinners by telling how your prayer saved us both. Simon—won't you testify?"

In the last glow of sunset, Anna May's uplifted eyes glowed and her sweet face was transfigured. Grimes forgot that girls like her were made to be kissed. "Honey," he promised, "I'm getting religion. Wheah is yo' father's camp meeting?"

"In Poison Well," answered Anna May.

Grimes' teeth gritted. Poison Well, of all places! But he was too stubborn to back down, and the girl's sincerity had touched him deeply.

SOME HOURS LATER, GRIMES' HAND WAS HALF CRUSHED IN THE STRONG GRASP OF Anna May's lanky father. The thin-faced evangelist's eyes glowed like coals in deep caverns as he thanked the boy.

"Shucks, reverend," stuttered Grimes, "wa'nt nuthin a-tall—"

"Don't say *reverend,*" corrected McDavid. "I'm not ordained. I'm not a preacher or parson or anything. I'm just trying to tell this wild country that there is something better than robbery and bloodshed and sin."

The evangelist's meeting was held in the two-by-four ballroom in the second floor of the town hall. The thin, fluting notes of the little melodeon Anna May played blended with the raucous voices and the squeaking fiddles in Poison Well's eleven saloons; but McDavid's deep voice blotted out sounds of riot and bawdy mirth.

Grimes, sitting up well to the front, watched the devout and the curious filter in. A few dirt farmers, store keepers, the local schoolm'am; none of the hard-riding, hard-bitten cattlemen of Poison Well were among the thirty or forty who planted themselves in the rickety chairs. Grimes was relieved. Then Hiram White, the fire chief, stalked in, head bandaged, and his one visible eye balefully glaring.

They exchanged nods, hostile stares, but the chief did not interrupt the services. Grimes, shaky inside, got up on his feet to testify. His voice almost failed him when he saw four members of the defeated fire company hobble in. Though still sore from their wounds, they were capable of using their belted guns.

McDavid's upraised hand commanded silence so that all might hear "Brother" Grimes' testimony. But the boy from Georgia could fairly taste the silence; a lot of it wasn't pious ecstasy, but the grim thoughts of tough jaspers who still hesitated at shooting up a religious service.

"So divine providence sort of give me a hunch," boomed Grimes. "So I follows this lovely gal, jest in case."

"Amen, brother!" intoned the harness maker. "Halleluiah!"

"An' then, when I heerd the riotin' and ungodly shoutin' of them lawless gents, I goes larrupin' in with a smoke pole in each hand—"

"Glory be to God!" bellowed the blacksmith; McDavid had aroused devotion in everyone who had a single lurking speck of it.

"But I says, I ain't killin' more people, not even skunks, so I shoves both plough handles back and sails in with both fists—"

"Amens" punctuated the testimony; but the fire chief and his four men chewed tobacco, spat and glared. The town marshal, shotgun in the crook of his arm, came in. He'd heard Grimes was in town, and there would be no outbreaks if he could help it.

"An' theah I was, on my back an' dizzy, an' that son of Belial stompin' toward me to blow my head loose afore I could git my jammed gun. But the dawg gonest luck—"

"The hand of the Lord, Brother Grimes," corrected McDavid.

"Anyway, the fuzztails bolted an' knocked the dirty skunk over the edge—"

"Praised be the Lord!" chorused the front row, eyes all agleam.

"So I'm taking that sign," Grimes was warming up to his theme. "I ain't killin' no one from now on, I'm plumb through with gunslinging."

He unbuckled his belt, draped his guns across the pulpit, wiped the sweat from his forehead. The fire chief and his companions gritted their teeth. Nobody but a low down polecat would take advantage of five wrathful gents and shuck his guns that way, so he couldn't be shot at. The town marshal sighed from his boots and walked out, puzzled.

Grimes' testimony was a success. But as the little gathering finally broke up, he became uneasy. "I'm gittin' out of this town. It's hostile. Ain't no sense lookin' fo' trouble."

He turned a deaf ear to McDavid's protests. In another moment, he was in the darkened doorway of the side entrance. Anna May tiptoed to kiss him. As they clung to each other, he saw the gleam of tears in her eyes. "Simon, darling," she sobbed. "Ever since you kissed me, I been feeling sort of—oh, I wish you could come with us—"

But Grimes remembered Flora. So did Anna May. Silently, she turned. He ducked to the back door of the livery stable, got his horse. "Yuh better slip out tother way," whispered the hostler. "They's ten jaspers waitin' jest outside of town on the Skunk Valley road tuh beat the pie-wadding outen yuh fer shuckin' yore guns. They claims yo're a ___ ____ coward."

GRIMES MADE A DETOUR. THUS IT WAS LATE THAT NIGHT WHEN HE REACHED SKUNK VALLEY to begin his thirty days of probation.

The hotel clerk, Clem Wiggins, blinked when the battered boy stalked into the lobby. "Simon—whut the hell yuh doing, runnin' around plumb naked—whar's yore guns?"

Grimes explained. Wiggins gulped, muttered, "Teched in the head!"

Grimes spent a tense day in his room. Then he revolted at hiding out. And while he had enemies aplenty, the friends whose bankrolls he had saved in the fire engine contest with Poison Well were there to protect him during his "running around plumb nekkid."

That evening, emerging from the Seven Skunks Tavern, Lem Frost, the post-master, accosted him. "Simon, that redheaded Doris Winfield writ yuh a postcard asking yuh tuh see her. I ain't got it with me, but I done read it in case I seen yuh after office hours."

Grimes thanked the inquisitive old chap and set out for the redhead's house. His horse was slightly lame, so he walked toward the outskirts of Skunk Valley. He whistled blithely. Tarnation, he'd been getting absent-minded, wasting all that time.

A light gleamed across the railway tracks. It came from the squatter shack which old Sally Winfield had defended, years ago, with a shotgun; the town had long since conceded the right that the owner of the vast *rancho* had disputed until he died and a corner of his partitioned estate had blossomed into the municipality of Skunk Valley.

And then dark figures cropped up out of the gloom. "Yuh kain't chuck yore guns and figger yo're duckin' us," growled one of the men who hemmed him in. "We ain't killin' yuh, yuh consarn' coward, but we're fixing yuh fer that slick work—"

He had an answer for that; a hard fist that spattered teeth all over an acre of prairie. Stubbornness, and wrath at their misunderstanding of his motives, kept him there. He stood and fought.

That is, he stood for a while, shifting, countering, pounded dizzy as he slugged against the odds. They knocked him flat, but he came up again, bloody, battered, raging.

A woman's voice shrilled above the grunts and gasps of the men from Poison Well. "Simon, you idiot! Ain't you got any legs!" It was Doris. She screamed, "You dirty low-lifed cowards—Simon—run—you idiot—"

He picked himself from the trampled ground. He cast aside the tradition that the Grimeses never fled. He remembered the great-great-grandfather Hezekiah Grimes had been a cross-country runner of distinction. So he made the most of the distraction. He bolted, and before the men of Poison Well knew what was happpening, the red-haired girl and their victim were high tailing for the house beyond the tracks.

"Come on out an' fight," they howled at the slamming door.

"Git out, you ornery polecats," screeched Ma Winfield.

The muttering outside drew back. The toothless squatter cackled, watched her daughter sponge the dirt from Grimes' face, then hobbled into the adjoining room.

Alone at last. . . . Doris did not say that, but her eyes meant it. She was shocked at Grimes running around without his guns, but she was glad. She brought out doughnuts, but he checked her when she started to make coffee. "Ef yo'all don't mind, I'd ruther have whiskey."

There wasn't a drop in the house, but Doris had better stimulants. She draped herself on his knee. Grimes did not hear the creak of the rickety lounge; he was too much interested in her. A glimpse of the breasts peeping from the vee of her blouse made him forget his bruises, until her avid lips found his battered mouth.

He drew her closer, felt the pounding of her heart. Doris was panting, "Simon—darling."

Grimes wasn't scairt, but he was trembling from thrills, first hot, then cold, that raced from the ear tickled by her red hair and all the way to his boots.

And then, for a while, they forgot everything but the warmth of kisses. It seemed rather odd to Grimes, as his arms closed about that throbbing bundle of love, that he'd gone to such lengths to win Flora—

A rock crashed through the window. "Come on out an' fight," howled the men from Poison Well. "Yuh cain't hide behind that gal's skirts!" They said a lot more, but Grimes was through listening. These were times when the mildest gent got sore, regardless of resolutions.

Then Ma Winfield came raging out. More rocks hammered the walls of the weatherbeaten shack. "Simon," she cackled, "what—?"

"Gimme a gun!" he stormed. "Gimme a axe—gimme—"

"You'll get killed," wailed Doris, as her mother entered the room.

But Grimes missed the length of shapely leg that was disclosed. Ma Winfield dug a pair of rusty six-guns from a locker. She tossed them to him, and he caught them in mid-air.

Grimes kicked the door open. Rocks rained about him. And then fire gushed from both hands. "Git out, yuh gol danged sculpins—"

Answering shots roared from the gloom. Lead spattered the windowpanes, chewed slivers from the door jamb. Grimes' guns were strange. They spewed lead wildly, and in the gloom he could not pick his mark. But he poured slugs at the flashes as he charged. The raiders from Poison Well yelled, broke; they ran, except for two whose gizzards had stopped a Boot Hill ticket in the gloom.

Grimes, panting and triumphant, turned back, slapped the smoking old .45s on the table. "This here resolution stuff is a snare and a dee-lusion," he announced, eyes flickering right and left as though looking for more enemies.

Ma Winfield took the hint. She cackled, hobbled to the rear.

"Oh—that was wonderful, Simon," cooed Doris. "They won't come back."

With Doris' voluptuous curves pressed against him in the gloom, he didn't care much who heard their kisses. Nothing like having a right smart gal setting a fellow right. Texas was a fighting man's country. . . .

A RAPPING AT THE DOOR AROUSED GRIMES. DORIS STIRRED LANGUIDLY IN HIS ARMS. HE must have fallen asleep because it was dawn, and the early light gilded her red hair, cast a lovely rose-flush over her legs and the white curves that rounded the top of her slip.

"Sounds like company," muttered Grimes.

He blinked, stumbled to the door.

He was looking at the rising sun—and at a sawed off shotgun that Sheriff Anson pointed at Grimes' shirt front. "Don't try it!" warned the grizzled lawman. "Got yuh covered."

That was gospel; and Grimes' borrowed guns might as well have been a mile away. Doris gasped. Grimes demanded, gulping, "Whut the tarnation hell, sheriff—"

"I got a warrant fer yuh. Shootn' Porky Willis and Slim—"

"Dad blame it!" He was outraged. "That was self defense."

"No go, Simon. Not after pertending yuh warn't slinging guns no more. Yuh might jest as well have drygulched them gents outright."

The sheriff herded Grimes to Poison Well, the county seat. The door of his cell had scarcely slammed when the town was abuzz with the story of his capture. The Poison Well Herald ran off a special edition: *Notorious Gunner Dragged from Arms of Red-Haired Sweetheart.*

Grimes cursed, stamped on the extra. Fat chance now of Flora hiring a smart lawyer. And because of the feud between the towns, no one in Skunk Valley would venture a jail delivery. A cordon of special deputies was posted to guard against that.

That afternoon, Anna May came to visit the prisoner. Grimes reddened to his ankles. The deputy said, "M'am, bein' as how yo're a ee-vangelist's daughter, I guess we kin let yuh in tuh exhort with the culpert. But don't yuh dast give him any more religion!"

"Simon, darling." The door slammed behind her. "Father's awful put out about your backsliding. He's coming later—"

"Honey, tain't no use. I ain't going to live long enough to need any sperityul consolation." He spat a jet of tobacco juice at a cockroach, looked up, appraising her trim ankles, the delightful flare of her hips and the soft roundness of her bosom. "Lot of things I ain't living long enough to need much of. They's sho' sot on hangin' me."

Anna May seated herself on the bench beside him, slipped a slender arm about his neck. She pressed close, kissed him until he gasped; and with the deputy looking right at them.

"One more like that," he whispered hoarsely, "and audience or none—! Any gent would look tother way—"

"I ain't no gent," chuckled the deputy. "Anyway, I heard how yuh kissed yore way outen the last jail."

And then Grimes learned things about Anna May's ardent embrace. She was slipping a file down his shirt front and whispering, "I'll try to have a horse waiting by that cottonwood next to the courthouse." Then, aloud, "I got to go now, darling. Dad's coming later."

GRIMES, HOWEVER, HAD LITTLE CHANCE TO USE HIS FILE. POISON WELL WAS CLAMORING for an immediate trial, so they could hang the prisoner before sunrise. The sheriff and a squad of deputies marched him across the square, to the weatherbeaten courthouse. The Poison Well fire department had turned out in full uniform. The town was in full fiesta!

The prisoner vainly scanned the crowd for one friendly face. He couldn't find

Anna May. He did not look for any other. The judge pounded his desk with the butt of a six-gun. Hank Hensley, clerk of the court and leading bartender, read the indictment.

"Whereas, the aforesaid Simon Bolivar Grimes, the same being the prisoner at the bar, did on or about sometime last night maliciously, feloniously and with pure dumb luck shoot the pie wadding outen Porky Willis and Slim Corrigan, the people of this yere county charges the aforementioned prisoner with murder and gittin' religion under false pertenses."

"Listen here, listen here, listen here!" thundered the bailiff, setting aside his half-drained pint. "The honorable court is here and now in session."

"Guilty or not guilty?" boomed the judge.

"I never said I'd got religion!" protested Grimes.

"The aforesaid prisoner pleads guilty!" declared the court. "Whar's yore attorney?"

The lanky juror who was spinning a lariat while waiting for the testimony to be presented gave Grimes the creeps. That rope wouldn't be playing much longer. Grimes' glance swept the court, seeking one friend who would slip him a gun so he could go down like a man, making at least a break for the plaza.

"Hell, jedge, I'm pleading my own case." The setting sun made the sweat on his forehead gleam like small rubies. It wouldn't be much longer. He couldn't think of a stall. He gulped, "Ef one of yo' would jest loan me a gun, I could sorta make a better argument—"

But his wry grimace did not win him a single chuckle; not a single grin that might help him turn the day. Once, he'd worked that gag. But this dang town was downright prejudiced. The judge's pistol butt whacked down. "Order, prisoner at the bar! This ain't no time fer levity!" He turned to the jury. "Yuh gents done read the evidence in the special mawnin' paper. Whut's yore verdict?"

"Guilty as hell, yore honor!" the twelve good men chorused.

It was grotesque; utterly unreal. But they weren't playing. The judge was rumbling, "Hanged by yore gol dang neck till yo're plumb dead, an' Gawd have mercy on yore soul. Sheriff, take the sculpin out an—"

Hoofs clattered across the plaza. Men whirled, drawing guns. A shriek from the doorway blotted out "do yore duty." Doris Winfield burst into the courtroom. In sheer astonishment, the spectators made way. Another scream of protest. Her red hair trailed after her as she ran down the aisle, bounded to the platform.

"Judge, you ornery skunk, you can't hang that boy! It ain't right—"

Her voice cracked hysterically. She laughed, clawed at her blouse. It ripped as she reeled, spun dizzily, sprawled at the prisoner's feet. "Order!" choked the amazed judge. "Bailiff, git that gal out— Sit down, or I'll fine every last one of yuh fer contempt of court!"

But Poison Well was not sitting down. Doris' skirt was bunched about her hips, and her hysterical writhing threw her half-bared breast into bold relief. Grimes gawked, flashed a glance at the window. But the way was blocked. The crowd was packed thicker than ever. One move, and they'd forget that shuddering white flesh.

They did. That was when the opposite window rattled up. A wicker basket catapulted into the crowded room. Seven furry black beasts with white stripes down their backs, bushy tails elevated, emerged from it when the lid rolled clear. An old woman cackled from outside, "Jedge, yuh coyote, see how you like my pet skunks!"

Maw Winfield's polecats did not like the court. They did not like Poison Well. They scattered. So did the crowd. Grimes was lost in the scramble. Men howled, coughed, clawed at their smarting eyes. Windows spattered to bits as stout gunmen plunged headlong through the panes.

"Simon—grab it and git—"

Doris' hysteria was over. From somewhere out of the tangle of her disheveled clothes, she pulled the rusty six-shooters. "My hoss is out there—git, Simon—"

He did. But he ran afoul of the saving skunks. They played no favorites. One deputy, breaking at the first alarm, stood his ground, pulling down with his shotgun on the scented fugitive. But both Grimes' borrowed weapons blazed. He whirled, sprayed lead into those who remembered they had guns.

That checked the rush. He never knew whose horse he mounted. He had to fork it on the run. Wild shots zipped about him. Then the rising dust fanned out behind Grimes and he headed for the open prairie.

"Gawd bless them polecats," he gasped, holding his nose. "Otherwise, she'd sho' never of gotten to me with them guns!"

FROM AFAR, THE LIGHTS OF SKUNK VALLEY WINKED AT HIM. BUT GRIMES SHOOK HIS HEAD, pinched his nose. "Kain't go back to Flora. Not this way. Anyway, they's been too dang much scandal . . . she'd never believe I done reformed."

• • • • •

Hungry Valley

SIMON BOLIVAR GRIMES WAS FROZEN NEARLY STIFF BY THE TIME THE SUN PEEPED OVER the hills and gave him his first look at Yavapai County. Wooded hills rose from the cactus-dotted plain. Their verdure was in striking contrast to the painted buttes that shimmered to the south.

"They may be gold in them hills," he grumbled, "but danged ef I wouldn't ruther find me some po'k sausages, and six aigs, and a dozen flapjacks, and a gallon of cawfee.

"An' I ain't seen a dang-blasted nugget yet. Somebody's been lying to me. . . ."

He saddled his pinto mustang and tightened his belt as he rode down into the valley. Grass was still scarce, and the cow critters looked like walking skeletons. His coffin-shaped face lengthened some more. There was hardly enough meat on any one steer to make a sandwich.

And then he sat back in the saddle and stared. A girl was riding from a shadowed chasm in the valley wall. Grimes reached for his spyglasses, and focused them.

His China-blue eyes brightened. He raised his hat, brushed back the straw-colored cowlick that reached well into his forehead, and forgot both gold and hunger. The powerful binoculars seemed to bring her within arm's reach. She was slim-waisted and supple; and, while her boots and riding skirt gave him no more than a suggestion of her legs, the vee-necked blouse was far more generous. The motion of her horse made her firm breasts quiver attractively.

Grimes spurred the pinto forward. But as he rode, he frowned perplexedly and shook his head.

"Whut in all git-out is that gal aiming to do?"

She had dismounted and removed the short-handled pitchfork tied to the saddle. Then she cut off clusters of needle-pointed yucca leaves with a hatchet, and touched a match to the lot. As they blazed up, she walked over to the nearest cactus with the forkload of fire and let the blaze lick the broad blades.

The lowing cattle came staggering toward her. When the fire died out, she took her hatchet and lopped off branches of cactus. The starved critters greedily ate that strange fodder.

"Ef this ain't the gol-dangedest country!" he muttered. "Feedin' roasted cactus fo' breakfast."

The girl did not perceive his approach. The low, slanting rays of the sun dazzled her. It brought ruddy copper glints from her wavy hair, and gilded the fine line of her throat.

"Purty as a picture," Grimes told himself.

And then something hit the pommel of his saddle and went whining into the air. Grimes took a nosedive for the ground, just as a second slug whacked over the mustang's back.

He landed with a gun in each hand, but that was wasted effort. The far-off smack of a rifle mocked him. The marksman was way beyond pistol range.

The girl heard his wrathful yell, and dropped her pitchfork.

"M'am," he shouted, rolling to the shelter of a boulder, "whut in tarnation's happening? Is them gol-danged range wars busted out again?"

For a moment, she regarded the lanky stranger with the bullet-riddled hat. Then she holstered the .38 she had drawn, turned her back on Grimes and faced the draw from which she had emerged. She waved her red kerchief and cried, "Yoo-hoo, dad! It's just a dumb-lookin' pilgrim." Her voice carried through the still air with the power of a hog-caller's.

Grimes reddened to his boots. He flared, "Listen here, m'am, I never fed cow critters toasted cactus! You'd oughta be ashamed of yo'self!"

"Come on from behind that rock." She smiled at his indignation, and, somehow, Grimes' wrath evaporated. "Dad's just naturally suspicious."

Grimes inched from cover. The bombardment had ceased, but he divided a wary eye between the lovely redhead and the lowing cattle. The girl added, "I'm Velma Crawford, and this is my dad's spread, as far south as you can see. Only, Gabe Yeager and his boy, Lem, are trying to run us out. That's why our critters are so starved. Nothing else to feed them but cactus."

"Yo' pappy crippled?" he wondered.

Her dark eyes became somber. "He had a hoss shot under him, and his leg isn't right yet. So I'm tending to things myself. If you burn the spines off the cactus, it's not such awful fodder."

So Grimes gave her a hand, using a forked stick instead of a pitchfork. And as they went from one cactus cluster to the next, he told her of his search for gold. Velma shook her head and said, "Simon, Aztec Hill's the toughest mining camp in Arizona."

"I ain't afeard of that," he declared. "Not after not eating for as long as I ain't et regular!"

A sudden drumming shook the mesquite at his right. Grimes drew his bone-handled Colt. Its blast blotted out the whirring of wings. A jet of feathers spurted from the sand, a yard clear of the brush.

One quail, slow in taking wing, had lost its crested head.

"Good heavens, Simon!" the girl gasped in amazement.

He leaned from the saddle and came up with the bird. He explained, "That's how I been eating fo' the last couple days."

Her eyes widened. "Don't you ever miss them?"

Grimes looked apologetic. "Well, yes, sometimes. The fool birds run like all git-out, but it ain't really so bad excepting when they got sense enough to take wing right away."

That left Velma incredulous but thoughtful, and when they finally rode into the draw, in the mouth of which stood a log cabin and barn, Velma said, "I wish you'd stay awhile and help me and dad.

"We own this spread. We bought it. From the Yeagers, the dirty crooks! Dan Yeager robbed a train and they sold this piece of ground to raise money to defend him. Then he busted out of jail a few months ago and a posse shot him full of holes. And ever since then, they've run us off all but this back corner, and our critters are starving—we can't keep any cowpunchers."

"Honey," Grimes cut in, "I'm a peaceable cuss, but I'm allus ready to slap leather on the side of law an' order."

"Oh, you're a darling!" They were past the low cabin, and leading their horses into the barn. Velma's arms slipped about Grimes and she arched herself against him, murmuring, "You'll help us, really?"

Her red lips set his blood to racing, and the warm contact of her lithe young form sent thrills racing all the way down to his boots. But when he drew her closer, she broke away, flushed and panting.

OLD MAN CRAWFORD LOOKED HARDBITTEN AND SATURNINE AS HE SAT THERE, A Winchester across the arm of his chair and one bandaged leg propped up on a soap box. He apologized, "Bub, yuh looked like that lanky skunk of a Lem Yeager, so I cut loose. I missed yuh, account of this game leg keeps me from gittin' set fer good shooting. But yuh look purty young tuh be a gunslick."

"Shucks, I ain't."

"I seen yuh knock off that quail with yore .45."

"Yo'd oughta see my grandpappy, back in Gawgia. I allowed I'd bring you a bit of a delicacy to tempt yo' appetite. I'm plumb sick of the dang things."

Soon, he was tying into the larruping flapjacks Velma heaped on his plate. Crawford was saying, "Them Yeagers is nacheral-born skunks. They's a barb-wire fence acrost the valley. I cut it, and got winged. Now we're getting starved out."

LATE THAT AFTERNOON, GRIMES RODE DOWN THE HUNGRY VALLEY. AT THE END OF AN hour, he came to a barbed-wire fence. Two men were repairing the extensive cutting done by Crawford. One of the cowpokes was short and stocky; the other, lean and hatchet-faced.

"Where yuh fixing tuh go, stranger?" demanded the short plug-ugly.

"Me, I'm lookin' fo' the boss of the Lazy Y," Grimes guilelessly answered, though he wheeled so as to put his horse between them and himself as he dismounted. "I'd sho' like to get myself a job."

"He don't need no riders," growled the taller of the two hardcases. "Where the hell you from, anyway?"

"Skeleton Creek, Texas." Grimes was sizing up the further stretch of cactus-dotted valley. It did not look much better than the upper portion, though it might furnish adequate fodder for Crawford's critters. "Ain't no harm axing him, is they?"

Slim snapped, "Better run along, bub!"

"Danged ef you gents ain't the most onsociable critters!" Grimes chuckled. "Shucks, I'll help y'all finish stringing this yere wire, and then yo' kin show me the way."

"Purty smart, ain't yuh?" They both eyed him. A glance flashed between the two cowpokes. Shorty said, "Grab a holt of this wire."

Grimes reached for the barbed strand, to put it into the stretching ratchet. But once his hands were full, Slim's gun flickered out. The trigger was filed off for fanning.

"Reach fer yore ears, hub! Shorty, git a riata and tie this jughaid. I reckon Yeager'd like tuh talk to him a little."

"Hey, whut the tarnation hell!" Grimes blinked, and his hands slowly rose.

"We seen yuh help that Crawford gal feed her critters this marnin'," Shorty said. "Yo're too all-fired dumb tuh live. Now git them hands down so I kin tie 'em."

Slim was grinning at the gangling boy. He had not seen him picking off a quail on the run.

Grimes' hands came down, but with a swiftness that no eye could follow. Both guns were out before Slim could thumb the hammer. Shorty's warning yell was swallowed by a thunderous drumming. He dropped the rope and made a dive for his gun.

But Slim was buckling. When he did get the hammer back, it slipped and fired a slug into the ground. Shorty bent in the middle as though kicked in the stomach. Once-twice-thrice—his body jerked as .45s followed it to the ground.

Grimes wiped the sweat from his forehead and sourly regarded the blood trickling from a crease in his calf. "Dad-blamed skunks ruinin' a pair of fo'ty dollar boots!"

What had given him confidence was Slim's filed trigger. A gun fanner depends on terrifying volume of fire, plus luck.

Grimes reloaded and holstered his guns. Then he strung the three strands of wire, closing the gap in the fence. For the time, it would keep Crawford's starving critters from straying and being killed. Once the Yeagers were well in hand, the barbed wire would be removed.

He loaded Slim and Shorty on his own horse and headed over the crest. He planted them under a heap of rocks. Thus, their disappearance would set the Yeagers wondering; whereas the discovery of the corpses would leave the boss of the Lazy Y with no doubt about their fate.

THAT EVENING, GRIMES CONTENTED HIMSELF WITH ANNOUNCING TO HIS NEW FRIENDS THAT the fence might as well stay where it was for the time, and that, in due course, he'd snoop around.

During the meal, Velma regarded him with wide, dark eyes. A question hovered on her red lips. And one was blazing in Grimes' mind. Every time her calico skirt shaped itself to her sweetly curved legs, or drew close enough to outline her pert bosom, the query became more urgent.

Under guise of helping her with the dishes, he drank in the scent of her hair,and thrilled from furtive, burning contacts whenever he brushed against her.

"Simon!" she snapped as he dropped the second saucer. "You're as clumsy as a bear cub! Run along and get out of my way."

He spread his blankets in the barn. In the darkness, he debated: "Resolved that Jawn Crawford oughta be deef instead of havin' a game laig."

Finally, he crept from between his blankets and slipped into his boots. She'd surely have sense enough to leave her window open. But as he reached the granary door, a spindle of whiteness came undulating through the gloom and past the horses.

"Honey," he softly said, "I been thinkin' a bit myself—"

"Simon!" She turned, and they found each other in the dark. "I was afraid you'd do something foolish. Dad's awful suspicious. So—"

"You came out to warn me?"

She could not answer. He had her in his arms. Only her frail night garments and trailing hair were between them. They were both gasping when they slowly relaxed from that clinging embrace. Then Velma said, "I saw your boot had a crease in it. And I smelled burned powder when you came in—"

"Shucks, honey. That wa'nt nuthin. Jest argufying with a couple of Yeager's gunslicks."

"Ohhh—what happened?"

Her upturned face was hardly more than a white oval in the gloom, but he caught the gleam of her eyes, felt the warmth of her encircling arms and the flattening of her breasts against his shirt front. Before Velma could repeat her query, he had drawn her into the granary.

"Simon, you mustn't!" she panted.

He kissed her breathless. A shudder of ecstasy rippled down her white length. She moaned softly, exhaled a sigh that had started as a half-articulate protest. But before Grimes could draw her down on his knees, Velma had slipped from his arms.

"Don't! Or I'll call dad," she gasped.

That outraged Grimes. "Gol blame it," he reproached, stung by such last minute heartlessness, "you done promised me—"

"You promised *me,*" she cut in, "to help us."

"Fo' two cents, I'd let the Yeagers run y'all out," he hotly flared. "If that's yore gratitude. . . ."

"Simon, darling," she pleaded. "Don't be hasty."

Velma was wavering, and the world looked better to Grimes. But not for long. The granary door jerked open. Crawford, dragging his game leg after him, had a lantern in one hand and a six-gun in the other.

"Git outen here, yuh young skunk!" he howled. "And yuh, yuh shameless hussy, git back in the house afore I whales yuh black and blue!"

He fetched Velma a hefty smack. She tried to duck it, but tripped over a sack of oats. The loveliest legs in Yavapai County reached for the ceiling and her flimsy gown flew toward her hips. But Grimes missed most of the fascinating scramble. He flared, "Gol dang it, me riskin' my neck, an' you sneaking up, spying!"

"I warn't spying, yuh young whelp!" stormed Crawford. "When that gal run yuh outen the kitchen, I knowed she was pertending! Yuh got jest enough time tuh get yore gun belt outen the hayloft and saddle up yore cayuse. And I'll be watching with a shotgun."

He hobbled out of the barn, dragging Velma with him.

A few minutes later, Grimes was saddled up. Crawford, good as his word, was sitting on the steps with a double-barreled ten-gauge Parker.

"You and yo' daughter kin stay here and eat cactus!" Grimes tossed over his shoulder. "Me, I'm going to Aztec Hill to find me a gold mine, and y'all are going to wish you was dead!"

GRIMES FOLLOWED THE OLD STAGE ROAD THAT HAD BEEN ABANDONED SINCE THE railroad had built a spur line to Aztec Hill. That morning, before he had decided to team up with the Crawfords, Velma had told him of that little-used route.

Finally he came to a fork in the trail. He paused there to size things up. She had not mentioned this detail. And before he had a chance to pick his way, a voice commanded from the gloom, "Lift your hands, or I'll blow you loose from your hoss."

Darkness concealed the lurker. Grimes was in full moonlight. He promptly obeyed, good humoredly observing, "Ef yo'all are looking fo' money, I'll do my dangedest to help."

A slight figure in Levi's emerged from cover. A kerchief hid his face and muffled his low, husky voice. "Who be you? Where you from? Where you going, and what are you aiming to do when you get there?"

"Me, I'm Simon Bolivar Grimes, from Kennesaw Mountain, Gawgia. I'm heading fo' Aztec Hill, and I'm aiming to dig myself a passel of gold."

The kerchief did not quite muffle a sniff of disdain. "I don't reckon you're the one I've been expecting." The gun was deliberately lowered. "The trail to Aztec Hill is over thattaway. You sure you'd know gold if you saw it?"

"My Uncle Jason," Grimes answered, "allowed I wouldn't know it if I fell over some."

"Light and set a minute," invited the stranger. "I'll show you some ore."

Grimes dismounted, grinned amiably, and advanced a few paces. Even in the moonlight, he looked as though he were about to stumble over his own feet. He was curious about the lurker. Somehow, it just did not make any too much sense.

The stranger fumbled in the pocket of a dudish-looking silk shirt and said, "Better strike a match."

The flame flared yellow. Grimes leaned forward for a closer inspection of the glittering object held in his accoster's hand. It was a brass cartridge case.

"Whut the hell—!"

Whop! A pistol barrel smacked down on his head. He grunted, pitched to his knees, and sprawled on the rocks, not quite face down. But the heavy crown of his Stetson had somewhat broken the shock. Furthermore, it took at least a caulking maul to do more than passing damage to a skull worn by one of the Grimeses of Kennesaw Mountain, Georgia.

Deft hands searched his pockets. Grimes was still groggy, but wrath and instinct moved him. The rock he clenched gave weight to his fist. He swung, and more swiftly than the stranger could duck.

His assailant crumpled and slumped across him.

Then Grimes did get a shock. That was when he felt the resilient contact of a firm but well rounded bosom.

"Fancy bandit!" Grimes muttered. He jerked aside the kerchief and exposed a face framed by the shimmering black hair that the broad-brimmed hat had thus far concealed. "Danged if she ain't a purty critter."

He got a long glimpse of the ivory curves that peeped from the open neck of the disarrayed shirt. "Built jest like that picture in Lafe Wiggin's saloon, back in Skeleton Creek. It's Gawd's blessing I didn't have a chanct to swap lead with her."

If this was a female road agent, she could have robbed him without tricking and sapping him. And if she had planned to kill him, she need not have given him the wrong direction to Aztec Hill—which is exactly what she had done, he now perceived. The other fork never could have been used by a stagecoach.

Something was going on down the line; something which apparently would interest an audience, Grimes then and there decided to investigate.

He took the *mecate* from his mustang's neck and deftly trussed the girl. Before he had completed his work, she began to stir, and her eyelids fluttered. Grimes, however, was riled by Arizona hospitality, so he carried on.

Her first cry of alarm was stifled by her own kerchief. He neatly gagged her, although he was relieved to know that her heavy hair had kept her from suffering any serious injury. Then he muffled his mustang's hoofs and led the beast, ready at any instant to pinch its nostrils at the first sign of a betraying whinny.

There must be a horse nearby. The masked girl could not have walked very far in those dainty, high-heeled boots.

Presently, he rounded a turn and emerged from the wooded section. The valley below was flooded by moonlight. In the thin Arizona air, the glow seemed almost a pallid day.

Two horses were cropping grass as they stood there, reins over their heads. A tall man slowly paced some fifty measured strides, then returned to the white rock on which his gunbelt lay. In his hands he held a forked stick.

He paused for a moment, slowly turned, then again advanced.

Grimes shook his head. "Looks like that gent's witching fo' water."

At least some of it made sense. His grandpappy, Gideon Grimes, had often used a hazel fork to pick the location of a well, though there were some who allowed peach was just as good.

He retraced his steps. The girl was writhing and struggling with the horsehair *mecate*. Grimes said, "Take it easy, m'am, and I'll let you loose. Danged ef y'all ain't the most onsociable folks I ever did see, setting aroun' waitin' to whop a gent so's he won't watch another gent witching fo' water."

"What's that?" she gasped, catching her breath as the kerchief was jerked loose. "Doing what?"

"Witching fo' water, m'am," Grimes repeated.

"Of course." She blinked "What'd you hit me with?"

"With my fist, m'am. Only, I had a rock in it. Watn't until you sort of tumbled right over me that I noticed you was a lady."

"Oh—" She made a hasty gesture, both hands reaching for the open neck of her silk shirt.

"I told you who I was and what I was aiming to do," he went on. "And seein' as how we done whopped each other, it's only fair fo' to even things off all around by telling me who—"

"I hit you," she snapped, "because you looked too pig dumb to shoot! It's none of your business who I am."

"I whopped you," he said, "because I didn't have a chanct to see how dang sweet a critter you are. But you ain't telling me who you are?"

"I am not!" She glared at him, lovely and defiant.

Grimes drew her to him before she could wriggle away. Her resistance served only to emphasize every sweet young curve from her knees to her collarbone. They were both panting when he found her mouth and kissed her until she gasped. "M'am, ef you don't tell me who y'are, I'm kissin' you some more. And I ain't— promising—when I'm quitting—"

Smack! One hand, wrenched free, fingerprinted his cheek. But Grimes got a fresh hold. A better one. And the curves pressed against him inspired his efforts. She tried to bite him, but that did not quite work.

Finally, she relaxed in his arms and looked up at him, eyes misty and wide in the moonlight. "I'll tell you, Simon," she murmured. "And if you'll promise to forget all about this witching for water, I'll do more than that."

Her eyes, the caress of her voice, the half-restrained abandon of her supple figure were all a fascinating promise. Stung by the ingratitude of the Crawfords, Grimes was ready to accept it.

"Honey, if it makes that much difference to you—"

"Oh—you will, won't you?" She was eager, and her nails sank into his wrist for a moment. "If my brother knew you'd gotten past me and watched him, he'd kill me. He'd be looking for you, and you'd probably kill him. The way you outwitted me—" She shivered. "I'm glad I wasn't a man!"

For a moment, he looked down at her, and told himself that she would be dazzling in feminine attire.

"I'll meet you in Aztec Hill. Go around the long way," she breathlessly continued. "Over that trail to the right. Wait for me at the Navajo Hotel." A long, clinging kiss, and, as she gently broke away, she whispered, "The name's Blanche, and hurry, before my brother comes over the hill. Hurry, Simon!"

SOME TIME AFTER GRIMES HAD LEFT THE ROAD FORK, A RIDER CAME TOWARD THE intersection. He had a lead horse. Before Blanche could accost him, he had whistled softly. She emerged from cover. "Any luck, Lem?"

He cursed bitterly. "Moon's shifted too much. Nary a sign of anything buried. Gawd, if that damn' posse hadn't kilt poor Dan afore he had a chanct tuh let us know whar he buried the loot!"

"Don't that hazel fork work?"

Lem spat. "Sometimes I reckon it's jest damn' superstition, trying tuh find gold er water with witchin' rods! Anybody pass by?"

She nodded. "A two-headed yokel. Too dumb to come in out of the rain."

"Whar—whut'd yuh do with him?" Lem's eyes flickered right and left.

Blanche laughed. "He was a stranger heading for the mines. So I made a date with him to meet me in Aztec Hill. He'll get killed off in that town afore he can say Jack Robinson. Before then, you'll find the cache of coin."

Lem dismounted. "Damn it, mebbe it'll take us weeks tuh find it. Why the hell do yuh reckon we fenced off that valley? When Slim and Shorty's hosses come in alone, I went out tuh look-see. That dang Crawford's hiring gunslicks! One of 'em kilt my boys."

As he spoke, he struck a match, crouched, scanned the earth. Another match . . . another. Then Lem cursed in a low, bitter voice. "I could knock yore head off! Lookit them hoofprints! The same cayuse that hauled Slim and Shorty away from whar they dropped."

"What?"

"Ain't no mistake! That towheaded jasper yuh figgered was so dumb kilt the two of 'em. I found their guns. They both was fired, but he outshot 'em. By gravy—!" He leaped to the saddle. "I'll git that young skunk—"

"Lem, for God's sake, don't!" Blanche pleaded. "If he outshot Slim and Shorty, you haven't a Chinaman's chance.

"I got a date to meet him, and I'll be there. He is pig-stupid, even if he is a freak with a gun. You catch him with me at the hotel and it'll be easy." Her eyes blazed venomously; the Yeagers were a poisonous tribe. "Defending my honor, see. No questions asked."

Blanche, riding back with her brother, told herself that Grimes could not have gotten the real point of Lem's moonlight search; that the young lout's southern gallantry would keep him from breaking his promise of silence.

He'd be dead before he saw the Crawfords again.

AZTEC HILL WAS LIKE A COWTOWN THAT CELEBRATES PAYDAY THIRTY TIMES A MONTH. Honky-tonk music blared. Girls with bare shoulders and half-exposed breasts

150

leaned from windows to hail Grimes as he rode up the ascent of the main street. Shills invited him into gambling houses, but he ignored the bait.

At the Navajo Hotel, he turned his horse over to a hostler and went into the bar to get a drink. Rather, he wanted a bottle. The long ride had cooled his indignation against the Crawford's. It hadn't really been Velma's fault. And he could hardly blame her crusty father.

He took his bottle to a table. The more he thought about Blanche and her brother, the more peculiar it seemed. Witching for water made sense, but the secrecy did not. He muttered, "Mo' I think about it, mo' it seems like they watn't so dang far from the Crawford spread."

The whiskey warmed him. It mellowed his wrath into half tolerance. But for his curiosity about Blanche, and a growing determination to learn more about her moonlight activities, he would have risked returning to the Crawford ranch.

A cat-footed fellow with restless eyes and long hair edged in through the swinging doors. His entire manner was that of a tomcat entering a strange alley. Yet he moved with a swagger; and his hands seemed ready at any instant to dart toward a pair of pearl-handled six-guns.

The rumble of voices and the tinkle of glass suddenly subsided. Only the raucous blare and whine of the orchestra remained as men glanced uneasily about. Speech was resumed, but a discreet mutter of voices from an adjoining table informed Grimes that this stranger was Red Eye McGee.

The town marshal came in, shotgun cradled over his arm.

McGee seemed to have anticipated that. He had his back to the bar. The man behind the star advanced and said, "Ain't got any Arizony warrants fer yuh, Red Eye. But step keerful in this yere town."

McGee spat ostentatiously. "Jest here fer ree-laxation, marshal. I don't reckon yo're *quite* hankering tuh try fer any New Mexico reward money."

He reached into a pocket of his embroidered vest, carefully unfolded a poster. He handed it to the marshal and added, "Here's one I picked up in the post office in Gallup."

The marshal snorted. "I reckon yo're not stayin' long enough fer me tuh git any extradition, huh?"

Grimes did not hear the answer. A gust of fragrance cut into the fumes from his glass and a soft arm slipped about his neck. An olive-skinned girl whose generous breasts peeped above her bodice was leaning a powdered shoulder against him; she was half on his knee, and the luscious curve of hip and thigh made Grimes catch his breath.

"You buy me wan dreenk, no?" she wheedled, making a theatrical gesture toward adjusting the tall comb that glittered from her high piled black hair.

He dumped the untasted chaser to the floor, filled the glass with whiskey. Carmencita tasted the blazing stuff. "Ohhh . . . and you dreenk it, like that!" Her dark eyes widened in admiration. "You are work in the mine, no?"

"I'm aiming to do a mite of prospecting."

"You 'ave the what you call grubstake?"

"Shucks, no. I'm payin' fo' my own digging."

"Maybe," Carmencita wheedled, "you come to my room? W'ere we can 'ave the quiet. I weel tell you of the good mine, w'ere you can buy the share. Ees my brother own the mine—verree rich, but—"

Her shoulders shrugged, and the ripe contents of the spangled bodice throbbed deliciously.

"You, there!" bawled a brusque voice. "You deaft?"

Red Eye McGee was addressing Grimes from the bar. The boy from Georgia blinked. He had to get his eyes in focus after lifting his glance from Carmencita's dimpled knee, and the garter peeping from the short skirt that had climbed upward, exposing olive-hued luxury.

"Bub," said a hoarse whisper from his right, "fer Gawd's sake, speak up! He's axing yuh tuh drink with him. Ee's bought drinks fer the house—"

"Who's deef?" Grimes demanded, thoroughly riled. "Listen, yo' skunk—"

"Why—yuh ornery, tow-headed son of—"

And then Red Eye's jaw sagged, and his hands froze. A gun was lined up with his cartridge belt. Grimes had drawn with one hand and swept Carmencita aside with the other, so that she sprawled in a frothy heap on the floor.

"Put 'em up, you two!" roared the marshal, his sawed-off shotgun covering the scene.

But it was Carmencita's upward-pointing legs that broke the tension. From exquisite ankles to luscious calves, the dancer had what it took to quell an incipient riot. Grimes lifted her to her feet. The marshal said, "Young feller, yuh better git outen here. He warn't expecting yuh tuh draw, or yuh'd be daid. An' gittin' the drop on Red Eye's plenty enough apology fer his slip of the tongue. But don't let it go tuh yore head, son."

So Grimes took his girl and his bottle from the barroom. When Carmencita wanted to take him to her quarters, he rebelled. "No, m'am, I'm hawg drunk, an' I got some impo'tant business tomorrow in this hotel, an' I aims tuh be here on time. . . ."

WHEN GRIMES AWOKE, IT WAS NEAR SUNSET. HE HAD A SPLITTING HEADACHE. CARMENCITA was gone, and so was his buckskin poke of gold pieces. Nothing remained but some silver. He tottered down to the general store, drank two cans of tomatoes.

As he was returning to the Navajo Hotel, he saw a familiar figure on the horse that was toiling up the steep street. Blanche was keeping the engagement.

Grimes ducked into the bar, took a double whiskey and followed it with half a bottle of Worcestershire sauce. Carmencita, peeping from the unpatronized dance hall, looked confused, then ran forward, saying, "Oh, Meestair Grimes, I 'ave the message for you—"

"Shut up!" he snarled, heading for the door.

As Grimes headed for the stairs to the second floor, he caught a passing glimpse of Red Eye McGee and a lean, lanky fellow in a huddle in the corner. But that fact scarcely registered.

Once in his room, he lathered his face and hacked the fuzz from his chin. The dozen cuts were wasted. He could have taken his time. Time stretched. He wondered what in tarnation was detaining Blanche. She'd said the Navajo . . . or had it been El Dorado?

He sat down to think it out.

Finally, there was a gentle tapping at his door.

Blanche, resplendent in shimmering coral satin, fairly floored him with heady perfume and tantalizing glimpses of white curves smiling through the frothy lace that made up the top of her decolleté gown.

So that's why she'd taken so long to show up!

She smiled at his incredulous admiration, and as she let him take her small hand, she murmured, "I wanted you to see me dressed up."

"Yo're so gawd-awful gorgeous," he gulped, "I feel plumb foolish."

"Nonsense, Simon!" She was in his arms, a scented length of beauty that clung to him like a coat of paint.

"I wisht yo'd put on yo' old clothes," he protested. "I feel like suthin'll get ruined ef I teehed you."

Nonetheless, he held her so close that she gasped, "Oh—that gun's hurting me! As long as we're not on the street, you won't need your weapons."

She slipped from his embrace, undulated across the room. He watched the ripple of her figure and gaped as he abstractedly shucked his guns and hung the belt over a chair back.

"All you can catch is fair enough," she tempted, edging back.

"Dawg gone!" He lurched after her—clumsily knocked her handbag from the dresser. As he retrieved it, he felt the stubby revolver that rounded it out. But he did not bother to snap the clasp. Not with that shimmering length of scented beauty extending its arms to him.

But, before he scooped her to his chest, she let out a scream that shook the shingles. She clawed at her gown, ripped it to the waist.

"Whut the tarnation hell?"

It was not a hornet that had inexplicably gotten into the upper reaches of that revealing gown. He learned that when the door slammed open. A tall, lean man was at the threshold. Blanche screamed, "Lem! Wait!" She did not quite succeeded in flinging herself clear of Grimes.

Lem's gun was out, but he could not yet risk a shot. And those deadly bone-handled Colts were far from Grimes' reach.

Lem! That registered. Lem Yeager! And a glimpse of the man behind Yeager clinched it: Red Eye McGee, his flickering gesture a blur of pearl and blued steel. He knew that he could cut things close.

But McGee did not know about Blanche's handbag. As his fancy gun twinkled into line, Grimes was moving in the opposite to the expected direction. McGee's shot no more than grazed the boy from Georgia.

The handbag spurted flame. Grimes had got his hand on the stubby revolver and fired through the bag's end. Lem Yeager's gunblast riddled the wall. He reeled, blocking McGee. The desperado had to shift to get in his next shot.

Blanche lunged to block the yokel who had blossomed fire when he had no right to. But she was too late. The smouldering handbag spurted doom.

McGee pitched forward. He had been riddled from front and rear. A woman screamed in the hall. Feet pounded up the stairs. Grimes leaped like a panther, sprawling Blanche across the bed, her ripped gown tangling with her ankles. When he saw who rushed across the threshold, he lowered his own gun. It was Velma.

But she kept the smoking six-gun as she cried, "Oh—darling—did he hit you—?"

"Nary a scratch!" But Grimes was wondering at the partnership between Red Eye McGee and Lem Yeager. He told of the witching for water—though he skipped a lot of details.

The marshal, behind her, cut in, "I bet he was looking fer loot from the train robbery. I seen those skunks with their heads together down in the bar."

He made a dive for the late Red Eye, and began going through his pockets.

"Honey," demanded Grimes, "how in blazes y'all git here?"

She ignored Blanche's whitefaced wrath. She said, "I got sore at how dad treated you, so I came to Aztec Hill to find you. A girl by the name of Carmencita said she'd seen you—"

"Uh—uh—gol dang it, don't you believe a word she says," gulped Grimes.

"So when I heard you had a business engagement," Velma went on, sweetly malicious, "with a girl whom she described as having had a heart to heart talk with Lem Yeager, I got worried. I came up just as—"

"Witching fer water, hell!" whooped the marshal. He waved a blood-stained sheet of paper. "It's a map showing whar the loot's buried. Plainer'n day, the hull mess. When Dan Yeager got shot, he'd given McGee a map tuh take tuh his sorrowin' relatives, who'd been spending some time hounding the Crawfords to cover up that diggin' around by moonlight."

"Simon," sighed Velma, pensively eyeing Blanche's ruined gown, "if I had clothes like that—"

"Honey," declared Grimes, "when I git my reward money—I mean, when we gits it fo' smokin' out them t'rantlers—"

"We'll buy Carmencita a dress, and then you hide behind the woodpile while I talk dad into common sense."

• • • • •

Nomad's Trail

"SIMON," PANTED THE RED-HAIRED GIRL, "YOU MUSTN'T—OH, YOU'RE TERRIBLE, TAKING advantage of me, this way—"

Velma Crawford wriggled out of his embrace. She was lithe and shapely, and the neat calico dress plainly revealed the rise and fall of her breast.

"Honey," protested Simon Bolivar Grimes, "y'all done took advantage of *me*. I was aiming to go to Aztec Hill with yo' pappy, but y'allowed yo'd be lonesome, so I stayed, an' I ain't been tuh town sence I shot Lem Yeager."

"You know the only reason dad left us alone here while he went to pay off the mortgage was because I'd promised him that I'd make you behave. And now—"

She raised a trembling little hand to the neck of her dress; it was still all awry, giving fascinating glimpses of curving, soft flesh. The gesture somehow made her dishevelment even more alluring. Grimes rose from the sagging couch in the corner. She was in his arms before she could fend him off.

He was deceptive that way; gangling, tow-headed, apparently always on the point of stumbling over his own feet, he somehow connected.

"Don't," she pleaded, vainly squirming and wriggling.

His first kiss missed her red mouth and reached her throat instead, but Velma was sweet and luscious all over. His arm tightened about her. The close embrace thrilled the half reluctant girl, in spite of herself.

"Simon," she moaned, "please don't—you know I like you to kiss me—only I oughtn't to—"

Then she began sobbing. Trickling tears salted the kiss. She relaxed, helplessly snuggling in his arms. Grimes knew he was whipped. Weeping, wailing females always upset him.

"Listen, I wan't aiming to git really rough."

"Oh, I'm so unhappy!" Velma buried her face in her hands.

Flinging herself on the sofa had brought her skirt well over her knees. Though shapely and well rounded, Velma's abject posture made her seem frail and helpless; to be consoled and protected, rather than to be aroused to an emotion that frightened her.

"Dawg gone it," he began impulsively, "I was jest fixing to axe yo'all to marry me."

He had not expected her to whoop with glee at that proposal, but neither did he anticipate a continuation of her grief. She sat up, blinking away her tears. "That's just it, darling. I can't marry you."

"Why—whut in tarnation—we think a heap of each other—"

"I know we do. But—but—you're a nomad."

The accusation made Grimes sit up straight. He flared, "Woman, you kain't insult me thattaway! My folks has been God-fearin' white people fo' years an' years. Not a tech of Injun er nuthin'. Listen heah, whut y'all mean, *nomad?* Anyway, I ain't one."

"You are too, Simon. Always wandering around. Like an A-rab or something," she explained. "And I want to marry someone home-loving and steady, not just brave and handsome."

No one had ever doubted the pig-headed valor of the Grimeses of Kennesaw Mountain, Gawgia, but neither had anyone ever hinted that any one of that coffin-faced clan was handsome. Grimes brightened. Velma sho' must be in love with him!

"Honey," he promised, "I'm goin' to be the home-lovingest jasper. Dang it, I'm takin' up a section of grazing land, an' building a house."

In the meanwhile, he was gathering Velma into his arms. When Simon Bolivar Grimes made up his mind, it stayed made up. In playing sweet and helpless, the redhead had momentarily disarmed him. Before she could rearrange her defenses, he was kissing her dizzy.

She had played her part a bit too well. She was helpless . . . and she liked it. . . .

THEY HAD LONG SINCE LOST TRACK OF TIME WHEN A SOUND OUTSIDE THE WEATHER-BEATEN little farmhouse startled them from each other's arms. *Clump-clop, clump-clop . . .* hoofbeats, but irregular.

Velma scrambled to her feet, fumbled for matches. Grimes already had a Colt in each hand. He checked her when she tried to strike a light.

"It's dad," she gasped. "Rover ain't barked. I got to have a light. To fix my hair. Go in the other room and pretend you're reading."

Grimes slowly holstered his guns. "That hoss's limpin' bad. Listen to that!"

There was a groan, a stifled oath; then a soggy thud. Far off, a coyote howled, blood chilling in its eerie mockery. A horse whinnied, and one answered from the barn.

Grimes, still cautious, crept to the front door. For a moment, he stared into the searchlight splendor of the full moon. Then he called back over his shoulder, "Start heating some water, and git some bandages. It's yo' pappy, shot fuller of holes'n a Chinese lottery ticket."

"Oh, Lord," she moaned, running to Grimes' side.

"Git back and do like I tol' you. I kin handle him."

The wounded buckskin horse was limping to its comrades in the corral. John Crawford's lean frame was a dark huddle on the hard-baked earth; a dark pool was reaching out.

156

Grimes knelt. Though gangling, his mountaineer frame was amply equipped with sinew. He gently lifted John Crawford from the ground, as easily as though it had been Velma. He laid the wounded man on the clean-scrubbed kitchen table, listened to the confused muttering that came from the bearded lips.

Then he looked at Crawford's holstered pistol. It had not been fired. Someone had drygulched him, left him for dead. Later, the ambushed man had somehow struggled to the saddle and the mustang had headed for home.

"Lucky," he muttered, as white-faced Velma handed him bandages and stood by with a steaming basin and a pair of scissors, "the slugs went plumb through. Don't have to wait fo' a doctor to probe. It's jest up to Gawd and guts whether he'll pull through."

"Will he?"

The boy from Georgia shrugged. "I hopes and prays. Anyway, he's been shot up afore now." Then he straightened up. "He was drygulched befo' he got to Aztec Hill."

"How do you know?"

"Fust, he ain't got his poke of gold. Second, he ain't got no receipt er nuthin' like he'd have ef he'd paid off. An' finally, they musta been some sculpin what knew about us gettin' money fo' them critters we shipped to Kansas."

He carefully inspected his guns and adjusted the holsters.

"Simon." Velma's flat, somber voice broke into a new tremor. "Where are you going?"

"To git a doctor," he gruffly answered. "I fixed my pappy and my granpappy up after heaps of feud shootin's back home, but I sho' ain't got a license to practice medicine."

His forced chuckle did not convince Velma. She clung to him, taut and trembling. "Simon, don't you lie to me. You're going for more than a doctor. You look just like you did when you shot Lem Yeager, and kept on shooting till he hit the floor."

He jerked her hands from his shoulders, thrust her away. It no longer meant a thing to him that the night breeze was whipping her flimsy skirt against her thighs. Grimes cut in as she swallowed and tried for a fresh start: "All right, I'm gittin' a doc and I'm gittin' me the hide of the skunk what dry gulched yo' pappy. I'll send a couple cowpokes out to run things, seeing me and him ain't working fo' a while."

Before leaving, he put axle grease on the bullet-grazed haunch of the old man's horse.

He followed Crawford's trail. Blood from horse and man made that easy in the moonlight. And dawn helped him, later. Grimes spent some time studying the scene of the crime. Considering that Crawford had planned to get to Aztec Hill before the closing of the bank that held the mortgage, it was not hard to figure the time element. And best of all, the boy from Georgia was practically a stranger in that tough mining town.

No one knew him except the marshal, and Carmencita, that dark eyed dancehall girl with a mouth always shaped for a kiss.

GRIMES, GEORGIA MOUNTAINEER, HAD ENOUGH INSTINCTIVE SUSPICION OF ALL PEOPLE TO equip two cautious men; and this despite a disarming boyishness and a straw-colored cowlick that did not make his face seem any brighter than necessary. His pappy had always allowed Simon looked too dumb for people to suspect him of any tricks. . . .

By midmorning, his horse was toiling up the steep ascent to Aztec Hill. Miners, cowpunchers, long-haired trappers and blanketed Indians thronged the terraced street. Painted women thrust bleached heads and bare shoulders from the windows of dives and invited the boys to come in for a good time. And, despite the hour, the gambling halls were hell-roaring as the saloons that outnumbered every other enterprise by five to one.

One of Aztec Hill's two medicos was in the Antler Bar. Grimes found the other one at his residence. He said to the frock-coated little man, "Doc, I'm payin' yo' in advance. An' I'm trustin' y'all not to tell no one who's hurt or nuthin'."

Doctor Warren wiped his spectacles, thrust the gold piece into his waistcoat pocket, and heartily agreed. Then he waited for Grimes to write a note and also tell him how to get out to the Crawford spread.

The boy from Georgia watched the sawbones head for the livery stable to get his buggy. He hoped Warren wouldn't read the note to Velma; it instructed her to keep the doctor from returning to town, even if she had to cut up the harness, turn his horse loose and steal his boots.

Grimes knew that in a place as hard-bitten as Aztec Hill, there was no sense in asking the town marshal to look for trouble. It would be a lot easier to prowl around himself until he found someone wearing narrow, extremely high-heeled boots; a man who had ridden a blue roan pony that had been freshly shod.

These signs had all been apparent near the ambush, but they were not proof that any lawman or court could use. That, however, did not worry Grimes!

He spent the day inspecting the hitching racks of Aztec Hill. Finally, he found a blue roan with new shoes. His own mount, a thoroughbred from home, was not any too well shod, so he went to the blacksmith shop to have the job attended to.

"Ef yo'all don't mind, suh," Grimes began as the farrier set to work, "I'd sho' admire having you tell me who that hoss belongs to what's in front of the Wigwam Saloon. That there blue one, suh."

The smith bit off a chew, quenched the glowing iron in the tub of water, and looked up the street. "Kain't say I know, bub. Seemed sorter new in these parts. Like dang nigh four outen every five jaspers in this yere town sence the mine opened. How come yo're interested?"

"I allowed mebbe I could trade this hoss of mine fo' his'n," Grimes plausibly explained.

"Yo're plumb crazy ef yuh do," grumbled the smith.

"Co'se, I'll git suthin' to boot, so I kin head fo' Californy."

"Wuss yet. Bub, when the railroad comes tuh Aztec Hill, yo're going tuh see a town what is a town. It's got a heap more'n mines."

They discussed the proposed railroad at length, though, thus far, it was a secret; all confidential information. And the talk shifted back to horses.

A shadow fell across the open doorway of the shop. Grimes whirled. A tall, hatchet-faced hombre regarded him with ironic eyes. He said, "That there roan's mine. I done heard yuh say yuh craved tuh swap."

That was awkward. The stranger's Levi's were sweat-stained, and so were his boots. He had the look of one who had specialized in keeping ahead of a posse. A salty jasper, and the soft, seasoned leather of his holsters hinted a readiness to add another to the notches that were cut in the butts of his walnut handled guns.

"I sho' said that, suh," fumbled Grimes, thinking fast. "Yes, suh, Mistah—" He paused, looked at his man in courteous inquiry.

"Bitter Creek Doane," the gunner announced with a vocal flourish.

It was no longer a question of slapping leather. This "long rider" might on a hunch have waylaid John Crawford. But, being a stranger, it was more probable that Bitter Creek Doane had been put on the job by local talent. Grimes did not dive for his guns. He wanted to learn who was behind Bitter Creek.

"Mistah Doane," he said, "ef y'all give me fo'ty dollahs to boot, yo' kin have my hoss. He's a tho'bred from mah Uncle Cahtah's stable, suh. My uncle'd lambaste me ef he ever got a holt on me, but I need mo' money."

"Let's have a drink," countered Bitter Creek.

He jerked his thumb toward the Navajo Hotel. Grimes didn't like that. Carmencita hustled drinks there. He said, "Ef y'all don't mind, suh, I'd ruther go to the Hoot Owl."

That amendment was accepted as proposed.

"Forty bucks is purty stiff," grumbled Bitter Creek, bellying up to the bar.

They had another whiskey, and the dickering continued. Bitter Creek seemed amused about something. Grimes reckoned that it must be the idea of swapping hosses with a boy from Gawgia. No matter; play it up, and finally get Mistah Doane bragging a little. . . .

In the bar mirror, Grimes saw the reflection of a voluptuously-shaped girl with olive-tinted shoulders. Her high-piled hair was blue black, her red lips were full and sensuous; though most of her allure came from the taper of her ample hips to her slender legs, and the way her bodice accented a breast that was firm as well as generous.

It was Carmencita, and he did not want her to blow off about the shooting party that had finished Lem Yeager, the no-good brother of an outlaw.

"Uh . . . um—Mistah Doane," gulped Grimes. "I jest remember I got to see a gent . . . uh . . . a gent I don't want to see account of some money."

Bitter Creek chuckled as Grimes gulped his whiskey and stumbled toward the side door.

It would have been a perfect getaway had Carmencita not recognized him. She was waiting for him in the alley outside the Hoot Owl Saloon. "Oh, Don Simon," she cooed, catching his arm, her warm curves blocking his way. "I 'ave quit the Navajo an' dance here. Eez nize, meet you thees way."

Her caressing fingers were telegraphing signals along his arm. She wanted him to go back with her and drink. Grimes protested, "Shucks, honey, I jest kain't . . . uh . . . I'm scairt of trouble."

She laughed. The sound was soft and tinkling; her bosom quivered under its tight bodice. "Don Simon, when 'ave *you* the fear of anyone?" Then a wise little wink and a reproving index finger. "Bot you do not fool me. Eez a girl you don' like to see, no?"

That he was dodging some dancehall lady seemed logical to Carmencita, and before he knew what was happening, she was edging him toward one of the shacks that lined the alley.

"Hey, wait a second," he protested. "I know y'all done me a favor onct, but yo' likewise got me hawg drunk and grabbed my poke."

"Por dios, I did not mean to keep the money. I take eet so wan othair girl do not get it!"

The over-sweet scent that billowed from her bodice began to make Grimes' pulse do tricks. After all, Bitter Creek wasn't leaving town in a hurry. Maybe Carmencita knew something about him.

He followed her into a room fixed up with mirrors and horsehair furniture. Negligee, hosiery, a filmy nightgown and a pair of gaudy garters littered the chairs and sofa. Carmencita planted herself, cocked one leg over the other. When she reached for the whiskey bottle, the skirt hiked up.

Grimes choked on his liquor. Carmencita laughed, coyly raised her skirt further to fumble with a pocket stitched to her garter. She produced a pair of twenty-dollar bills, and laid them on the table.

"Now, w'at I told you?" She drew him to the arm of her chair.

"Uh . . . shucks, that's paper." Grimes had never convinced himself that stuff like that was money. A lot of people had, but somehow, it had always seemed a bit silly, and grandpappy Gideon Grimes had always told him that during the war, a bushel of that stuff wouldn't buy a pound of sugar.

"Listen, honey, they's suthin' I want to ask you."

Carmencita could think of only two things Grimes or anyone else would ask for, and he'd already had a drink. She looked up, uncorked all the glamour in those magnificent eyes and shaped her mouth for a kiss.

Then the door slammed open. Carmencita made motions of getting her skirt down over her knees. Grimes jumped as though he'd touched a hot rock, and landed on his feet. Bitter Creek Doane was in the doorway, and he looked like his name.

"Bub," he growled, "yuh look too dumb tuh know whut yo're playin' with."

Being surprised with an armful of girl always had embarrassed Grimes, though this wasn't the first time it had happened. Carmencita looked annoyed and confused.

Bitter Creek exploded, "Yuh no-good greaser, whut yuh mean, giving that squirt my money? I'll—"

He hefted her a backhanded slap that plumped her across the arm of her chair.

Carmencita's legs flailed skyward. She screamed, *"Chinga'o cabron,* don' I dance weeth you all las' night—don' I—"

She had no chance to enumerate the various ways in which she had been amiable. Grimes planted Bitter Creek a wallop that lifted him into the sofa. "Next time yo' lay hands on a lady—"

Carmencita screeched, *"Cuida'o!"*

Bitter Creek snatched a derringer from a wrist clip, a treacherous and deadly draw. Grimes pivoted. His hands darted like snakes heading for a hole. For two endless seconds, the frail room shook from the steady blasts of his .45s. Powder flecks from the derringer's twin barrels half-blinded him, but as he blinked his eyes clear, he saw Carmencita on the floor, her legs and arms threshing from either side of the overturned chair.

Bitter Creek was gurgling, kicking the planks. Then he slumped flat. Grimes jerked Carmencita to her feet. She was screaming and massaging her hip. Her injuries were not mortal; they'd not even interfere with her dancing.

"Gol dang it, yo're a hoodoo! Now I kain't axe that gent nuthin'!" he growled disgustedly. "Who is he?"

"Ees wan generous *caballero* weeth plenty money."

Grimes hastily went through Bitter Creek's pockets. He had a handful of paper money and some silver. According to that, he hadn't robbed John Crawford.

"I got to git going."

With all this publicity, he had become conspicuous.

Then the marshal came clumping up, a Colt in each hand. Grimes' hands rose. The lawman jerked back, teetered on the balls of his feet when he saw the scene within. When he heard the story, he said, "Simon, I reckon it's self defense. But it's shore tough, yuh gunning out Bitter Creek."

"How come?"

"He's a detective. Suthin' like a Pinkerton man."

"Lawd," groaned Grimes, "I ain't never shot a lawman afore."

They'd not been able to convict him, but he might spend a smart spell in jail. These powerful eastern agencies that sent men to track down train robbers and cattle thieves would raise tunket; the authorities of Aztec Hill had to make a show of doing something in such an exceptional case.

"I'm afeard I got tuh run yuh in, Simon. Jest fer a matter of form."

"He workin' fer anyone in town that'd be real hostile?"

The marshal knew that Grimes would not pull down on him, even if there was a chance; which there was not. He answered, "I reckon he was. Jud Eagen's powerful important."

Grimes' face lengthened. Carmencita's sudden glance nailed him. Her eyes had become black points, and her lips moved silently. But whatever she was trying to say, her pantomine didn't register.

"Marshal, yuh better take my smoke poles an' I'll go to the hoosegow. But it was self defense. Lawdy, I never been in jail afore. If my pappy knew—"

The marshal was convinced by the boy's misery, his utter abjectness. He holstered his guns and reached for Grimes' belt.

That was a mistake. The edges of Grimes' hands cut down like descending sabres, and momentarily, the effect was just as deadly. His height and swiftness had made it easy.

The marshal was knocked cold by the shock at the base of his brain. As he telescoped, Carmencita gasped, "That ees what I try to tell you. Bot I don' theenk you can do."

"Listen here, honey! Who's Jud Eagen?"

Carmencita shrugged. *"Muy malo.* Wan tough hombre. But he own the big mine."

"Where's he live?"

She told him. And without waiting to hear her advice about leaving town, Grimes bounded to the door. "Y'all tell the marshal," was his farewell, "I sho' hated to treat him thattaway, but I got to hurry to Californy."

"California?" she echoed. "Why—"

"I'm jest a gol danged nomad," he answered bitterly.

Dusk had enveloped the hell-roaring town. As far as he could see, nobody but the marshal had paid any attention to the gunplay. After all, no one but a lawman was paid to waste his time on such matters: Aztec Hill was that kind of a town. Grimes went to the main street to get his horse.

The old blacksmith wondered how the trade had come out. Then he wanted Grimes to take a message to his brother in California.

JUD EAGEN'S HOUSE WAS SOME DISTANCE FROM THE MINING CAMP, AND A BIT BEYOND the residence of Baldy Farrell, the banker who held the mortgage on the Crawford spread. Just how the late Bitter Creek Doane tied in with Eagen and the dry-gulching of Velma's father was beyond all fathoming. But since Eagen lived near Farrell's place, maybe the banker could put out a shred of gossip.

"Damnation, it's jest my luck, shootin' the evidence." Grimes somberly shook his head. "No wonder I'm a gol dang nomad critter."

He hesitated for a moment. Jud Eagen's house was dark, but there was a light in the banker's residence. He dismounted, left his horse in a clump of shrubbery a hundred yards from Farrell's place, then set out on foot for a look-see. Things had gone past the point where he could blunder along. It would not be long before the marshal regained his wits, and that goat-whiskered gent would be fit to tie!

A woman's scream made him start. It was abruptly choked, but that momentary cry of terror sent shivers racing down his spine. When a girl shrieked that way, something Gawd-awful was happening. Without stopping to consider the consequences of getting mixed up in something spectacular, the boy from Georgia stretched long legs toward the lighted window.

What he saw inside the bedroom was beyond believing. A blonde girl was lashed hand and foot to a chair. A masked man was readjusting the gag that had slipped enough to permit that one shuddering scream. Another stood by; he was stocky, square shouldered, and likewise masked.

162

The girl had been snatched from her bed. She wore only a filmy nightgown. Her futile struggles threw her shapely body into bold relief. Her breast quivered with her agonized writhing. A muffled moan seeped through the towel that masked all of her face, except those fear widened eyes.

"Now, look-ee here, m'am." The tall man's voice trembled. "We ain't aiming tuh hurt yuh onless yuh jest makes us. Tain't no use hollerin'. Yore pappy ain't coming back fer a right smart spell. Air yuh tellin' us whut we axed yuh?"

She shook her head. Her slim fingers convulsively gripped the arms of the chair. The short man was swarthy, judging by the hand that reached suddenly out, ripped the frail nightgown off one shoulder. He struck a match, held the flame close to the soft flesh that swelled above her breast.

She cringed, her horror-struck eyes glued in fascinated terror to the flickering flame that seemed to lick greedily toward shrinking white flesh. The lanky man snatched his partner's wrist and growled, "Bernal, yuh kain't do that—"

"Shut up!" snarled Bernal, enraged at the pronouncing of his name.

"Y'all hist 'em up," Grimes cut in, hurdling the sill.

Bernal whirled. He dropped the blazing match and went for his gun. The tall man cursed as he slapped leather. Grimes flung himself aside. His guns were out, but he held his fire for that precious instant he needed to avoid driving .45s through the girl, whose twisting body was directly behind the two ruffians.

Pistol flame lashed the room. Grimes felt the biting stab of a slug that raked his ribs. The shock spun him. But he landed out of line with the girl.

The startled invaders had shot in panicky haste. For an instant, Grimes steadied himself, recovering from the shock. Then his guns roared, and Bernal and his partner learned that pausing to spot their shots had been fatal.

The tall man lurched athwart the Mexican. Grimes followed through, the drumming Colts riddling Bernal. He crumpled beside his companion, smoking gun skated across the floor. The two lay huddled in a red, quiverin' heap.

The girl stared, frozen by the murderous instant during which crossfire had threatened to cut her down. Grimes slashed her bonds and drew her to her feet. She clung to him, alternating sobs and incoherent cries.

"Y'ain't hurt a bit, m'am," he assured, extricating himself from her hysterical embrace. "What in tunket—I never seen ornier gents—"

As she calmed down, he learned that she was Sally Farrell, the banker's daughter. A headache had sent her to bed early. "There's been a lot of ill feeling about mortgage foreclosures," she concluded. "And those ruffians were going to torture me until I told them where Dad's strongbox is. A lot of those loans were personal, and so he didn't keep the papers at the bank, like he ought."

Grimes retreated a pace. His face hardened. He knelt, jerked the masks from the two he had cut down. The Mexican, Bernal, probably was an employee of the tall man who lay there, still gripping his Colt.

"M'am," he said, slowly rising, "fo' the fust time in my life, I'm kind of sorry I had to shoot the gizzards outen a couple gents. I ain't blamin' you fo' what yo' pappy done, and roastin' anyone right on the hoof ain't right. But them po' devils—I reckon they's had hard luck, like me."

Sally's eyes widened. This sudden grimness of her rescuer had taken the breath out of her. She stood there, quite unaware of her torn gown and the play of the lamplight on white skin that shone through the rents. Fresh tears rolled slowly down her cheeks; she seemed to understand that this was another one who had been beaten into desperation by a mortgage. She advanced a pace, laid a soft hand on his arm.

"I wouldn't tell *them*. But if *you're* in trouble—oh, Lord, how I hate all this business! I'll give you anything in the house."

That came from her heart. Grimes' wrath faded. Impulsively, he drew her toward him, stroked her hair as her tears soaked his shirt front. Sally had been through some tough moments; no wonder she was cracking.

"Honey," he said, trying to swallow the heart that suddenly rose to choke him, "since yo' feel that-taway, mebbe I ain't plumb sorry I hosed them gents with lead."

"I'm so glad you don't hate me," she gulped, quivering against him. "You were wonderful."

"Yo're sort of wonderful yo'self," he blurted, inspired by Sally's close-pressed curves. His hand slid up her arm, over her curving back.

"Oh," she gasped, breaking away and trying to pull together the edges of the tore gown. "Heavens, I was so upset—"

She hurried to a closet, found a robe and drew it about her. But Sally's slim legs were exposed enough to make Grimes vividly conscious of the loveliness she had concealed. With difficulty, he got his mind back on business. "Lookee here, Sally. Yo' pappy knows all about business in Aztec Hill. Mebbe y'all kin tell me about Jud Eagen."

"Oh, that's easy." She beckoned, then picked up the kerosene lamp to lead him out of that blood-spattered room. "Jud's a speculator."

"You mean, mining shares and sech like?"

"No." She had paused in a room somewhat to the front. As she knelt to fumble with a trapdoor under the rug of what seemed to be her father's library, Sally explained, "There's a railroad coming to Aztec Hill, and it's got to lay its tracks up Hungry Valley. Eagen was fixing to buy up some of Dad's mortgages. So he can make the railroad pay plenty for the right of way. Otherwise, they'd have to dig awfully expensive tunnels."

That began to clear things up. Crawford's spread was in the proposed right of way. The drygulching probably had not been plain robbery, but an attempt to keep him from paying off the debt he owed Baldy Farrell.

"Why'd yo' pappy sell the dang mo'gage?" he suspiciously demanded.

"He needed money to put into a mine he was interested in," Sally answered, producing a small strongbox from the crypt in the floor.

She found a ring of keys in the oak desk. Grimes leaned, looped an encircling arm over Sally's shoulder, watched her unlock the box. He eagerly reached past her and seized the sheaf of legal documents.

"Take what you want," she said. "It's little enough to repay you."

Women were funny, Grimes allowed as he thumbed over the papers. Here Sally had faced hell and high water, defying a pair of desperate ranchers, and now, just out of gratitude, she was giving him his choice.

He found the one covering John Crawford's range. As nearly as he could figure it out, Baldy Farrell had been bargaining for the lot. He was glad that the skunk he was after was Jud Eagen, not Sally's father.

"Honey," he said, "I'd shore crave to meet this Mistah Eagen afore I leave Aztec Hill. Y'all reckon he's to home?"

Something about his voice must have betrayed him, or perhaps it was the deadly glitter of his China-blue eyes. Sally caught his arm and said, "No, you mustn't, Simon. You'll get killed."

He tried to shrug her loose, but she would not let him get to the door. He said, "I done took care of them two gents in yo' room."

"Oh, but you don't understand," she cried. "Those were just two cattlemen. But Eagen has professional gunslicks. He's never without them. You'd be cut down before you had a chance."

Her arms reinforced her plea. She clung to him, trying to melt his stubbornness. Her kisses burned his mouth, and every curve of that ripe young body conspired to shake him. "Don't, Simon," she begged. "He's got all kinds of influence. Even if you killed him, they'd hunt you down."

"One of his gunslicks kilt a friend of mine," he growled; but he wavered, overwhelmed by Sally's extravagant caresses.

"You saved me," she murmured, feeling the relaxation of his efforts to shake her off. "You risked your life. Darling, if you'll promise to forget this silly idea of revenge—you've got your pardner's mortgage—if you'll just be sensible—"

Her lids drooped, shading her misty eyes. They contained a promise that her half-parted lips had not yet spoken. A flush was creeping across her upturned face, and the very hand that tugged at his arm told him that she was offering a sweet substitute for vengeance, and maybe John Crawford wouldn't die, after all.

Sally was whispering, "Dad's down at the Hoot Owl Saloon, dickering with Jud Eagen. He won't be back till late."

In the hallway, he wavered. With the marshal hostile, there wasn't a chance of getting to the Hoot Owl to settle with Eagen. The speculator, hearing of the death of Bitter Creek Doane, would be on guard. Sally snuggled closer and whispered, "You'll stay, Simon? Maybe I can persuade Dad to help your friends, so they can carry over till better times. He'll he grateful for what you did for me." Her arms twined about his neck, her lips sought his.

He had gotten way past the thinking stage. Sally did not know that Grimes had hopelessly committed himself by sapping the marshal. And when he followed her across the threshold of a darkened room, he forgot that she had left the lamp burning in her father's study, that the Crawford mortgage lay on the desk beside the opened strongbox.

"I'm so glad, Simon," she sighed as his arms engulfed her in a clinging, ardent caress. . . .

GRIMES WAS THE FIRST TO BE AWARE OF THE OPENING OF THE FRONT DOOR, THE CREAK OF A floorboard, the muttering of men's voices. As he leaped to his feet, Sally's terrified whisper told him, "Dad's come home!"

"Gol dang it, Jud," rumbled a voice intended to be subdued, "lookit that strongbox!"

Sally felt the sudden tension of Grimes' arm. Jud Eagen was in the other room. Baldy Farrell bellowed, "Sally! Whar in tarnation are yuh?"

Grimes bounded down the hall. One long leap brought him to the library. "Eagen, yo' gold danged skunk," he shouted; "fill yo' hands!"

No doubt which was Baldy Farrell; his glistening head identified him. The other had a shaggy crop of black hair. But before anyone could fire, Sally had overtaken Grimes. She flung herself in front of him. "Don't shoot!" she shrieked.

Things had popped up too fast for thought: first, the rifled strongbox, then the lanky gunner in the doorway, then Sally in the trailing robe that exposed all but the bits her town gown still covered. Eagen did not know whether he had barged into an ambush, or whether the banker was his companion in trouble. He shouted, "Frosty! Mike! Cover the back!"

From outside came answering yells and pounding boots. Eagen's gunslicks were on the job.

All that in split seconds. Grimes lashed out, knocked Sally sprawling into the library. His left hand gun came out. "Steady, Baldy!" he yelled to the banker, but the blast of the .45 blotted the warning.

Eagen's gun cleared leather. Baldy Farrell, fearing for his daughter's safety in a general exchange of lead, lunged for the table. The lamp spattered to the floor, but darkness was not quite quick enough to stop the show. Eagen dropped, missing his chance by an instant. His slug chunked into the door jamb.

For a moment, the gloom was broken only by the flickering lampwick. Then the spilled kerosene flared up, licking the curtains. As Grimes lunged, Baldy popped one shot, then held his fire. His swiftly-moving target had landed in the corner with Sally. Baldy dared not shoot.

Grimes hurled his gun. It caught the banker full in the face, stunning him. Sally recovered, ran screaming to her father, who lay just short of the smoking yellow flames.

"Git him to the front door," shouted Grimes.

The gunslicks, who had covered the rear, were now charging in through the back, ready to join the riot. Grimes rolled the desk athwart the hall door. The room was dense with smoke; the blaze was licking up the dry woodwork.

Seconds counted. Grimes and the girl tripped, rolled down the front steps with their half-conscious burden. Grimes kicked clear of the scramble, and beat out the smoldering patch that was eating into Sally's gown.

166

A buckskin poke had fallen out of Baldy Farrell's pocket. During the tangle, Grimes had noted its metallic tinkle and weight. He snatched it. By the flames, he recognized John Crawford's pouch of gold pieces.

"I got to shake a hock, honey," he panted. "You' pappy ain't shot, jest knocked silly."

As the gunslicks tumbled out of a side window, Grimes was heading for the further shadows. For half a dozen leaps, he ducked lead. Then Jud Eagen's gunners realized that the leaping flames made them good targets.

Grimes piled into the saddle and headed up the trail. Below him, somewhat to the left of the flaming house, winked the lights of Aztec Hill. Once he cleared the first crest, he sighed, jingled the buckskin poke.

It was clear now: Eagen's gunslick, Bitter Creek Doane, had shot and robbed Crawford, and given the gold to his employer in exchange for some new-fangled paper dollars. Eagen, dickering for the mortgages in Hungry Valley, had handed the golden loot to Sally's father to bind the wholesale transaction.

"Gawd," the boy from Georgia muttered. "Baldy Farrell's sho' to be riled at me. And the marshal. Kain't go back to Aztec Hill, nor Hungry Valley, neither. Best I kin do is to ship this yere poke to Jawn Crawford by express from Californy. Anyway, that mo'gage is plumb burned up by now."

He swallowed, blinked as he remembered Velma's kisses and her qualms. He sighed, "I reckon she was right. I'm jest a gol danged nomad."

$$\bullet\ \bullet\ \bullet\ \bullet\ \bullet$$

Order these and other titles from our website.

ADVENTURE FICTION FROM BLACK DOG BOOKS

CRIME FICTION FROM BLACK DOG BOOKS

HORROR FICTION FROM BLACK DOG BOOKS

SCIENCE FICTION FROM BLACK DOG BOOKS

Visit www.blackdogbooks.net for more information,
or write to info@blackdogbooks.net.

Made in the USA
Charleston, SC
22 March 2011